BEST WISHES

BOOK FOUR

HOW TO BE THE BEST DAMN FAERY GODMOTHER IN THE WORLD (OR DIE TRYING)

HELEN HARPER

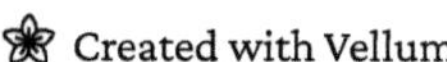 Created with Vellum

Someone was following me. I knew it from the indescribable itch at the back of my neck and the flicker of a figure in my peripheral vision when I turned left down the side street, away from the main thoroughfare containing Colchester's bustling shops.

There was a good chance it was one of Ethan's trolls; after all, he'd set his people onto tailing me before. I shouldn't worry. Despite recent events between the faery godmothers and the trolls, they meant me no harm. They'd even helped me. But I was no longer a faery godmother and something about my latest shadow felt different. It wasn't necessarily a malign presence, but it was good to be wary. These days, it was always good to be wary.

I checked my watch. Time wasn't on my side. The last thing I wanted was to be late for my appointment. I had an appearance to maintain and that didn't include a lack of punctuality. I pulled back my shoulders, set my expression into a grim mask, and ducked through the double doors of the small arthouse cinema on my left.

The spotty bloke behind the counter, who looked more like

a child than someone who should legally be allowed gainful employment, smiled. 'Good afternoon!'

I managed a small smile in return. Whether I was under extreme stress or not, I could still be polite. I strode purposefully towards him. 'I'd like a ticket to your next showing, please.'

'Is that for *Badenhaus*, the German thriller? Or *Sunlight*? The...' his mouth turned down in an expression of disgust '... romance?'

He could sneer all he wanted. For my part, I fervently wished that I had some romance in my life. Since I'd effectively humiliated Jasper, the Devil's Advocate, in a bid to save his job from the Director's machinations, there were going to be zero hearts and flowers coming my way any time soon. I had no-one to blame but myself but that didn't mean there wasn't a stab in my chest whenever I thought of Jasper's glittering emerald-green eyes and warm-hearted nature. And that happened only about a thousand times a day.

I glanced out towards the pavement. It remained empty for now, but I doubted it would stay that way for long. 'The romance is fine,' I said, yanking out a crumpled ten-pound note and crossing my fingers that he'd be quick about the ticket.

'Really? Because I can highly recommend *Badenhaus*. It's...'

My efforts to remain polite only went so far. 'Just give me the ticket,' I snapped.

The light in his eyes turned icy cold. 'Would you like to upgrade to one of our luxury seats and receive free popcorn with that?'

I dropped the money onto the counter. 'Just the ticket.'

He sniffed and picked up the note, holding it between his thumb and forefinger as if afraid he might catch some cheesy romantic disease, and made the transaction. I tapped my foot, repeatedly checking behind me for signs of my tail. When the kid finally held out my cinema ticket, I practically snatched it from his hand and whirled round in the direction of the screen.

'Wait!' he called out. 'Your change!'

I waved a dismissive hand and charged ahead. 'Keep it!' While I couldn't afford to lose the cash – and he certainly didn't deserve a tip – I was running out of time. I shouldn't have left home so late. I'd spent far too long carefully selecting my outfit, taming the unkempt frizz of my hair and avoiding Pumpkin's attempts to chew my shoes. I was paying for all that now.

Cursing under my breath, I jogged down the darkened aisles. A couple were necking in the back row and a homeless guy was asleep in one of the seats at the far side. I ignored all of them and swung round the front row of plush, velvet-covered chairs, my feet crunching on a few errant pieces of popcorn from the previous showing. Then I burst through the fire door marked Exit and back into the outside world.

This time I was in a closed off alleyway. There was only one way out and it was on the other side of the cinema and away from the street I'd been on previously. Whoever was following me wouldn't catch me easily now. I gave myself a self-satisfied pat on the back and marched quickly down the narrow street. I'd only lost a few minutes' time; I wasn't going to be late even if I was now slightly off course.

Alas, no sooner had that thought crossed my mind than the silhouette of a towering figure appeared at the end of the narrow street, blocking my exit. Fuck a puck. Any chance that this was merely some random passer-by was immediately negated by the magical vibrations emanating from its tall body – not to mention the way it began to stride purposefully in my direction. When it drew closer and I could see who was in front of me, my heart sank further. This was definitely no human out for a stroll.

I stared at her. While there was no doubt that she was some

sort of magical conjuration, she was unlike anything I'd ever seen or could have conceived of. For one thing, she was naked from the waist up, wearing nothing but a leather skirt made out of pointed flaps of material and thigh-high boots. She had thick, glossy, blonde hair and glowing red eyes that sparked with anger. And her white teeth were painfully sharp looking, though it wasn't her dentistry that caused my mouth to drop open. It was the fact that she had three very pert and very bare breasts bouncing on her chest. Okaaaay then.

'Aren't you cold?' I asked. 'It is almost November, you know. There are some great shops around the corner where you can buy yourself a T-shirt. Or a coat.'

Unsurprisingly, the conjuration didn't speak. I knew from my own experience in stirring up similar visions that intelligible speech was an impossible task. After all, you couldn't enchant a terrifying creature into existence and then expect it to make small talk. Illusions such as this one weren't sentient; they were brought into being to serve one purpose only and that was to carry out the wishes of their creator. Judging from the way the three-breasted monstrosity was fixed on me, her purpose was to stop me in my tracks. And quite possibly swipe my head from my shoulders at the same time.

I didn't stop to think about who was behind the conjuration. Frankly, it could have been any number of people. Whoever had created the monstrous woman would be close by but I had neither the inclination nor the time to find out who they were. Not right now. Instead I focused on what was important – getting out of this alley unscathed so I could get to where I needed to be.

The one good thing was that I no longer required a wand to call upon my own magic. While there were always limitations, my recent acts had broken the natural barriers within me that kept my inherent magic at bay. I could flick my fingers and summon any number of spells – it was simply a matter of choosing the right one.

As the woman reached me, her massive frame preventing me from sidling past her and making a run for it, I twisted my left wrist. Meet fire with fire, I decided. It was the best way.

The molecules in the air cracked and snapped, pulling the energy in the very atmosphere together to provide me with what I needed. I stepped back as a monster of my own appeared. The difference was that this one would do what I wanted – and it was at least twice the size of the bizarre woman.

Something about my wandless magic allowed for greater details and flourishes. Once upon a time bulging muscles, gleaming green skin and breath that could knock out most living creatures at a hundred paces would have been more than enough colour to my conjurations; now there were also thick pulsating veins, sprouting black wiry hairs and unspent, fathomless fury. The woman had no chance.

My monster advanced, fists up and teeth bared. The woman stood her ground, her lack of conscious thought also giving her a complete lack of fear. That worked both ways, of course, and when she calmly produced a long sword with a sharply gleaming tip, my green-skinned creation didn't falter.

He threw back his head, roared and flew straight at her. Her sword clattered to the ground before disappearing in a puff of smoke. Then the two of them were rolling around on the grimy cobblestones, biting and kicking at each other. Unfortunately for me, they were also still in my way. In fact, now there was even less chance of me skipping past them and making my escape.

Grimacing, I glanced upwards, wondering whether I dared try a ninja-inspired wall run above their heads. I had the magic to sustain one but I wasn't quite so convinced about my ability to beat gravity. I was powerful but I wasn't omnipotent.

I hissed and looked back at the cinema's fire exit. I could always re-enter the building, head back out through the main doors onto the same street as before. But if my opponent had any nous, he or she would be waiting for me to do just that. No. It was get past the two writhing conjurations, or get caught.

I twirled my fingers, forcing my monster up to his feet again and back towards me. The woman also sprang up, smiling prettily at us both. I rolled my eyes at her expression and gestured to my green-skinned creature. He hunkered down, the muscles in his back bulging, then he grabbed the woman and lifted her up by the waist before holding her body in the air and spinning it backwards. In theory, she'd land behind me and I'd get the opportunity to sprint out of the alley. In practice, she resisted just enough that his aim was off. Rather than arcing through the air and falling several metres away from me, her foot connected with my head and we both tumbled to the ground, my body sprawled underneath hers.

I wriggled out as she pushed herself away. My back was aching where I'd hit the ground and the sharp throb of pain in my wrist suggested that I'd fallen badly enough to break it. I cradled it against my stomach and ducked my head then I dashed blindly away, leaving the two magical creations behind.

My own monster would vanish into the ether in less than a minute, just long enough to allow me to get away. What happened to the three-breasted woman was no longer my concern. I'd managed to escape and that was all that mattered.

ALTHOUGH I DIDN'T HAVE the magic to heal any major injuries, my powers were enough to heal the fracture in my wrist. There would be plenty of unsightly bruising to mark the spot and no doubt a lot of lingering pain but I wouldn't lose the use of my hand, so things could have been worse.

What I couldn't do much about were the muddy stains all down my expensive suit. I dried them off as best as I could but I didn't have the time to extend my magic to the skills of a dry cleaner. So, when I walked into the prefab hut on the abandoned industrial estate, I knew I looked more like a bedraggled beggar than a potential new employee. Or old employee, depending on how you looked at it.

'Saffron!' Jacob was already waiting and extended his arms in an effusive greeting. 'Have you been mud wrestling on your way here?'

I had no choice but to brazen it out. 'Let's say that I was somewhat waylaid and leave it at that.' I offered my old boss a sheepish grin.

'Ah, that will explain why you're late, then.'

I winced. Only by five minutes or so. All the same, I hated that I'd kept him waiting. I desperately wanted to make a good impression and remind Jacob of what an outstanding employee I'd been when I'd worked as a dope faery. 'I'm very sorry,' I told him. 'It was unavoidable.'

'Knowing you as I do,' he said with a broad smile, 'I have no doubt about that.' He pointed towards his office. 'Would you like to come in?'

I exhaled and nodded, grateful that he wasn't about to chide me further. 'Thank you.'

Several other dope faeries were milling around. As we passed, they all looked up and smiled at me with genuine pleasure. I'd forgotten what it was like to work somewhere without worrying about the knives at my back. I could get used to this. I grinned at them then settled on the chair in front of Jacob's desk, waiting while he closed the door to afford us some degree of privacy.

'You're looking good,' I said, meaning every word. 'Have you lost weight?'

He patted his belly. 'I've been eating a lot of green stuff lately,' he admitted. 'Apparently vegetables are better for you than doughnuts.'

I smirked. 'Who knew?'

'Who indeed?' He leaned forward, his expression growing more serious. 'Anyway, it's good to see you, Saffron. I wasn't sure our paths would cross again. However, I've been following your progress at the Office of Faery Godmothers with some interest.'

'Mmmm.' I scratched my neck awkwardly. 'Things didn't work out there quite as I'd hoped they would.' That was putting it mildly.

Jacob regarded me implacably. 'I did try to warn you. The faery godmothers might have a golden reputation but all that glitters isn't gold.' He rarely let a good idiom pass him by. It was good to see that some things hadn't changed.

'Their reputation isn't quite so unblemished now,' I murmured.

'No.' He eyed me curiously. 'The Devil's Advocate has certainly made his opinion of the entire office very clear. From what I hear, his report has set the cat amongst the pigeons.'

I had a burning desire to know exactly what Jasper's report contained. 'I don't suppose you happen to have a copy?' I asked.

Jacob raised an eyebrow. 'I thought from what you said on the phone that you'd left the Office of Faery Godmothers behind you and their future no longer concerned you.'

Heat flared in my cheeks. 'I did say that,' I admitted. 'And I meant it. Call it professional curiosity. It would be interesting to see whether the Devil's Advocate's assessment matches my own.'

And to know what the Director was doing about it. I didn't believe for a second that she would simply roll over and accept whatever Jasper recommended. Not after the lengths she'd gone to when she'd tried to put a halt to his audit. The only way I'd been able to stop her plan was to make sure that Jasper publicly denigrated me and put an end to our association so that his reputation remained unblemished. No matter how much it wrenched at my heart to end it, my relationship with him had been putting him in danger.

Jacob chuckled. 'Relax, Saffron. I'm not trying to put you on the spot or to call you out. I was young and ambitious once, you know. Strange as it may seem.'

This was exactly the opening I needed. 'Speaking of ambition,' I began.

Jacob held his hands up, palms outwards, pre-empting me. 'Let me guess,' he said, his eyes no longer dancing with humour. 'You'd like your old job back.'

I bit my lips and twisted my fingers together in my lap but I maintained eye contact with him. Nervous or not, I wasn't here to play games.

'Yes,' I said. 'I would.' I drew in a breath. 'I was always proud of my achievements as a dope faery. I did the very best by my clients. Now that I've had the opportunity to work at the Office of Faery Godmothers, I'm certain that I've gained new skills that I can put to good use. In fact, if I can tell you about some of my recent experiences then I'm sure you'll see that—'

Jacob grimaced and interrupted me. 'I'm going to stop you right there, Saffron.'

Uh-oh. I had a bad feeling about this.

'Unfortunately,' he said, 'you've become a victim of your own success. When word got around that a dope faery had been promoted to the faery godmothers, we were inundated with applications. There are scores of faeries out there who now see our enterprise as a stepping stone to greater things. Whether that will prove to be true I can't say, but we are stuffed to the gunnels with talented faeries. Much as I would love to have you back, there simply aren't any job openings at the moment. I can't afford you.' He gave me a sympathetic look. 'Maybe in another six months it'll be a different story.'

A wave of desperation flooded my veins. 'I'm prepared to work on a reduced salary,' I said. 'I understand that I can't just swoop in and expect to be reinstated at the same level as before.'

Jacob shook his head. 'I'm truly sorry.'

Fuck a puck. I dropped my head. Fuck. A. Puck. 'I understand,' I mumbled, trying not to think about the growing pile of bills sitting on my coffee table. 'Thank you for your time.' I got to my feet, stumbling slightly as I turned away.

'Saffron, wait,' Jacob said. 'I can still help. I have it on good authority that the dream faeries are recruiting.' He reached towards his desk, opened a drawer and took out a slim envelope. 'I've taken the liberty of writing you a recommendation. I'm sure that, with your experience, they'll be delighted to have you on board. I've arranged for you to meet Winkie Santorini tomorrow. She's their head and an all-round good faery.'

I stared at the envelope. The dream faeries. That didn't sound so bad. It wasn't a million miles away from the other work that I'd done. It might even be fun helping to conjure up sweet dreams and vicious nightmares that would allow humans to make sense of their day-to-day realities. I could be good at that. Hell, I'd be awesome. I was Saffron Sawyer. Right?

I swallowed. 'Thank you, Jacob.'

He nodded at me. 'You're welcome. You have a lot to offer the faery world, Saffron. Don't let anyone tell you otherwise.'

I let myself back into my flat. Before I'd even stepped across the threshold, Pumpkin rushed me, barking and yelping in delight at my return. I bent down and scooped him up, letting him lick my face. Until recently, both of us would have recoiled from such closeness but now the dog and I had reached an understanding, and I liked to think that we both welcomed it.

'Thank you, Pumpkin,' I mumbled into his fur. 'I needed that.'

Vincent wandered out of the kitchen, wearing one of those comedy bodybuilder aprons that displayed a muscular bare chest and tiny red shorts. It looked remarkably incongruous against his scrawny frame. 'Well?' he asked. 'When do you start?'

I put Pumpkin down on the floor and avoided his gaze. 'I didn't get the job,' I said. 'They don't have anything available right now.'

'Oh, Saffy,' he said. 'That's shite.'

Yeah. It was. I sniffed and tilted up my chin. 'It's okay.

Jacob's given me a personal recommendation for the dream faeries. I've got an appointment with them tomorrow so I'm sure something will turn up there.'

'Dream faeries?' he asked dubiously. 'While I can imagine what they do, won't that mean you'll be working nights?'

I shrugged. 'That's okay. I can sleep during the day.'

'Sure. You'll have an outstanding social life too.'

'I need a job, Vincent. I can't afford to be choosy.' It wasn't like I had much of a social life these days anyway.

'You have enough trouble sleeping as it is, Saffy. Those bags under your eyes are so big that you could pack them for a weekend away. I don't think working nights will improve anything.' He shuffled his feet. 'I can pick up more shifts and help out. I'm starting to enjoy being a courier. It's not all that different from drug dealing when you think about it. I run around town and deliver stuff to people in return for money. It's even legal.'

My gaze softened. 'That's very kind of you. But you already do enough shifts and I'm not going to accept your charity.'

'I'm not saying that I'll do it for free. I can give you some of my money and in return you can give me … things.'

'Wishes, you mean.'

'Sure.' He gave me an arch grin. 'If that's all you have to barter with, that's what it'll have to be. I can make the sacrifice.'

'I'm not granting you random wishes, Vincent. It wouldn't be right.' I wagged my finger at him. 'You have to make your own way in the world. You can't rely on magic. It's another form of dependence that will do you more harm than good in the long run. Look at what you've already achieved without making any wishes. You've got a job, steady income, new friends. You're now a functioning member of society and you achieved that all on your own merits.'

'Is that why you won't magic yourself up some money?' he enquired. 'Because you want to prove you have merits too?'

'Using magic to improve my situation would be wrong,' I said primly. 'I have morals.' Well, I tried to have them though recent history might suggest otherwise.

Vincent gave me a long look. 'Morals don't fill your belly. They're sugar free, calorie free and therefore entirely pointless.'

'You don't believe that any more than I do.'

'I'm a drug dealer!' he protested. 'I have no morals! I've got a criminal record longer than Pumpkin's tail to prove it!'

I glanced down at the tail in question. Yes, it was wagging enthusiastically. It was also incredibly short and stubby – and Vincent knew it. 'Go you,' I murmured. 'I won't change my mind though. I'll get a job with the dream faeries and all will be well.'

Vincent sighed. 'I've heard that sort of thing before.' He unhooked the apron from round his neck and hung it up behind the door. 'Anyway, I've cooked you some of my special Bolognese for dinner. All you have to do is heat it up and cook the pasta. I've got to head out to work. Pumpkin has been walked and watered. I'll pop by again tomorrow and take him out when you're off with the dreamy ones.'

I might have had a crappy morning but I suddenly felt the cockles of my heart warming. 'Thank you, Vincent.'

'I'm your slave,' he answered with a fake pout. 'I have to do it.'

I sighed in mock exasperation. 'You're not my slave. The magic that binds you to me only works when I make a direct request of you. And I didn't ask you to make me dinner. You did it because you're a good guy.'

He looked alarmed. 'Hush! Don't say that so loudly! Someone might hear you.'

I grinned and reached forward to hug him. 'Thank you,' I repeated. I meant it wholeheartedly.

'You're welcome,' he murmured into my ear. 'And when you change your mind about granting me a wish…'

I drew back and nudged him away. 'You don't need any wishes. You're doing great all on your own.'

For a moment his expression remained serious. 'Only thanks to you, Saffron.' Pumpkin whined. 'And you, dog.'

I smiled. 'Love you, Vinnie. You're the best.'

He winked at me. 'I know.' He ambled to the door and opened it, peering out. 'Your new neighbour has finally moved in next door,' he said. 'I bumped into him in the hallway earlier. Seems kinda shifty. Don't worry, though – I warned him off. He won't be bothering you.'

Oh no. 'Vincent,' I demanded, 'what did you say?'

He turned his head, blinking innocently. 'I'm just looking out for you, Saffy.'

I passed a hand in front of my eyes. 'I can look after myself.'

'Not right now you can't,' he replied pointedly. Then he grinned. 'Catch you tomorrow!' He shoved his hands into his pockets and sloped off, whistling.

I looked down at Pumpkin, who was pawing at my leg in a bid for more attention. 'I guess we'll have to go round and make amends to the new bloke for whatever Vincent said to him.'

Pumpkin gazed up at me with his large chocolate-brown eyes.

'You're right,' I agreed. 'We'll do it later.' I deserved a cup of tea first. Followed by several stiff shots of tequila. It was gone midday, after all. I closed the door and headed inside.

THREE SHEETS to the wind later, I tripped outside with Pumpkin in tow. The wee dog was good for more than one thing. No matter how much ill-advised booze I tipped down my throat, I couldn't loll around on my sofa and feel sorry for myself all afternoon before slipping into a drool-fest coma. Not when Pumpkin needed his walkies.

It was just as well. Drinking alone accomplished little more than making me feel very bad about myself. I'd yelled at the wall, thrown around a few cushions and allowed myself several noisy sobs. I should have stuck to tea. But then there were a lot of things I should have done recently and I'd not managed any of them.

'Well, hello there,' drawled an unfamiliar Home Counties voice as I stumbled towards the stairs. 'You must be Saffron. I didn't expect to have a new neighbour quite as lovely looking as you. I'm Ben.'

Pumpkin immediately sprang into action, launching himself in front of my feet in a bid to protect my shoes before baring his teeth in a sharp growl. I blinked blearily, trying to work out whether the bloke was taking the piss about my appearance because I looked like a dishevelled drunk. Was he trying to suck up so that I'd happily spend the rest of his neighbourly tenure collecting his post for him? Or was he merely being nice? Probably the former, I decided, as he reached into his pocket and pulled out a dog treat. That was handy.

Pumpkin immediately ceased growling and began to dance at my feet in expectant joy. Capricious mutt.

'Hi.' I peered at my new neighbour as he gave Pumpkin the treat. He was younger than I'd expected and considerably better looking. That didn't endear him to me but, for the sake of neighbourly harmony, I supposed I ought to stick with my earlier plan and play nice. 'Sorry about my friend earlier. I hope he wasn't rude to you.'

'You mean Vincent? Goodness, no! He was perfectly charming. What a lovely chap.'

Alright: if I hadn't been suspicious before, I was definitely suspicious now. I loved Vincent to bits but he was about as far removed from charming as a rattlesnake.

Ben also seemed enamoured of the word 'lovely'. I was not feeling any loveliness, not at this particular moment in time. I was, however, feeling woozy and rather pathetic.

I straightened my shoulders. I wouldn't let this situation get the better of me. I was Saffron Sawyer, faery extraordinaire. I would continue to fight fire with fire and dance rings round this man.

'Good,' I said, in an overly loud voice. 'I think you'll find we're all lovely round here. You seem lovely yourself. You'll fit right into this lovely building with all its lovely people.' Then I grimaced. I was pretty certain I was slurring every second word and swaying from side to side. I tried to force myself to maintain my balance. 'Lovely,' I finished lamely.

If Ben was put off by my inebriated state, he didn't show it. 'You're definitely my kind of person,' he beamed. 'We're going to get on like a house on fire.'

I stared at him. Either he'd sprouted two heads, or I was seeing double. I squinted and shook my head slightly but it didn't help. 'As long as it's not this house that's on fire.'

He threw back his head and laughed. 'Indeed, Saffron! Indeed!'

Good ol' Ben was far too cheery.

'So tell me,' he smiled, 'what do you do? Do you work from home?'

The last thing I wanted to do was chat about my lack of employment. 'I'm between jobs,' I said. I lifted my chin. 'But I have an interview tomorrow.'

He clapped his hands. 'Fantastic! For what?'

'Er, you won't have heard of them. It's a company that helps people ... sleep.'

His grin spread even wider. 'Lovely!'

Yep. Definitely too cheery.

'Well,' I said, as the clickety-clack sound of another pair of shoes at the far end of the hallway reached my ears, 'I've got to get this one out for some fresh air. Have a ... lovely day.' I half-turned, caught sight of the new arrival and frowned. Now I really was seeing things.

'Good afternoon, Saffron,' Alicia called. She tossed her gleaming blonde hair like a model in a shampoo advert and smiled at me. I backed up, staggering against Ben as I did so.

'Tell me,' I muttered in a low voice, 'is there a scary-looking blonde woman heading this way?'

'No,' he answered, his eyes wide. 'There is a gorgeous-looking blonde woman, though.'

Fuck a puck. A hallucination would be preferable. I forced myself upright again and managed a fake smile. 'Alicia, what a wonderful surprise. Don't tell me you're moving into this building as well.'

A look of horrified disgust crossed her face. 'Don't be ridiculous, Saffron.' She glanced down at Pumpkin. 'Hello again, dog.'

Pumpkin arched his head towards me with an anxious whine. He clearly wasn't happy about this bizarre turn of events. Neither was I. Ben, however, was ecstatic.

'Well, hello there!' He thrust out his hand in Alicia's direction. 'I'm Ben. How lovely to meet you! You must be a friend of Saffron's.'

Alicia's lip curled and she gazed down at his outstretched hand until he withdrew it.

'Don't mind her,' I told him. 'She's got a terribly contagious flesh-eating disease, so she has to avoid physical contact with others at all times.'

Ben blinked. Alicia rolled her eyes. 'I see your attempts at humour are continuing, Saffron. I suppose I should take that as a good sign.' Then her nose wrinkled and she leaned in, sniffing the air. 'Have you been drinking? You smell like a brewery.'

What I did in my own time had nothing to do with her. 'Yesh.' I cleared my throat and tried again. 'I mean, yes. So what? I'm an adult, Alicia, I can do what I want. It's not like I have to be at work,' I added pointedly.

Ben's head swung from Alicia to me and back again. 'I've got boxes to unpack,' he said, his expression clearly stating that he'd decided it was safer to get out of this conversation while he still could, despite the glamorous vision that was Alicia. 'I'd better get on. It really was lovely to meet you both.'

'Lovely,' I muttered.

'Lovely,' she said, her face suggesting it had been anything but.

He smiled, raised his hand and waved an exuberant farewell before disappearing towards his own apartment.

I waited until he'd gone before quirking an eyebrow at Alicia. 'What can I do for you?' I asked. 'Because if you're here on the Director's say-so then—'

'She's got nothing to do with me being here.' Alicia reached into her designer handbag and drew out a heavy, embossed envelope. 'I merely popped round to give you this.'

I gazed stupidly at the envelope, wondering if it contained some sort of poison. 'What is it?'

'An invitation. Take it.' She thrust it at me, giving me no choice.

I held it gingerly between my finger and thumb. The scent of rosewater wafted upwards. Maybe it had been applied liberally to the paper to disguise the smell of arsenic. Or whatever.

Alicia tutted. 'It won't bite you,' she said. 'It's for a soirée my family is having on Saturday night. I would like you to be there.'

I looked up at her in astonishment. 'Why?'

'Because I wish for you to attend, Saffron,' she explained as if I were incredibly dense. 'I came round in person, as I suspected you would ignore it if I simply posted it. It's important that you come along and I expect to see you there.'

Several responses popped into my head, none of them polite. 'The Devil's Advocate is not my boyfriend, Alicia,' I said. 'So if you're hoping that by inviting me you'll encourage him to attend, you're sadly mistaken.'

Her brow wrinkled. 'This has nothing to do with that man. Come alone. Or come with someone else. I don't care. I just need you to come.'

My life was bad enough at the moment without having to go to a party hosted by Alicia. 'I'm really very busy right now. I doubt I'll manage to make it.'

'You will come.'

I folded my arms, crumpling the invitation in the process. 'I will n—'

'If you won't come for me,' Alicia interrupted, 'come for Figgy. Before she died, she invited you to a party that she never had chance to hold. So come to this in her memory instead.'

I immediately swallowed my words. That wasn't fair. Figgy might have been Alicia's best friend, at least at the Office of Faery Godmothers, and she might have been killed as an inadvertent result of my actions, but Alicia couldn't hold her death over my head. Not for a damned party, anyway.

She had already begun to walk away, her job seemingly done. 'Oh, and Saffron?' she called out over her shoulder. 'It would be a good idea if you were to leave the dog at home and arrive sober.' She wiggled her fingers in a gesture of farewell and clickety-clacked away. 'See you there!'

I looked down at Pumpkin, who was gazing up at me. He raised a tentative paw in my direction. 'Don't look at me,' I told him. 'I don't understand it any more than you do.' I sighed and shoved the envelope into my pocket without opening it. 'Come on,' I said, putting the bizarre encounter behind me and moving once again, narrowly avoiding a collision with the wall as I did so. Walking in a straight line really is a lot harder than a person might think.

CHAPTER

THREE

A normal person might well have felt remorse for spending the better part of the previous day with little more than a dog and a bottle of tequila for company but I had far weightier things to regret. Getting pissed and making a fool of myself with my new neighbour didn't come close to my other recent actions. Given that I'd somehow escaped even a vague hangover, and I'd woken early enough to tame my usual frizz into compliance while also washing, drying and perfectly ironing yesterday's suit, I wasn't going to fret about my behaviour.

Today was a new day. I would dazzle the dream faeries with my brilliance and start a whole new chapter of my life. Pumpkin seemed to agree, giving me an enthusiastic lick before I left home. The job would be a shoo-in.

I wasn't sure what to expect of the dream faeries' headquarters. The Office of Faery Godmothers was all high-end glamour and sophistication, with gleaming marbled floors and opulent furnishings. The dope faeries, who were drastically underfunded, were housed in far less salubrious buildings hidden away at the back of a derelict building site. I imagined that the dream faeries would be somewhere in between, in a large building neither as luxurious as the godmothers' nor as rundown as the dope faeries'.

What I hadn't expected was to find myself navigating dark, subterranean tunnels underneath the busy Colchester streets. And I certainly hadn't envisioned needing a guide to find my way. However, the quiet dream faery who'd been waiting for me at the first tunnel's entrance assured me that I'd no hope of reaching the inner sanctum on my own. Once we began winding our way through various gloomy twists and turns, I realised she was right. The place was a warren of caverns, both large and small, and there were no helpful markings or sign-posts to point the way.

When I asked why they didn't rent somewhere that allowed for fresher air and brighter light, all I received was a baffled shrug. Honestly, the echoing sound of random drips splashing into black puddles was already driving me mad.

After what seemed like an interminable journey, although when I checked my watch it was less than a quarter of an hour, we reached a nondescript stainless-steel door. It opened apparently of its own accord as we approached, revealing a surprisingly comfortable interior. While there still wasn't any natural light, the place was suffused with a warm glow. The air was scented with lavender and I was amused to note that there were several day beds and hammocks dotted about, probably to add a reminder that the dream faeries' work demanded sleep.

My guide led me to the front desk. The man behind it was wearing a blue-and-white striped suit. If it hadn't been for the embroidered name tag on his chest, I'd have assumed he'd simply forgotten to get dressed that morning.

'This is Saffron Sawyer,' my guide said. She nodded once, remaining stubbornly taciturn even with her colleague, before departing.

'Hey!' He gave me a warm smile. 'I'm Bryan. We've been expecting you, Saffron. Please take a seat and someone will be with you shortly. Can I get you a drink while you wait?'

This was more like it. I smiled at him. 'Coffee would be great.'

Bryan winced. 'Caffeine isn't allowed, I'm afraid. We have herbal tea and hot chocolate, though.'

I didn't miss a beat. 'Oh, I'd been hoping for decaf coffee,' I said, knowing that I wouldn't touch the stuff if I were given a choice. But I was prepared to drink hot milk with a cookie like a child if that's what it took to make a good impression. 'But chamomile tea would be amazing.'

Bryan relaxed almost immediately. 'I can see why you think we'd serve decaf,' he said kindly. 'But Winkie thinks that the psychological effects of decaf coffee are almost as bad as the physical effects of *real* coffee, so we steer clear of it. Don't worry, I'll rustle you up a wee chamomile brew in moments.'

I murmured my thanks and sat down on the nearest chair. It was covered in a soft, soothing material and was so squishy that I could feel my body sinking into it. Everything about this place was designed to be as soporific as possible. It was disturbing but only, I decided, because it was unfamiliar; I could get used to anything if I had to. I desperately needed a job and I was more than prepared to throw myself into the world of dreams if it meant I could pay my bills. Besides, there was something so calming about this place that I reckoned it would do wonders for my equilibrium.

I'd almost finished my tea and was growing drowsier by the second when a tall woman appeared. She was holding a clipboard and possessed a business-like air that totally contradicted the onesie she was wearing. I was liking the dream faeries more and more.

'Saffron Sawyer?' she asked, in a faintly Irish accent.

I threw myself upwards. My display of energy was out of place but there was no way I was getting out of that chair without a serious burst of effort. I smiled widely. 'Yes! That's me!'

She smiled at me in return, her eyes crinkling at the edges. 'I'm Laura, one of the Assistant Managers around here. I'm sorry to have kept you waiting.'

I reached forward and shook her hand. So far so good. 'It's lovely to meet you. And please don't apologise. It's been no time at all. Thank you so much for this opportunity.'

I was being entirely sincere and Laura seemed to recognise it. She squeezed my hand briefly in gentle reassurance before releasing it. 'We're ready for you now. Please follow me.'

I bobbed my head enthusiastically and tripped after her as she led me down a narrow tunnel. I could see rooms to my left and right, each of which contained an assortment of beds, comfortable chairs and hammocks. Some were occupied by twitching faeries who were slumbering as they wove their magic, but most were empty.

'We don't tend to be busy at this time of day,' Laura told me, noting my interest. 'But there are more people than you'd think who require attention. Night-shift workers, anyone who's sick, that sort of thing.'

I craned my neck to peer round each doorway. 'So dream faeries have to be asleep to weave their magic?'

'Oh yes.' She shot me a side glance. 'A lot of new starts seem to think that it's easy because you have to doze off in order to do your job – but it's not restful. Far from it. Everyone you see who is under is working tremendously hard.'

'I like working hard,' I said honestly. 'I find it fulfilling.'

Laura grinned. 'Then I'm sure you'll fit right in.' She turned left and walked into a smaller room set up with a desk, several chairs and a narrow bed. Laura pointed me towards one of the empty chairs facing the desk and she took her place next to two other dream faeries.

'This is Saffron,' she said by way of introduction. She gestured to the others. 'This is Mark, the other Assistant Manager, and Winkie.'

Winkie, who had one of those timeless faces that suggested she could be anything between forty and seventy years of age, nodded at me. 'It's nice to meet you, Saffron. You come highly recommended. Jacob had nothing but good things to say about you.'

I breathed out and reminded myself to smile. 'Thank you. I appreciate that.'

'So why don't you tell us why you're interested in working for the dream faeries?'

I swallowed hard and met her eyes. 'I won't pretend that it's always been a lifelong dream,' I said carefully, unwilling to lie. 'But I've always admired your work and the service that you provide. In a sense, what you do combines all the skills that I've learnt in my previous jobs. I truly loved helping my clients when I was both a dope faery and a faery godmother, and the dedication that the dream faeries clearly have is something that fills me with joy. It's obviously a careful balance between psychological care and wish fulfilment.'

Winkie's brow furrowed. 'How so?'

'Dream faeries walk into that subconscious part of human beings that they're often not even aware of themselves. You use your magic to help them sort through their previous waking hours, which is what the dope faeries help with, and to prepare for the next hours – which is essentially the work the faery godmothers do.'

Her expression cleared and she smiled in a way that told me I'd said exactly the right thing. 'That's an interesting way of looking at things,' she murmured. 'And quite accurate.'

The male faery leaned forward, resting his chin on his hands. 'Some faeries find our offices claustrophobic and struggle to work effectively underground.'

I was prepared for this; I'd had some time to think about it while I'd been waiting in reception. 'Actually,' I said, 'it makes perfect sense. The twisting journey here is a clever reminder of how we have to weave through darkness before we can wield our magic.'

He exchanged a glance with Winkie, who nodded approvingly. 'There aren't many faeries who understand the symbolism of that. Well done.'

This was going far better than I'd hoped. I opened my mouth to continue but, before I could breathe a word, there was a knock at the door. Bryan, the faery from the front desk, popped his head round. 'Winkie, there's someone here to see you.'

'Ask them to wait. I'll be out once we're done here.'

His face twisted. 'Actually, I think you should come now,' he said, without looking in my direction. 'Your visitor is ... important.'

There was something ominous about the note in his voice and I felt an uncomfortable shiver run down my spine. All the same, I smiled pleasantly as Winkie got to her feet. 'I won't be long,' she promised, then stepped out of the small room.

There were a few beats of silence. I could tell that Laura and Mark were curious about what was going on. They weren't the only ones.

In a bid to break the awkward atmosphere, I started to babble. 'I'm far from fault free,' I said, 'but I do learn from my mistakes and I'm very much a team player.'

Laura pulled her eyes away from the door and fixed them on me. 'That's important,' she said. 'Dream faeries will often find themselves paired up when we have more complex clients to deal with.' She gestured towards the bed. 'How do you feel right now? Will you be able to sleep? We have a test client ready and waiting. We don't expect miracles, but it would be good to see how you'd approach someone and what your instincts are like.'

It was just as well I'd not had that coffee. I nodded and stood up, hoping that I'd drift off fairly easily so that I could enter the dream world and show them what I was capable of.

'If you lie down and close your eyes,' Laura instructed, while pulling out an unvarnished but clearly well-worn magical wand, 'I'll direct you to where you need to be. It feels a bit strange the first time you do it, but you'll soon get used to it.'

I did as she instructed, my eyelids fluttering shut at the very moment I heard the door open again.

'You don't need to do that,' Winkie said. Her voice was tight. 'I think we've got everything we need for now.'

I opened my eyes and sat up. She looked pale. 'Is everything alright?' I asked.

'It's fine. We'll look over everything and be in touch in the next week or so.'

Both Laura and Mark looked surprised and Winkie was avoiding my gaze. Fuck a puck. What had gone wrong? I'd barely started.

'I'll escort you out,' Laura said.

'Winkie,' I began. 'If I can just...'

'Thank you for your time, Ms Sawyer.' She turned away and my heart sank.

Standing up and inwardly cursing, I traipsed after Laura as we headed out to the main reception area. At first I could only see Bryan, his back ramrod straight and his expression serious. Then I spotted the other figure in the room.

'Good day, Saffron,' the Director intoned. 'What a surprise to see you here.'

I stiffened. Clearly, it wasn't any surprise at all. 'Hello,' I said, folding my arms. 'How are things with you?' And then, because I couldn't help myself, 'Are you enjoying implementing the recommendations from the Devil's Advocate's report?'

Fury sparked in the Director's eyes but she masked it quickly. 'The Office of Faery Godmothers will always aspire to be the best it can be. It's why we only have the crème de la crème of faeries work with us. We don't allow failures.'

If she was trying to suggest that was the reason why I was no longer a faery godmother, she was forgetting that I'd resigned. I hadn't been sacked. 'Yes,' I murmured, 'you do indeed have genuine success stories working for you.' I spoke without a trace of sarcasm but I knew she'd got my message from the way her spine stiffened.

Sensing that the situation was about to get out of hand, Laura stepped in hastily. 'The exit is this way, Saffron.'

I wanted to stay where I was. The desire to make a scene and get into the Director's face was overwhelming. She was obviously the reason why I was being thrown out of the dream faeries' domain before my interview had even really begun. The Director was determined to see me firmly squashed into the dirt for not acceding to her blackmail.

I took a deep breath. And then I remembered that I was a better person.

'Thank you, Laura,' I said. 'I can find my own way out.'

I ignored the flash of triumph in the Director's eyes and walked away. I wasn't defeated, I told myself. I wasn't going to lose my head over this. I'd beaten her at her own game before and this war was still far from over.

CHAPTER
FOUR

Harry was worried. I could see it in the way he spoke to me and the expression in his eyes. Hell, his concern was all but seeping out of his pores. 'There might be something coming up with the rainbow faeries,' he said, twisting his fingers together anxiously.

Both of us knew I didn't have the temperament to be a rainbow faery. They were all sweetness and light; my edges were considerably harsher.

'It doesn't matter,' I muttered into my almost empty glass. 'Whatever job I try to get, the Director will put a stop to it. Clearly all it takes is a few well-placed words and,' I clicked my fingers, 'hey presto! I'm out on my ear. Jacob probably lied to me and was under pressure to keep me out.'

Harry shook his head. 'He wouldn't have recommended you to the dream faeries if that were the case.'

'It's not paranoia,' I said softly, 'if they're really out to get you.'

He ran a hand through his hair and sighed. 'Why would the Director care? It's all over with. You left.'

'I'm the one who put a stop to her scheming,' I answered.

'She could have avoided Jasper's report if it hadn't been for me. She wants her revenge. And she has to be the one who sent that damned three-breasted abomination after me.' A shiver ran down my spine. 'She's that kind of person.' My shoulders sank. 'The trouble is that she's winning. All the other faery departments kowtow to her. I bet even the sewage faeries won't take me now.'

'Go to Jasper,' Harry urged. 'Tell him the truth about what happened.'

'Should I tell him that I can now use magic without a wand, just like he can?'

'Yes!'

'And,' I said, 'should I tell him that I lied to him? That I pretended I didn't want to be with him because I wanted to protect him? Because if I do that, I should also tell him what the Director is really like. And you know what he'll do then.'

Harry reached across the scratched wooden table and took my hands. 'He's the Devil's Advocate. He can look after himself. He would want to know.'

'If I tell him the truth, he'll confront the Director. And you and I both know that she'll already be prepared for that eventuality. She'll do whatever it takes to bring him down and I will *not* allow that to happen. He might have powerful magic but he's far more vulnerable than he lets on. Jasper,' my voice cracked slightly when I said his name, 'needs to be protected.'

'He's not a child, Saffron,' Harry said.

'No,' I interrupted. 'Neither am I. I need to adult up and deal with my problems face on. Without involving Jasper. If the Director won't let me pick up the pieces of my life and move on, then I need to take action against her.'

A faint look of alarm crossed his face. 'Is that wise?'

I sniffed. 'I was always going to do something about her. I just didn't know what and I was biding my time until an effective solution presented itself. Now she's forced my hand. If she's trying to ruin my life, I'll work harder to expose her. Then Jasper will understand everything that's happened and everything I've done.' I lifted up my chin and acted like I didn't care. 'And if he doesn't, so be it.'

'Saffron, you know I'm on your side. I will *always* be on your side. But she's the Director of the Faery Godmothers. She's got every resource at her fingertips. Maybe you need to let it go.'

I drained my glass and slammed it down hard onto the table. 'I don't have a job. I don't have any prospects. That means I've got all the time in the world. I either use it to continue getting sloshed out of my mind in the middle of the day, or I use it to bring down the Director. I'm going to make sure she pays for what she's done.'

I forced a humourless smile in the direction of my best friend. 'Watch. This. Space.' Then I nodded farewell, stood up and walked out of the Stagger Inn. I'd start now. There was no time like the present.

As soon as the cold air hit me, the futility of my situation smacked me in the face. My only friends were a powerless rainbow faery, a chubby Jack Russell and an ex-drug dealer. I was on the periphery of the faery world and my situation was dire. The Director had power and influence and I had ... nothing.

Uncalled magic crackled at my fingertips and I bunched up my fists and stuffed them under my armpits. I was like a cornered animal. I'd been racking my brains for the last few weeks, trying to think of a way to bring the Director to justice. I wouldn't do it by feeling sorry for myself, however. I was...

The back of my neck started to prickle again. Fuck a puck. Not this. Not again. I bared my teeth in a snarl. Well, if the Director was sending magical conjurations after me in a bid to end my existence, maybe I could turn the tables and use them against her. I'd wanted proof of her nefarious scheming.

Perhaps this would do the trick. It was dangerous – but it could be worth it.

The traffic lights at the crossroads ahead changed and a few cars trundled towards me. A couple, heads bowed together as they giggled, were strolling along the opposite side of the street. This was not the place. The alleyway I'd been in by the cinema had been the perfect opportunity but I'd not been in a position to take it. Now I had all the time in the world.

There were no deserted side streets in this area. There was, however, an old cemetery not too far away. It would be the perfect spot.

Grimly determined, I veered left, mapping out what I knew of the cemetery in my head. I'd always found it quite a peaceful spot rather than a depressing one, and I'd often stopped there to take a few minutes out of my day. I knew there was a large tomb in the far corner and an ancient willow tree not far from it. Both of them would provide all the cover I needed to set my trap.

Picking up speed, I crossed the road and jumped over the low railings. In this dim light, the gravestones were casting long shadows and there was an eerie glow from the moon. In theory, I was cornered and pretty much defenceless. Only Vincent and Harry – and possibly Mrs Jardine – knew that I no longer required a wand to use magic. The Director might have her suspicions after I'd bested her bizarre conjuration yesterday, but I doubted she genuinely expected me to possess the magic that I did. This was my chance to take full advantage of that ignorance.

I wove my way along the uneven path and ducked down in the shadows to wait between the tomb and the tree. All I had to do was capture whatever magical beast was after me and find a way to bind it to prevent the Director from either recalling it or destroying it. Then I could take it to other faeries as evidence that she was attacking me. They'd be able to trace its conjuration back to her. It wouldn't be absolute proof of her manipulations but it would certainly plant a seed of doubt. Right now, that was the best I could hope for.

I didn't have long to wait. A few minutes after I'd hunkered down on the cold ground, a shape appeared at the cemetery gates. I squinted through the gloom, trying to make out what it was and what sort of fight I could expect. Whatever this conjuration was, it wasn't endowed with any great sense. It took a while to work out that the railings were low enough to jump over and spent an inordinate amount of time fiddling with the rusty catch on the cemetery gate. When it swung open with a grating creak, I was more than ready.

The Director was obviously hedging her bets with this incantation. It might be dark but she had to be wary that her spell would be spotted by some passing humans; that was the reason she'd created something that looked more normal.

The thing was wearing a baseball cap and a long coat. No doubt as soon as it was sure we were alone, it would sweep off both and reveal its true nature. Whether it was the creature from the black lagoon or a vicious, sharp-toothed Yeti, I would deal with it.

It stepped forward, its breath clouding as it huffed and puffed in the cool night air. I tensed my shoulders. No doubt it could sense that I was near, even if it couldn't see me. All I needed was for it to draw a little closer...

My fingertips were already tingling, the magic threatening to spill forth at any moment. I held my nerve. Come on, little monster. Just a few more steps.

The figure shuffled forward, its head swinging every which way as its eyes tried to pierce the darkness and locate me. It wasn't as tall as the three-breasted abomination but that didn't mean it wasn't dangerous. I waited until it was less than five metres away, then I sucked in a breath and flicked my wrists.

This wasn't something that I'd practised before but I was reasonably confident that I could make it work. Within a few heartbeats, a glowing net of pure magic arced upwards, billowing out over the creature's head. I twisted my index finger and the net dropped like a stone, encasing the figure from head to toe. It let out a sharp cry and fell forwards, writhing in a bid to free itself. The net held fast, pinning it to the ground.

I gave a self-satisfied nod and stood up. That had been easier than I'd expected. Then, however, the creature spoke. 'Get off me! Get off me! What the fuck is going on?'

I squinted and frowned. Surely not. I tilted my head. 'Rupert?'

'Saffron, help me! Something's trapped me! I'm in serious danger!' he yelped, still squirming to get free. His voice rose, matching his panic. 'You have to save meeeee!'

Huh. I didn't take Rupert seriously, either as a threat or as a faery, but I wasn't entirely stupid. Until I knew exactly what was going on and why he was following me, I wasn't taking any chances.

I strode forward, being careful to stop before the toes of my shoes reached the edge of the magical net, and looked down. 'What are you doing here, Rupert?'

'Get me out of heeeeeere!' He was reaching fever pitch. The more his arms and legs flailed, however, the more entrapped he became. He couldn't even stretch down to reach his wand. The net wasn't designed for a faery but it was good to know that it worked this effectively.

I allowed myself a pleasing image of the Director snared in the same fashion before re-focusing. 'Stop struggling, Rupert,' I told him calmly. 'You'll only make it worse.'

He stared at me wild-eyed. 'Saffron,' he gasped. 'Something

did this to me. You should run before it gets you too. Leave me here and save yourself.'

I blinked. Well, I certainly hadn't expected that. 'I thought you wanted me to save you.'

'You don't have a wand. You're completely powerless. There's nothing you can do except abandon me to my fate.' A tear trickled down his cheek. 'Tell my parents that I love them. Tell them I died a hero.'

Oh for goodness' sake. This was too pathetic for words. I rolled my eyes and flicked out a burst of magic to remove the net.

Rupert didn't appear to realise that he was free. 'My little brother can have my car,' he said mournfully. 'It's the only thing I have that's of any value and I know he covets it.'

I sighed. 'Rupert...'

'My sister can have the portrait of me that's hanging in my room. She can use it to remember me by.'

'Rupert, look around yourself. You're free. The net's gone.'

'I want to be cremated,' he continued, blithely unaware of what I was telling him. 'I wasn't meant to be confined in a coffin and used as worm food. Not with these cheekbones.'

I gave him a quick but sharp kick in the ribs.

'Ow!' He curled up, protecting himself while glaring at me. 'Why did you do that? I'm about to die and you're making it worse! You're taking advantage of...' His words trailed off and he glanced round, finally realising that the net had gone. 'Oh.' He leapt to his feet and brushed himself off. 'I'm free!'

'Yes, Rupert,' I said drily. 'You are.' I stepped towards him. I wasn't about to let him wander off again. I needed answers. 'Now, let's start again. What are you doing here and why were you following me?'

Rupert stretched out his arms and spun round, savouring his liberty. Then his eyes widened and he quickly took out his phone to check his appearance. He spent a good few moments fiddling with his supposedly artless fringe before nodding and looking at me.

'We should be careful, Saffron,' he said in all seriousness. 'It's spooky here and something is after me. You don't have to worry. I'll protect you.' He glanced behind him and let out a delicate shudder. 'Whatever threw that net over me is probably still nearby.'

I tapped my foot. 'Rupert, I swear that if you don't start answering my questions, I'll feed you to the next beastie that comes along.'

He evinced total surprise. 'What's got your goat?'

'Why are you here?' I bit out.

'I wanted to talk to you. You're not an easy person to track down, you know. I tried to get hold of you yesterday but you ran away.'

My eyes narrowed. 'What do you mean you tried to get hold of me yesterday?'

He shrugged. 'I sent out an incantation. I couldn't be sure if worked properly. I'm using my grandfather's old wand,' he swished it in the air for effect, 'but it's not always reliable.'

'You sent that ... woman after me?' Suddenly it was starting to make sense. If I'd stopped to think about it, I might have worked it out for myself. Who else would create something that had three breasts?

'Yes.' He nodded proudly. 'Wasn't she amazing?'

The least said about her, the better. Something else occurred to me. 'Wait,' I said, 'why aren't you using your own wand?'

He splayed out his hands. 'I thought you knew. I've been sacked.' He motioned towards me. 'Both of us are the same. We're both victims of the Office of Faery Godmothers.' He leaned in. 'It's because we were both trying to modernise the place. The sexism there is rife! Obviously it's so far ingrained that the Director preferred to sack me rather than deal with the truth.' He shook his head. 'I was fired simply because I tried to encourage everyone to use the word godfather where necessary. This world has no space for equality. It's a sad, sad day, Saffron.'

He looked me up and down. 'I have to say,' he said, changing tack abruptly, 'you look sexy as hell in that outfit. More cleavage would be better though.' He reached towards my blouse as if to undo a few buttons. I stepped back in the nick of time. Unbelievable.

'Shit.' Rupert's face fell. 'I'm so sorry. I'm trying really hard not to do that kind of thing but old habits are hard to break, you know?'

'No,' I snapped. 'I don't know.'

He appeared even more dismayed. 'I'm a fuck up.' His head dropped.

I wasn't going to argue with that. Besides, I had far better things to do than worry about Rupert. This had been a complete waste of time. 'I have to go,' I said. 'Don't bother me again, Rupert. You were fired but I resigned. We don't have anything in common except that we're both unemployed. No more conjurations, no more following me home. Just stay away. Got that?'

He gazed at me and his face crumpled. 'But ... but...' His bottom lip was quivering. 'I'm all on my own. I can't go home. My parents already think I'm a failure. When they found out I'd been relegated to the Adventus room and I wasn't allowed to have my own clients, they were mortified. If they find out I've been sacked, they'll disown me.'

'Rupert, I'm sorry about that but there's nothing I can do—'

'Let me hang around with you for a while!' He clutched at my arm. 'You're strong and powerful and you don't care what other people think. If I can learn to be more like you, maybe I can face my parents with the truth.'

Even if I trusted what Rupert was telling me, I didn't like him enough to have him following me around like a horny puppy. Truthfully, I didn't like him at all. 'Rupert...'

'It would only be for a couple of weeks,' he begged. 'Until I sort myself out. You're the only person who's ever been honest with me, Saffron. You called me out for being inappropriate in the office and I've learned so much from that.'

He hadn't learned enough, otherwise he wouldn't have sent that half-naked conjuration after me and wouldn't have made that sleazy remark less than a minute earlier.

Rupert seemed to know what I was thinking. 'I know I can be even better,' he said earnestly. 'To prove myself, I brought you something I thought you'd like.' He reached into his coat pocket and pulled out a wad of paper. 'It's the report. The one the Devil's Advocate wrote. I thought you might want to read it.'

I did. I moved to take it from him but he snatched it away. 'You can have it if you let me be your friend for a while.' He sniffed loudly. 'I don't have many real friends.'

I folded my arms and told myself that I didn't feel sorry for him. Rupert had made his own bed and was responsible for his own actions. Besides, I could probably get a copy of Jasper's report elsewhere if I tried hard enough. I didn't have to rely on Rupert to satisfy my curiosity. But there was something about the hangdog look in his eyes that wrenched my heart... Not much, but enough to make me a soft touch. When it came down to it, it seemed I was more of an idiot than he was.

'Fine,' I said. 'You can hang around for a couple of weeks.' His face started to transform. 'But,' I said quickly, 'you do everything that I tell you. *Everything*. Got that?'

He nodded eagerly. 'Of course, Saffron.'

I was probably going to regret this. I had enough problems without collecting waifs and strays along the way. Rupert moved forward, his arms outstretched as he attempted to draw me in for a grateful kiss. I held up my hands, barring his approach. Scratch that.

I was definitely going to regret this.

'No touching, Rupert. No touching me, no touching anyone else. Not unless they touch you first – and even then you have to think about what you're doing and not overdo it.'

'Okay.' He nodded vigorously. 'No touching. I can manage that.' He muttered it under his breath several times like a mantra. 'No touching. No touching.'

It really wasn't that hard to remember. 'Can I have the report, Rupert?'

'Yes.' He passed it over, his fingers brushing against mine. He leapt back. 'Sorry!'

I frowned at him. His eyes had a glint of mischief that told me everything I needed to know. Rupert wasn't as dumb as he pretended to be. Or as needy. For some reason, though, I believed that he was trying to improve himself. Or maybe I just wanted to believe that.

'Can I come home with you now?' he begged. 'I really need some rest.'

Whoa. 'Can't you go to your own home?'

His mouth drooped again. 'I live with my parents. I've been doing my best to avoid them but sooner or later I'll have to talk to them. If they see me, they'll ask me how things are going at work and I'll have to tell them I've been fired. I can't lie, Saffron.' He clasped his hands together as if in prayer. 'Please? I can sleep on your sofa. You won't know I'm there.'

I doubted that very much. But Rupert might have his uses. If he continued to send magical conjurations after me and tail me through the streets, maybe it was better that I knew where he was so I could keep an eye on him. Maybe I deserved this after the havoc I'd wreaked on the office … but I had to draw a line somewhere.

'No. You cannot stay with me.'

'But…'

'Keep arguing,' I said, 'and I will wash my hands of you entirely.'

Alarm flashed across his face. 'Don't do that! I'll find somewhere else to crash. It'll be fine. Just don't change your mind. I want to learn from you, Saffron. Really I do. Help me be a better faery.'

Something odd shifted in his expression and his voice changed from whiny to serious. 'I get it, okay? I get that I'm annoying. I get that I overstep the mark time and time again. I'm immature and often unpleasant. But I really do believe that I have it in me to be a better man.' He looked away. 'Otherwise I might as well give up on everything now. You're going after the Director and I want to help with that.'

My spine stiffened. 'I'm not going after the Director.'

He snorted. 'Of course you are. And the reason I know that is because I want to do the same thing. Once upon a time I dreamed of being a good faery godfather. I wanted to help people and grant wishes. I guess I've been veering off track for a long time. I've seen plenty of the Director's less-than-salubrious methods and I've let them slide without comment because it suited me. I've been wrong.' He smiled without humour. 'It turns out that you're the kick up the arse I needed. '

For the first time, I felt as if I were seeing the real Rupert. It didn't mean I suddenly liked him but there was a glimmer of hope.

'Meet me outside my flat at nine o'clock tomorrow morning,' I told him. 'And we'll take things from there.'

CHAPTER

FIVE

'I still don't understand why we're here,' Rupert said, frowning at the wide street with its large expensive houses and well-kept driveways. 'What are you hoping to find?'

'I don't know,' I said honestly. 'But if there's any proof inside that house that the Director is corrupt then I'll find it.'

Rupert rubbed the small of his back. 'I'm all achy from my mate's lumpy sofa. We could have done this later on in the day.'

As I tugged on Pumpkin's lead, I caught sight of a cat on the pavement opposite and hoped that he wouldn't notice it. 'Well,' I said absently, 'you're perfectly welcome to leave and go back home and have all the lie-ins that you like.'

Rupert looked at me, his face filled with anguish. 'Why would you say such a thing, Saffron?'

'I can't begin to imagine.' I sent him an arch glance. 'And I thought we were past the histrionics.'

Guilt flashed across his face. 'Old habits really are hard to break.' He looked at the house. 'I can do it, Saffron. I will go in and look around. At least I've got a wand with me, so I'll be more likely to break in without anyone noticing.'

I didn't trust Rupert enough to give him such an important task. Or to tell him that I was now more powerful without a wand than he was with one. 'No, it's better if you stay out here.'

I took out a hair band and tied my curls into a tight bun. It didn't make me look more badass but I didn't know what sort of anti-intruder magic the Director might have in place and the last thing I wanted to do was leave behind any tell-tale DNA in the form of a few errant hairs. 'Now, you understand what you have to do?'

'I've got it. I'm to keep watch and alert you if anyone shows up.'

'And don't let Pumpkin chase after any cats,' I added, passing over the lead.

I glanced at Rupert. If he proved himself, his ability to wield magic from behind the scenes could be invaluable. And if he *did* betray me, at least I'd know where I stood.

Pumpkin's presence would help. The wee dog and I had reached a mutual understanding and I knew his loyalty was absolute. If Rupert tried anything, I had no doubt that Pumpkin would use his sharp teeth to good effect. He didn't appear particularly thrilled by the prospect of being left alone with my handsy ex-colleague but I ignored his plaintive whine.

'Yeah, yeah.' I clapped a hand on Rupert's shoulder. 'This is important work,' I told him. 'I couldn't do this without you. Knowing you have my back makes all the difference.'

Almost immediately, Rupert straightened his shoulders and puffed out his chest. 'Really, Saffron?'

I smiled. 'Really.'

'You might not find anything.'

I nodded. 'I know – but I have to start somewhere.'

'Good luck.'

'I won't be long,' I promised. I looked at him meaningfully. 'I trust you to keep me safe, Rupert.'

'I won't let you down,' he answered fervently.

We'll see, I thought. I smiled again, as much to reassure myself as to make Rupert feel good, and crossed the road after double-checking that the coast was clear.

My skin felt shivery. For a moment, I was tempted to flick magic at myself to ensure that I was invisible to all but the most talented eyes. Rupert still didn't know that I could perform magic without a wand, however, and I wasn't convinced that it was something I wanted him to know. The more people who were ignorant of my newfound abilities, the better. At least for now. It would be far better if he believed I was some sort of breaking and entering expert. Safety first, I reminded myself.

I padded up the gravel driveway, taking care not to leave footprints on the loose stones. The Director certainly reaped the rewards of her position; her house was massive and located in one of the more well-to-do areas of Colchester. Its red-brick façade against the dark-green fir trees in the garden, not to mention the pretty sash windows and smartly varnished front door, made it look very appealing.

Would I have been happier if she'd lived in a gothic mansion painted black to indicate her villainous nature? Would I have looked more kindly on her if her wealth wasn't displayed so extravagantly? The truth was that, regardless of how much I despised her, I knew that her motivation was to keep the Office of Faery Godmothers as strong as it could be. Her interpretation of that strength was very different to mine, and her methods were appalling, but they didn't make her a pantomime villain. She was far more complex than that. Sadly, we all were. But I was still going to make her pay for her actions, and breaking into her house to find evidence of her wrongdoing was the first step towards achieving that. I should have done it long before now.

Having already used Google maps to check out the building

and examine it for weaknesses that I could exploit, I knew there was a garage attached to the right-hand side of the house. I was banking on there being an inner entrance somewhere, which I could use as my entry point. It would be easier than jiggling with the front door and potentially leaving traces of myself.

I strode round the perimeter. The Director lived alone; at this hour, she'd be at the office. In theory I had plenty of time to snoop around but I didn't want to spend more time than I had to. It would only increase my chances of getting caught.

As soon as I reached the garage door, I flicked a bolt of magic towards it and released its catch. It opened easily enough, springing upwards by a few inches, so I doubted it had been locked. I hastily pulled on a pair of gloves, reached down and pulled it up so that I could duck underneath, then I took care to close it behind me in case a postman or neighbour happened by.

I looked round and spotted the door in the far corner. Ah-ha. I was right. I knew that if the garage entrance was unlocked there was a good chance that the door into the house would be both bolted and warded. If I wasn't careful, I'd set off an alarm, a trap, or quite possibly both.

I advanced slowly, flicking my eyes this way and that for any signs of magic. When the coast seemed clear, I placed the palms of my hands flat against the door and closed my eyes to concentrate my senses. I couldn't feel even the faintest buzz of magic. Maybe the Director was simply less wary than I'd expected? She was definitely arrogant enough to think that no-one would dare break into her house.

Then a thought occurred to me and I reached for the door-knob and twisted it. The door immediately sprang open. Huh. It hadn't been locked at all.

I paused on the threshold, wary that I was being led into a trap. Try as I might, I couldn't sense any danger, magical or otherwise, so, with my heart in my mouth, I stepped into the Director's perfectly designed kitchen.

Nothing happened.

I remained where I was for another beat, unwilling to move until I was absolutely sure that this wasn't a set up. I flicked my eyes from left to right in case there was a camera filming my every move, which the Director could then use as evidence of my criminality, but there appeared to be nothing. I shook my head. Anyone could wander in here any time they wanted to. It was baffling that she could be so blasé.

Licking my lips, and aware that my palms were sweaty, I took another step. Then another. Before long it appeared that I was being overly cautious. I pursed my lips. It was time to begin my search.

I started by opening cupboards and drawers. There was nothing out of the ordinary, just stacks of plates, neatly arranged glasses and an inordinate number of tins of Heinz baked beans. I moved to the fridge freezer and gazed at the photos on its door. The Director holding a trophy. The Director sitting behind her desk at the office. The Director grinning at the finish line of a marathon. I was sensing a theme.

I opened the freezer; it was empty except for a bag of peas. I opened the fridge; it contained a few bottles of champagne, half a carton of milk and some butter. She ought to re-think her diet; maybe some decent food would make her less of a vicious harpy.

Abandoning the kitchen, I went into the expansive hallway. It was very beige – that was probably the kindest thing I could say about the Director's taste in interior design. I swivelled round, wondering if the sickeningly kitsch painting at the far end might hide a safe where I'd discover her diary that offered up all the evidence I needed to prove her manipulations.

Suddenly I heard a faint sound coming from the next room.

I froze. Had I imagined it? Then I heard something else – a muffled clunk. Perhaps the Director had a cat, a fluffy white cat that she stroked while she spun in her chair and made evil pronouncements. Except her work clothes were always pristine and I'd have noticed stray cat hairs. No: the only possible conclusion was that I wasn't alone.

My mouth dried and I raised my hand, preparing to magic myself into invisibility. Unfortunately I was a fraction too late. From out of the open doorway a figure appeared, clothed in black, wearing gloves – and very grim faced.

'Jasper!' I blurted before I could stop myself.

For a strange moment, I thought that he'd moved in with the Director and was conducting a rampant love affair with her. Then I registered the horrified, guilty expression that flashed across his face. It probably mirrored my own.

'What are you doing here, Saffron?' he ground out.

I scrambled for a response. 'I might ask you the same question,' I said. So this was why I'd been able to waltz in so easily: Jasper had already broken in and disabled any magical alarms. The idiot. Didn't he realise how much of a risk he was taking by coming here?

He took a step towards me. 'You shouldn't be here.'

'Goddammit, Jasper. Neither should you! The Director...' I grimaced and flailed. Even now, I wasn't sure I could tell him the truth about her. 'Just leave, Jasper. You can't be here.'

'But,' he said softly, 'I already am here. As are you.' He hesitated before drawing in a breath and continuing. 'Tell me one thing, Saffron. I've had a lot of time to think over the last few days and it's been puzzling me a lot. Why did you resign your job? You went to incredible lengths to keep it, then you simply walked out.' His eyes held mine, tearing into my soul and refusing to let go. 'Why?'

My jaw worked uselessly as I tried to find the words.

'You goaded me into that argument in front of the entire office,' he said. 'I was too furious to realise it at the time, but you engineered the entire situation. You wanted me to say publicly that I thought you were unfit to be a faery godmother.'

The intense green of his eyes deepened. 'I revealed myself to you and told you things I'd never told anyone before – and you flung it all back in my face. Were you manipulating me from the start, or is there more to it? Are you sneaking around here for the same reasons?'

I dropped my gaze. I couldn't look at him any longer. It hurt too much. 'The truth is,' I mumbled, 'that…'

'Saffron!' Rupert's disembodied voice hissed through the air. 'Someone's coming! You need to get out of there!'

Jasper's eyebrows snapped together. 'Is that Rupert?' he asked, disbelief colouring his words.

'He's keeping watch outside.' I reached for Jasper's hand, yanking him towards me. He pulled away as if he'd been burned.

'And here was me thinking that I might have got it all wrong and that you had good reasons for doing what you did.' His lip curled. 'If you think that your star will rise by attaching yourself to Rupert of all people, you're crazier than I realised. Or is he the best you can do, now that I'm out of the picture?'

This wasn't the time or place for this discussion. 'We have to get out of here,' I told him. 'Let's talk outside.'

Voices floated in. More than one person was outside and, from the jangling sound, they had a set of keys and were preparing to enter. Fuck a puck.

Jasper's face closed off. 'I can leave whenever I want to,' he said. 'I doubt you can say the same.' He raised his hands and I knew he was about to invoke his own transportation magic. I might well be capable of doing the same, but without experimenting first I was unwilling to attempt it unless I had to. Goodness only knew where I might end up.

'Wait,' I said desperately. 'Jasper, can we just...'

He snapped his fingers, his body clouding away as the magic did its thing.

I heard the front door open. So much for my stealth operation. I spun round and ran out the way I'd come.

Without knowing what magic wards the Director had invoked to protect the sanctity of her home, I couldn't replace them. All I could do was get the hell out of there while I had the chance. I flew through the kitchen and into the garage, sending a flash towards the garage door so I could roll underneath it and escape. Within seconds I was out on the street, slowing to a walk and moving away.

Rupert, who was still on the other side of the road, peered anxiously at me while Pumpkin jumped up in the air excitedly.

I re-joined them. 'There was no time,' I said in frustration.

'I'm sorry, Saffron! They pulled up in a car. I think they're cleaners. I tried to give you enough warning but they were looking at me and I had to turn away and...'

'It's not your fault.'

Rupert wrung his hands. 'I tried really hard.'

'It's fine.' I sighed, then caught something out of the corner of my eye. Looking up I spotted Jasper, enough of a distance away to be safe but staring hard in my direction. His eyes narrowed. Even from a hundred feet away I could feel his ire.

'Is that ... is that the Devil's Advocate?' Rupert asked, his voice rising. 'Oh shit. We're screwed now. I'm going to be jailed for this. I'm going to be put in a cell. My parents will kill me. I'll be shunned for ever more. I'll...'

I ripped my eyes away from Jasper. 'Relax,' I snapped. 'He won't say or do anything.'

'How do you know?'

I looked back but Jasper had already vanished. I felt a twist of depression. 'I just do.' My shoulders dropped. 'Come on. Let's get out of here while we still can.'

CHAPTER

SIX

Four days later, I wasn't any further forward. My revenge fantasies were growing more and more elaborate – and more and more unrealistic. I'd debated returning to the Director's house but I knew deep down that, even if she hadn't noticed the intrusion, Jasper would already have found anything incriminating – assuming there was anything to find.

I tried tailing her from the office but I had to keep so far back to avoid being spotted that I lost her within minutes. If I was going to uncover proof of her wrongdoing, I needed to be a lot smarter. And that was more easily said than done.

What was equally unclear was what to do about Jasper. I lost count of the number of times I picked up my phone to call him and then chickened out at the last moment. I spent hours poring through the audit report, trying to see if there was any clue about Jasper's suspicions about the Director and any reason why he'd have broken into her house. I didn't find anything; nothing in the report was unexpected. It was damning, to be sure, but as far as I could tell he placed the blame for the state of the Office of Faery Godmothers on historical issues rather than pointing the finger at the Director for running an inept ship filled with back-biting.

As well as detailing the sordid nature of the office politics and the unpleasant working culture, he advocated changing the old-fashioned recruitment guidelines. He also concluded that the way clients were dealt with had to be altered; there should be less emphasis on single-wish fulfilment and more on improving their overall lives.

There was nothing to suggest that Jasper believed the Director had played a role in Figgy's death, or that she was less than impressed with the trolls' existence. There was no whiff of corruption or hint that the Director was prepared to sink to blackmail and lies to achieve her own ends. But Jasper had to suspect something was rotten or he wouldn't have sneaked around her house like I had.

The trouble was that I knew how far she'd already gone to try and destroy him. If he wasn't careful, she'd try again and next time she might succeed. If I'd sacrificed everything to save Jasper only for him to dance right back into the danger zone, I would be mightily pissed off.

The only bright spot on the horizon was that I'd found some gainful temporary employment. Unfortunately, as I was persona non grata in the faery world, it was an entirely unmagical job. I was on a zero-hours contract providing holiday cover and earning a whole penny over the minimum wage, but the interview had been perfunctory and they'd not requested references. I had bills to pay and, while I'd never get rich working the checkout at my local supermarket, it meant I wouldn't starve either.

Obviously I now had less time to concentrate on my plans to destroy the Director but, given that I had to feed both Pumpkin and myself and keep a roof over our heads, there wasn't a whole lot of choice.

The bonus, as well as my wages, was that my co-workers were genuinely good fun. The drawback was that there were some unpleasant tasks I was forced to take on, such as getting down on my hands and knees to clean up toddler vomit. It was amazing, I reflected, as I tried my best to reach the last few far-flung drops under a heavy shelving unit filled with tins of tomatoes, just how much liquid a small child could contain inside their body.

'Are you alright down there?' asked a quavering voice as I used my cloth to wipe down the last section. 'Do you need some help?'

I stood up, pocketing the cloth in my apron and smiling. 'No, it's all done, sir,' I beamed. I was a downright whizz at customer service. 'Watch your step. The floor is still a little slippy.'

The old man, who was wearing a dapper tweed suit and had to be pushing eighty years old, looked disappointed. 'Never mind then.' He smiled at me. 'Can you tell me where I'll find the loose tea?'

I squinted as I tried to remember, then pointed behind me. 'Aisle four,' I said. 'About halfway down.'

'Thank you.' He stayed where he was, still smiling despite the anxious light in his brown eyes. 'Nice weather we're having for this time of year.'

Was it? I glanced out towards the window. It looked like just another day to me. And didn't he want to fetch his tea? Then it hit me. He was bored and lonely and wanted to make conversation with someone, even if it was a stranger working in a supermarket.

'Yes!' I said, agreeing with him with a touch more enthusiasm than was appropriate. 'It truly is!' I stuck out my hand. 'I'm Saffron.'

He seemed delighted, taking my proffered hand and shaking it vigorously. 'Albert. I've not seen you here before.'

'I'm new,' I told him. 'This is only my second shift. I'm here to cover for a few people who are away on holiday.'

'That explains it.' He leaned in, dropping his voice conspiratorially. 'I have to say that I hope you last the course. You have a lovely smile. We could do with more friendly faces around here.'

I glanced into his shopping basket. A lonely lemon, a couple of onions and two meals for one. My heart contracted. 'Do you live nearby?'

'All my life. I've been coming to this supermarket for years, you know.'

I translated that to mean he knew exactly where to locate the loose tea. He'd just needed a reason to strike up a conversation. 'And your family?'

Albert's face fell. 'I have a son. He's terribly clever but I don't see much of him these days. He lives in Australia. He wants me to visit him but it's a long way to go.'

'It is,' I said quietly. There had to be a way for me to help him but I couldn't make Australia move any closer – and his son might not thank me for magically forcing him to return home. 'You must be very proud of him.'

'Oh, I am, I am.'

A bell rang and the tannoy sounded. 'Clean up required in aisle nine. Clean up in aisle nine.'

Fuck a puck.

Albert reached across and patted my hand. 'No rest for the wicked. You'd better go.'

Yeah. I sighed and offered him a sad shrug. 'Maybe I'll see you again.'

'I'm sure you will. It's been wonderful to talk to you.' He shuffled off.

I watched him go then turned and headed for latest mess, sucking thoughtfully on my bottom lip. Some hapless shopper had dropped a bottle of wine before making a hasty exit. I grabbed a broom and started sweeping up the glass. Albert needed a friend, I decided. While I could try to fill that role, I suspected he'd prefer someone of his own age – and someone who was less of a hot mess. All I had to do was find the right person.

Unwilling to let the grass grow under my feet, I looked round to double-check that no-one was watching me. When I was sure that the coast was clear, I allowed myself a sneaky grin and snapped my fingers Mary-Poppins style. In the blink of an eye, every shard of glass had vanished and the wine puddle was gone. Using magic like this was cheating but I'd allow it under the circumstances. After all, I had an old man to help.

I returned the broom to its place and marched through the supermarket. I rejected the slightly dodgy-looking bloke wearing a grubby trench coat, on the off-chance that he was some sort of flasher who could send Albert into an early grave. I also discounted the trio of university students hunting out cut-price bargains. I almost plumped for a young mum and the little girl sitting in her trolley until her partner joined her. Their bowed heads as they chatted and their happy smiling faces told me that they were too wrapped up in each other.

Then I spotted the perfect person. She looked to be about Albert's age and she was holding up a chicken tikka masala as if trying to decide whether the portion was big enough for one. She was ideal.

I craned my neck. Albert was at the furthest checkout, bagging up his shopping with slow and deliberate care. I didn't have long to make this happen. I was no longer a faery godmother but that didn't mean I couldn't still weave some fabulous magic. Go, Saffron, go.

The woman walked down towards the end of aisle and into

Albert's line of sight. I silently urged her to move more quickly. 'Come on,' I whispered. 'Come on.'

The moment she rounded the corner, I took action. I had to be careful – I didn't want any broken bones on my conscience. Using my left hand, I jolted out a tiny jet of magic, making the woman slip and slide backwards. With my right hand, I swirled enough force into the air to cushion her fall. She fell onto the cold supermarket floor with a loud thud, which was amplified when I flicked my fingers.

I could already see Brenda, the assistant manager, scurrying over in alarm. That wouldn't do. I needed Albert to get there first. Sending Brenda a mute apology, I used more magic to topple the stacked bushels of apples in front of her, effectively barring her way.

A moment later, Albert was at the woman's side and helping her to her feet. 'Oh my goodness,' he exclaimed. 'Are you alright?'

'Yes, yes.' She shook herself, clearly stunned that she'd lost her footing so suddenly but none the worse for wear.

I darted over. 'Oh no! Are you okay?'

She nodded at me. 'I think so.'

'You should sit down for a while.' I looked up. 'Maybe we can offer you a free cup of tea at the café?'

From behind the fallen apples, Brenda gave me a thumbs-up. Keep the customers happy; she'd impressed that on me during my first shift. In some ways, working at the supermarket wasn't that different from being a faery godmother, albeit with more stock rotation to worry about.

'You shouldn't be alone.' I made a show of glancing at the apples. 'I'll have to pick those up. But Albert, maybe you could...' My voice trailed off. This was his chance.

His expression transformed and he offered the woman his arm. 'It would be my pleasure to keep you company.'

She smiled at him. 'Thank you. I don't know what happened. One minute I was fine and the next...'

'It's so easily done at our age,' he said. 'Come on. I'll treat you to an iced bun and you'll be right as rain in no time.'

I bent down and helped Brenda pick up the apples. When I was done I stood up, checking on the pair of them and hugging myself happily as they sat down at the round table in the corner of the supermarket café. I'd done all I could for now. What happened next was up to them. Even if they didn't form a close friendship, I'd at least provided a diversion from their usual routines and given them both someone to chat to for an hour or so. Loneliness could be a killer, but not on my watch. And not in my neighbourhood.

'Well, well, well, Saffron. You *are* being a naughty faery.'

I jumped, startled by the sound of Billy's voice. I spun round and caught sight of him with his little black book. He mimed making notes and raised his eyebrows. 'I'll have to report this, you know.' He tutted. 'Tripping up random human beings. And wielding wandless magic too. I didn't believe Miranda when she told me you could, but it appears that she was right.'

Good as it was to see him, I felt my stomach drop at his words. My feelings must have registered on Billy's face because he smiled. 'Don't worry, I'm only teasing you. I saw what you were really up to. And if you're concerned that Miranda is blabbing your secrets to the world, she was very clear that I wasn't to breathe a word to anyone else. She only told me because she knows we're friends. I'm certain she's not mentioned it to anyone else.' He looked at me sympathetically. 'I take it something terrible happened to break your magical barriers?'

'Yeah,' I muttered, unable to meet his gaze. I couldn't tell him that I'd inadvertently killed Art Adwell by sending such an explosive thrust of magic towards him that he'd toppled out of a window. It wasn't Adwell's death that I was ashamed of – it was that moments before he had murdered Figgy and I hadn't been able to stop it. How could I explain that? I hadn't even shared the worst of the details with Harry, and I usually told him everything. I couldn't imagine what Billy's reaction would be.

'You don't have to talk about it, Saffron. You don't have to tell me. But I'm here and prepared to listen if you ever need me to.'

Unexpectedly, my eyes welled up with tears. I coughed loudly to cover the rush of emotion. 'Thanks.' I swallowed. 'You're a good friend, Billy.'

He nodded. 'I really am. In fact,' he continued, 'I'm such a good friend that I've even accepted an invitation to go to a party hosted by Alicia.'

I blinked. 'What?'

Brenda walked into my line of vision so I squeezed Billy's arm and nipped over to ask her if I could take my break. Then I scooted back and hauled him outside to the rear of the building where we could talk in private.

'Let's start that again,' I said. My voice rose. 'What?'

He smiled faintly. 'She persuaded me to say yes. Alicia Beauchamp has never invited me to anything. Ever. And now she's demanding that I show up to a party at her house and informed me that you'll be there too.'

Huh. I wasn't sure what to say to that. 'Maybe she wants to pretend that she's a super-nice person. Or she's planning to throw the biggest party the world has ever seen so she's invited every single person she knows – even the people she desperately hates.'

'Or,' Billy said, 'she's planning to douse us in pig's blood at the very first opportunity.'

It wouldn't surprise me and I knew that I'd deserve it –

along with so much more. 'To be honest, Bill,' I said, 'I'd forgotten all about it. I'm not planning to go.'

'She's also invited Ethan.'

I couldn't stop myself from recoiling in shock. 'Ethan? The troll?'

'Do you know any other Ethans?'

I passed a hand over my forehead. 'What is she up to?'

He shrugged. 'Beats me. But whatever it is, I think you need to be there.'

I swallowed. Maybe I did. I hated to think what Alicia was planning. It couldn't be good.

'I miss you, you know,' Billy said suddenly. 'Things at the office are horrible now. The Director is closeted away in meetings all the time and doing everything she can to stall the changes required by the audit. Everyone's walking on eggshells. She's fired a whole bunch of people.'

I grimaced. 'So I heard.'

Billy raised an eyebrow. 'Yes, I bumped into Rupert this morning. In fact, he's the one who directed me here to find you. Tell me the truth, Saffron. Is he really your new best friend?'

'Not exactly.' Not at all, if I were truthful.

'Hmmm.' He scratched his chin. 'If you say so. He was only sacked when he stood up for you, you know.'

I stared at him. 'Rupert stood up for me?'

'Yeah. He said, and I quote, that you were top totty and that we needed you back. The Director fired him on the spot. Then Angela said the same thing – without the top totty part, of course – and she lost her job as well.'

'Angela?' My mouth dropped open in astonishment. The HR faery had never liked me much and now she'd lost her job because of me? I shook my head.

'Naturally, the Director is saying that because the office

can't run properly on a skeleton staff, she'll have to wait before making any more of the changes the Devil's Advocate wants.'

So the Director was still looking for a way to maintain her authority. I felt sick. Nothing Jasper had recommended was bad, not in the long run. The fact that the Director was continuing to dig her heels in smacked of power-hungry idiocy.

'I hope you're not planning to do anything stupid like argue my case,' I told Billy. 'I resigned. I was in full control of my actions. No-one is to blame but me.'

'I'll keep my mouth shut if you promise you'll come to the party,' Billy said. 'You can't let me go there alone. Not if Alicia is up to something.'

I sighed. 'Billy...'

He took my hands. 'Please?'

I met his eyes. 'Alright.' I gazed heavenward. 'But if Alicia goes full psycho and the shit hits the fan, I'll be sprinting out of there.'

He grinned suddenly. 'Don't worry. I'll be right beside you.'

SEVEN

I had no idea if what I was wearing was appropriate or not. It wasn't like I spent a great deal of time hobnobbing with the Beauchamps of this world.

There wasn't a single part of me that was convinced attending Alicia's daft soirée was a good idea. She'd told me to come along without Pumpkin and I'd done just that, leaving him at home with a meaty bone for company. But that didn't mean I was arriving without back-up. I wasn't taking any chances. Not in this tight black dress.

The taxi pulled up outside a grand mansion on the outskirts of the city. If I'd thought that the Director's house was posh then I hadn't been using my imagination. Alicia's ancestral home was virtually a palace. It certainly paid to be a faery from a good family, I thought, stepping onto the neat driveway and gazing upwards. The loud buzz of voices and gentle strains of violin music filtered out from inside.

Vincent whistled. 'Nice place.'

I sent him a warning look. 'Keep your hands to yourself,' I told him. 'No pilfering the family silver.' I glanced at Rupert. 'And you keep your hands to yourself as well.'

Rupert very deliberately put his hands in his pockets. 'I'll be on my best behaviour. No touching.'

'I'll believe it when I see it,' I said, as another car pulled up beside us and Ethan's familiar figure stepped out. I wasn't the only one arriving with an entourage; he had Melissa and Finch in tow, both of whom had grim expressions. It appeared that none of us were at ease.

Ethan nodded at me and walked over. 'Saffron,' he said, inclining his head. 'How are you doing?'

'Good,' I said. 'Great. Now I'm no longer a faery godmother, I'm footloose, fancy free and loving life.' I forced a smile.

He raised an eyebrow. 'Now say it like you mean it.'

I grimaced.

Melissa's eyes flashed in my direction. Whether I was unemployed or not, she clearly didn't trust me an inch. Generations of hatred towards faery godmothers was not an easy prejudice to break. 'You're here too,' she said flatly. 'How wonderful.'

Ethan clicked his tongue at her in quiet disapproval. 'Do you know what this is about?' he asked me. 'Why we've been invited?'

I shrugged. 'Beats me.'

'If this is another chance for us to be criticised...' Melissa began.

Ethan shot her a narrow-eyed look and she lapsed into silence.

'Who's been criticising you?' I asked.

'Let's just say,' he said, 'that the Director is being somewhat underhand.'

'She's being a bitch,' Melissa muttered.

Concern flitted through me. No matter what I thought of the Director, relations between the faery godmothers and the trolls were too important to mess with. The thought that she was upsetting the still-delicate thread of peace was worrying indeed.

'I've spoken to her on a few occasions recently,' Ethan said. 'She's not been unpleasant but I suspect she is goading us towards a fight.'

'You can't let her do that! Ethan, I know how most of the trolls feel about us but we've come too far to turn back now. She's only one person.'

'You of all people know what it took to pause our feud, Saffron. And I did warn you at the time that it might only be temporary. I don't want war but I will take us there, if need be. The only reason I'm holding back is because I think she *wants* me to make a move against her.'

'She doesn't like you,' I burst out. 'She doesn't like any of you. She won't make the first move because she doesn't want to look bad. But if you take up arms against the faery godmothers, she'll claim the faeries are victims and assemble them all against you. You'll have no chance.'

'We can only be pushed so far. Without saying it directly, the Director has implied that we are weak, dirty and without honour. She repeatedly returns to her apology as if that makes her the bigger person and we should bow down in gratitude for the fact that she said sorry. Never mind that her apology was for a faery godmother error that resulted in the deaths of most of our kind.'

'Maybe Jasper...'

'Maybe Jasper what?'

I swung round, my eyes immediately meeting Jasper's hard emerald gaze. No-one had told me he would be here. I was so taken aback that all I could do was stare. He was wearing a tightly fitted tuxedo which only added to his usual dangerous and aloof air. By comparison, I felt drab and pale and very small.

'Satan!' Vincent exclaimed. 'Long time no see! Give me a hug!'

Jasper folded his arms. In that moment he really did look like the incarnation of Lucifer. 'Hello, Vincent.'

Rupert moved closer to me and hooked his arm through mine. I glared at him. I thought we'd been through this already. What the hell was he up to?

'Devil's Advocate,' he murmured. 'How lovely to see you again.'

Jasper didn't give anything away. 'Rupert.' He shook Ethan's hand, kissed Melissa's cheek and nodded at Finch. It hurt tremendously that he refused to greet me. I couldn't blame him – this lack of acknowledgment was what I'd worked for – but the remaining scraps of my pride wouldn't permit me to take his attitude lying down.

I cleared my throat. 'I was going to suggest,' I said loudly, 'that you could act as a conduit between the faery godmothers and the trolls. It might help to smooth ruffled feathers and avoid any unnecessary … misunderstandings.'

'Well,' Jasper replied, 'I certainly could do that, but I don't think the trolls see me as an unbiased party. They're no more likely to trust me than they are to trust the Director. I might not be a faery godmother but I *am* a faery.'

'They're having problems with her, Jasper,' I bit out, shaking off Rupert's arm irritably when he began to stroke my hand. 'As someone who helped broker peace, you should be prepared to step in and keep everyone happy.'

His eyes flashed. 'Thank you for telling me how to do my job, Saffron,' he said sarcastically. 'It's much appreciated.' He paused. 'And you will address me by my title. As far as you're concerned, I am – and always will be – the Devil's Advocate.'

Ethan coughed. 'Actually, Saffron, the Devil's Advocate has already suggested intervening but we turned him down. We can't rely on someone else forever. Either there is peace or there isn't. And he is right about one thing – he's still a faery. He will always be loyal to your side.'

I was prepared to overlook the spitting fury emanating from Jasper and inform Ethan that, as Devil's Advocate, he was above reproach. Jasper would always be even-handed and fair in all his dealings. I didn't get the chance, however, because Alicia walked out and drew all our attention.

Last time I'd seen her, she'd been cowed by grief over Figgy's death. Now she had returned to her usual gleaming self. She was wearing a silver dress and self-confidence was exuding from every pore.

'You made it! I'm so pleased to see you all. Thank you for coming.' She spread out her arms in greeting. 'Please do come in and help yourselves to a glass of champagne.'

Rupert reached for my arm again. I slapped him away while the others strode up to greet Alicia. 'What are you doing?' I hissed. 'No touching, remember?'

'It'll make him jealous if he thinks we're together,' Rupert whispered back. 'He'll try and fight me for you. He'll win. You can waltz off into the sunset together. You want him, right?'

I folded my arms. I had enough problems without Rupert making them worse. 'Not like that. And he wouldn't fight you. And we're not in high school. And this isn't some kind of game. And…'

'Are you joining us, Saffron?' Alicia called out. 'Billy seems anxious. I think he was worried that you wouldn't show up.'

I forced a smile in her direction. 'On my way.' I left Rupert where he was. 'You have a lovely home, Alicia,' I said politely.

'Thank you.' She glared at me. 'Why did you bring Rupert with you? And that despicable excuse for a human?'

'You just told me not to bring my dog,' I said innocently. 'Why did you invite Jasper?'

'I thought you might enjoy his company,' she returned with a sneer. 'I can't think of anyone who will enjoy the company of that pair.'

I glanced round her and noted Vincent downing a glass of champagne in one gulp before immediately grabbing another. Perhaps bringing Rupert and Vincent along had been a bad idea but it was too late now. Then I shivered at the thought of an entire evening with Jasper glaring at me. 'Actually, I think you're right. It's not appropriate that they're here and I over-stepped the mark by including them. The three of us should leave.'

Alicia's hand snapped out, encircling my wrist with surprising force. 'Their presence is unexpected,' she said, 'but I can adapt. Perhaps it's better that they're involved from the beginning.'

I stared at her. 'The beginning? The beginning of what?'

Alicia released me, reached behind to scoop up a glass and pressed it into my hand with a perfect hostess smile and a flick of her blonde hair. 'Have a drink, Saffron. Make some new friends. Once the party is in full swing, we'll have a chat and everything will be fine.'

I sincerely doubted that.

Twenty minutes later and I was desperate to make my escape. Standing around Alicia's staid drawing room and making stilted conversation with an old faery who was extolling the virtues of birch wands over mahogany ones, while Jasper refused to look in my direction and Vincent was guzzling his fourth glass of champagne, was becoming far too much. Even Billy's presence wasn't reassuring enough to make me want to stay.

Melissa kept shooting daggers in my direction. I didn't

know why we were here but I was damned if I was going to stay. There were too many people and I was starting to feel claustrophobic. I'd eaten all the canapés I could find and champagne was not the tipple of my choice, even if Alicia was paying for it.

My resolve hardened when Angela walked in, followed by Mrs Jardine, their eyes searching the crowd before resting on me. This was getting too uncomfortable for words.

I carefully placed my glass on the nearest table and raised my chin. When I stood on my tiptoes I could see the door. If I left now, there was a good chance I could catch a taxi that was dropping off a latecomer. I'd be home within the hour. Vincent and Rupert would have to fend for themselves.

I mumbled a farewell to the wand-obsessed faery and sidled out, narrowly avoiding knocking over several well-dressed people. I felt eyes burning the back of my neck as I edged my way to the exit but I didn't turn around. I didn't have it in me to engage in staring matches, especially when at least one of them would probably involve Jasper.

I was almost at the door and could actually smell my freedom when Alicia appeared, seemingly out of nowhere. She somehow managed to leap in front of me and effectively bar my way. Fuck a puck.

'Fabulous party,' I said. I touched my temples lightly. 'Unfortunately I've got a terrible migraine coming on. I should probably go.'

Her expression didn't change. 'Nice try. You're not going anywhere, Saffron. We still need to have our chat.'

I couldn't think of anything I wanted to say to her. 'No,' I told her, 'we don't. I'm going.'

'Not yet you're not.' She took hold of my elbow and started to propel me away from the fresh air of liberty towards a closed door. 'Trust me. If you still want to leave in ten minutes' time, then that's your prerogative. However, you owe me that much time first.'

I wasn't aware that I owed Alicia anything but I wasn't willing to make a scene. Thanks to the Director's machinations, I already possessed a bad enough reputation.

'Fine,' I muttered under my breath, allowing her to push me towards the door. Part of me hoped this was some kind of crazy ambush. I could do with a real fight.

When we entered the room, Angela, Billy and Mrs Jardine were already there, somehow having managed to skip ahead of me. A second later Ethan, Vincent and Rupert joined us. We stood there in awkward silence, fidgeting and smiling uncomfortably. This was not fun at all.

Vincent cleared his throat. 'Am I the only human at this party?' he asked no-one in particular. 'Because I have to say, that's kind of cool. But I don't want to end up on some sacrificial altar with my bowels cut open as a gift to one of your faery gods.' He paused. 'Do you worship any gods?'

Mrs Jardine clicked her tongue. 'What is he doing here?'

'He's linked with Saffron,' Alicia said. 'He might as well hear this now rather than later.'

Ethan folded his arms. 'Hear what? He might be the only human but, as one of only a handful of trolls, I have even more concern than he does about having my bowels cut open.'

Alicia rolled her eyes. 'There will be no cutting open of anyone's bowels. Honestly, you lot are a suspicious bunch.'

'With good reason,' Ethan muttered.

I sighed. 'Maybe you should get to the point, Alicia.' Assuming there was one.

'Fine.' She glanced around then lifted a small silver frame from a table and held it up. The photo it contained was of Alicia and Figgy, both grinning broadly at the camera. 'This,' she declared, 'was taken the day Figgy and I became faery godmothers.' She pointed at Mrs Jardine. 'In fact, Miranda, I think you were the photographer.'

'Yeah.' She shrugged. 'So?'

'You might remember how giddy we were that day. It was the culmination of everything we'd dreamed of and worked for. It might have escaped your notice, but none of those other guests out there are faery godmothers – although you can bet your sweet pixie arses that they all wish they'd had the chance to be. It's supposed to be the best job there is.'

Ethan let out a loud snort and made for the door. 'I don't have to stay here and listen to this.'

'I think you should. It won't take long.' Alicia sent the troll leader a hard look. He hesitated for a second and then halted. Despite my uneasiness, I was impressed. Alicia didn't take any prisoners.

'Anyway,' she continued, 'as I was saying, being a faery godmother is supposed to be the pinnacle of achievement. It's the dream. But everyone in this room knows that it's often closer to a nightmare.'

I started. I hadn't been expecting that.

'We're overworked,' Mrs Jardine agreed. 'But it's hardly a nightmare. Things aren't that bad.'

'Aren't they?' Alicia's gaze was direct. Mrs Jardine held her eyes unflinchingly but she didn't argue. 'Saffron, what really happened to Figgy?'

I sucked in a breath, taken aback by the question. 'Uh...' I fumbled. 'What do you mean?'

'You know,' she said quietly. 'I saw it in your eyes after she died. Tell us the truth about what happened.'

Nobody knew that I'd been there when Figgy was killed. Nobody but Vincent.

'I'll tell you,' he declared, striding into the centre and spreading out his arms. 'I was there.'

The small assembly gaped at him. 'But you're a human.'

'Yeah, Vincent,' I said, 'you're a human.'

He turned and looked at me. 'You can order me not to say anything, Saffron, and because I'm your slave you know that I'll have to obey. But they deserve to know the truth. Everyone does.'

Angela frowned. 'You're her slave?'

'Yeah.' He shrugged. 'It's not sexual or anything. Unfortunately. But he,' he pointed at Ethan, 'made us link together. I have to do what she says.' His eyes widened for effect. 'Forever.'

Mrs Jardine let out a loud gasp. 'You invoked that magic?'

'There are benefits,' Vincent said with a lazy smile. 'For example, I can do this.' He slapped himself hard across his own cheek and pain snapped through my skull.

'Ow!' I glared at him. 'Stop that!'

Alicia blinked rapidly. 'I had no idea such a thing was even possible. He'll do whatever you say?'

'Yep.' I was tempted to do a show-and-tell to prove it. As entertaining as making Vincent do the can-can would be, however, the magical binding was only there because Ethan was anxious that Vincent knew about the faery godmothers. I wouldn't demean him just to raise a giggle or two.

Billy was fascinated. 'It's a wonder more faeries don't have humans bound to them to do their bidding. The possibilities could be endless.'

'As the man has already shown,' I said drily, 'there are drawbacks.'

Vincent fluttered his eyelashes. 'Shall we get to the point?' he enquired. 'Will you let me speak?'

'Are you threatening me if I don't?' I shot back.

'As if, Saffy babe,' Vincent said. 'But you know you can't hide the truth forever.'

My jaw clenched. Unfortunately he was right.

'Well, now that's settled,' he said, 'I can tell you that your friend Figgy was murdered by Art Adwell. He shoved a magical wand through her neck.'

If he'd expected his words to be met with a drum roll or gasps of astonishment he was sorely disappointed. Alicia just frowned. 'We know that part,' she snapped. 'But I fail to believe that she was working with Art Adwell simply to get some extra money. I know he was offering a million pounds to anyone who could provide him with proof of the existence of faery godmothers, but she wouldn't have done that. For one thing, she didn't need the money. For another, she would never have betrayed the office.'

'Oh.' Vincent's face cleared. 'Yeah, she had a note on her desk from the Devil's Advocate ordering her to help Adwell.'

This time everyone really was shocked. 'No way,' Billy exclaimed, while Ethan's expression darkened thunderously.

Angela stared at me. 'Is that why you and he stopped talking? Because he's the real traitor in all this?'

'He didn't write the fucking note,' I said irritably.

'It's true,' Vincent interjected cheerfully. 'He arrived at the scene of crime and was more shocked than anyone. We don't have any proof, but we think the Director forged his handwriting and sent your Figgy to Adwell. Your boss was trying to discredit Saffron and pin the blame on the Devil's Advocate. That's the theory, anyway. Art Adwell admitted that he'd made a deal with your Director.' He looked at me. 'Right?'

Mrs Jardine was growing paler by the second. 'That's not...' she stuttered. 'She wouldn't...' She looked down at her feet. 'Shit.'

'Speak up, Miranda,' Alicia said grimly. 'I bet you know where the bodies are buried.'

Mrs Jardine refused to look any of us in the eye. 'Some of them,' she admitted. 'I knew the Director was trying to get rid of Saffron, but I didn't think she'd go that far and allow one of our own faeries to be killed. Or make a deal with that bastard of a politician.'

'She didn't expect Figgy to die,' I said quietly. 'That wasn't in her plan. I don't know if that makes it any better.'

Alicia folded her arms. 'That my best friend was killed because of a mistake? No, Saffron,' she said coldly, 'it doesn't make anything better.'

I bit my lip. 'Sorry.' My apology sounded lame but there was nothing else I could offer.

'Look,' Ethan said loudly. 'None of this is surprising to me in the slightest. I already knew the faery godmothers were corrupt. You always have been and you always will be. All that power has gone to your heads. However, this strikes me as your problem, not mine.' He paused. 'Unless you're expecting to use the trolls as an instrument of war to force the Director out of business, this is not our fight.'

Surprisingly it was Angela who answered him. 'It's your fight as much as it's ours,' she said. 'The Director is constantly poisoning us against you and your trolls.' Her eyes slid away. 'It's not difficult,' she admitted. 'You've done some bad things to us and there are a lot of hard feelings. But she's using the threat of your kind to distract us from what *she's* doing. Sooner or later it will end badly for all of us.'

Ethan didn't look surprised – but he didn't look happy, either.

Rupert interjected. 'So we tell the Devil's Advocate. It's his job to deal with this sort of shit. Not ours.'

Mrs Jardine was still looking down. 'She'll be prepared for that. The second he makes a move against her, she'll do her best to destroy him. His report was bad enough, at least,' she hastily amended with a sidelong glance in my direction, 'as far as the Director is concerned. She's stalling against actioning virtually all of his recommendations. And you have to remember that nobody has evidence of her wrongdoing. If I said anything, it would be my word against hers. The same goes for all of you. She's more clever than you give her credit for. She's prepared for everything and she'll defend herself to the death. And she'll take the entire Office of Faery Godmothers down with her, if she has to. All the other faery departments are on her side. If the Devil's Advocate tries to remove her for any reason that's not iron-clad, there will be civil war. I guarantee it.'

Angela nodded vigorously. 'Without absolute proof, he can't lift a finger against her and he knows it.'

I had to agree. Jasper's job was to keep the faery world in a state of relative harmony. After him, the Director was the most powerful faery in the country. No matter what his suspicions about her were, he was powerless to act unless he could prove she was corrupt. To do otherwise would be to invite disaster into every faery home in the land. The repercussions could destroy us all.

'It's down to us,' Billy muttered. 'We have to find evidence to prove she's not fit for office. That's when we get the Devil's Advocate on board.'

Mrs Jardine's reluctance was obvious. 'I didn't know about her hand in Figgy's death but I can tell you that it shook her. She's been ... calmer since then. Quieter. This might be the making of her.'

I was surprised that she was sticking up for the Director and I hissed through my teeth.

Alicia's face spasmed with fury. 'She's delaying the audit recommendations. She's created a culture of fear. She's stirring up hatred against the trolls. And,' she spat, 'she's responsible for Figgy's death. Quiet now or not, it won't be long before she's conniving and manipulating again.'

'She can't delay the audit recommendations for ever,' Angela pointed out.

'Which means,' Billy said sadly, 'that she'll put the Devil's Advocate out of business before too long. She's tried once and she'll try again.'

Rupert straightened his shoulders. 'We confront her. All of us against her. There's more of us.'

'She's got plenty of others in her pocket,' Mrs Jardine said. 'Believe me.'

Alicia nodded grimly. 'And who are we, anyway? I might be a Beauchamp but compared to the Director, I'm just another faery.'

Angela seemed to agree. She pointed at me. 'Will anyone take the word of the faery who caused half of the mess that involved Figgy in the first place?' She looked at Ethan. 'Or the word of a troll?' She moved round the room. 'A human drug dealer? A spoiled rich girl overcome by grief? A rule-obsessed jobsworth? A sexist fuck-up? An HR manager who everyone hates? Not one of us has a leg to stand on. No-one will believe us. And at the end of the day, the Director is smarter than all of us. We're fucked. We might as well give in now and let her do her thing.'

Alicia threw back her head and laughed. 'But those are all the reasons why we can bring her down. On paper we're fuck-ups but in real life we're stronger than anyone gives us credit for.'

'With no evidence,' Mrs Jardine began.

Alicia interrupted her. 'We don't need evidence of what the Director has done in the past. All we need is to lure her into making a grievous mistake. Why do you think I invited you all here?' She smiled. 'I've got a plan. It won't be easy to implement, given that not of all us can use magic now. I can try and get hold of a few spare wands – you'll certainly need one, Saffron.'

Mrs Jardine raised her eyebrows. 'Saffron doesn't require a wand any longer. She can click her fingers and use magic as she wishes.'

What the—?

The faery receptionist shrugged. 'They might as well know what you can do. We're all friends here, Saffron.'

'Since when?' I growled.

Alicia looked delighted. 'That's wonderful news! I wasn't sure that inviting someone of your social standing was a good idea, Saffron, but you might be useful after all.'

Unbelievable. I folded my arms and glared at Mrs Jardine. So much for keeping that little titbit quiet. 'Go on then,' I said, sourly. 'What's this plan?'

EIGHT

I walked out of the room with my head spinning. It was galling that Alicia was the one who'd come up with a plan to reveal the Director's true nature but I couldn't deny that it had potential. And Alicia had the financial means to pull it off in a way that I'd never have dreamed of. Until now, I'd felt like I was fumbling around in the dark. She'd just provided a lightbulb – and all the others were going to help her screw it in.

'Light at the end of the tunnel,' I whispered. Then I lifted my head and saw Jasper's muscular frame leaning against a wall nearby, his sharp green eyes watching me.

'Well, well, well,' he said, with only the tick of a tiny muscle in his cheek revealing his tension. 'Have you been having a secret meeting?'

I met his eyes. How easy it would be to tell him the truth. To let him know that, while I was as much of a fuck up as every other faery godmother, nothing I'd done had been deliberate. That I'd only been trying to keep him safe and do the right thing. But even if Jasper believed me, it wouldn't be a good move. He was the kind of guy who lived on the straight and narrow. His past had led him to be direct and honest. If I told him what I knew about the Director and the way she'd tried to manipulate me against him, he'd confront her.

I also knew she was prepared for that. For his own good, and for that of the whole faery world, he needed to keep out of any investigations into the Director until we had proof of her wrongdoing.

'I suppose you'll find out sooner or later,' I said, with what I hoped was an easy smile. 'After our little tiff…'

He pushed himself off the wall, his face darkening. 'Little tiff?'

I waved a dismissive hand. 'Yeah, the argument we had in the office. After that, I realised that I had no chance of success while I stayed there. So,' I shrugged, 'I resigned and now I'm in phase two of my plan. That's why I was in the Director's house. I was looking for any helpful documents to borrow to help move things along.'

'What things?' he growled. 'What are you talking about?'

'It's a wonder no-one's ever tried it before,' I said airily.

'Saffron…'

'A new agency,' I declared. 'We're setting up our own firm.'

Jasper blinked. 'Pardon?'

'I was going to suggest we call it Make A Wish,' I continued, 'but apparently that's already been taken. Instead it will be called Wish Inc.'

Billy took that moment to wander out of the room. His eyes widened when he saw us and he hastily retreated again. I pretended not to notice. 'Freelance faery godmothers,' I said proudly. 'That's us. No more Adventus room. No more contrived wish system. We will seek out new clients who need us and transform their lives. In five years, we'll be bigger than the Office of Faery Godmothers. Just you wait and see.'

Jasper continued to stare at me in astonishment. 'You can't do that,' he said.

'There aren't any rules against it,' I pointed out. 'Billy's involved. If there was a rule against establishing a new faery godmother business, he'd know about it. This way,' I purred, 'I get to be in charge. No more kow-towing to others.'

'You can't set up on your own, Saffron. Where would you get funding?'

I smiled. I had friends in high places – or ex-colleagues with a common enemy. 'Alicia and Rupert's families will provide it.'

'And supervision? Where will that come from?'

I scratched my head, as if that hadn't occurred to me. 'Hmmm. Well,' I said, 'it's early days. We'll worry about that when we come to it.'

Jasper held himself stiffly upright. 'There are procedures. Paperwork. Complex concerns that you don't seem to have thought about. I don't care what Billy knows or doesn't know, I'm the Devil's Advocate and I'm telling you that you can't do this.'

I stepped up to him, wishing I didn't feel so nauseous about the entire conversation. 'Show me the rule book that says we can't.'

'You...'

'Ethan's involved. We will be an inclusive organisation and ensure that there are no catastrophic errors – such as the whole troll race almost being wiped out by accident! There will be a troll representative included at all times. Or rather,' I said, proudly, 'a troll godmother. We've thought this through. It will be wonderful.' I leaned in. 'And far, far better than the Office of Faery Godmothers could ever be.'

Jasper shook his head. 'Impossible.'

'Not in the slightest,' I said cheerily.

He gritted his teeth. 'Even if this were to be allowed to happen, I would have to be involved from the beginning.'

'Hm.' I sucked on my bottom lip. 'I'm not sure that's a good idea. You're welcome to come in once we're established – we want to be transparent. But it's better if you wait a while.'

'You can't establish a new agency just like that, Saffron!'

A small group of faeries fell out of the drawing room, glasses in hand and giggles on their lips. They couldn't fail to hear Jasper's angry tone. One by one they fell silent and looked at us, their mouths opening with almost rabid curiosity.

Jasper muttered something under his breath, took hold of my elbow and propelled me outside where we could continue our conversation unheard. 'If you're going to do this,' he ground out, releasing his hold on me, 'and I *strongly* advise against it, then I have to be involved from the outset.'

Bingo. 'You're a busy man,' I said. 'You have a lot going on and you're clearly prejudiced against me...'

'I am perfectly capable of remaining professional,' he said, his jaw tight.

'Do you really have the time to oversee the establishment of a freelance faery agency?'

Jasper put his hands in his pockets. 'I'll make time.'

I tried very, very hard not to let my relief show. Our intention in setting up an agency was to unbalance the Director and draw her out into the open. Her ego wouldn't cope with competition, regardless of how small and insignificant that competition happened to be. But I could kill two birds with one stone; if Jasper spent his next few weeks focussing on the rights and wrongs of our new enterprise, he wouldn't have the time to follow up his own suspicions about the Director. If he wasn't investigating her he'd be safe – and that was the best outcome that I could think of.

'Well,' I said, as if it were a heavy burden for me to bear but one that I'd put up with if I had to, 'it's your funeral.'

'Apparently so.' He pulled his hands out of his pockets and crossed his arms over his broad chest. 'What's happened to you,

Saffron?' he asked eventually. 'You're not the same person I met a few months ago. The Saffron I met burst into hysterical giggles at sharing a lift with me. She was funny and sweet and wanted to change the world for the better. That Saffron was bright and optimistic and had a good heart.'

'And now I'm sad and downbeat and evil?' I returned, unable to help myself. 'Maybe this is who I've always been.'

'No.' His clever gaze continued to sear into me. 'You're still hiding something from me. Whatever's going on with you and Rupert, there's more to this – to you – than meets the eye. You might think I'm stupid but sooner or later I will get to the truth.'

I had to hope that it was later. 'Nothing's going on with Rupert apart from this new agency,' I answered truthfully. 'I still want to change the world for the better. I still want to be the best faery godmother the world has ever seen. That's not changed. I'm only going about it in different ways, Jasper. There's nothing wrong with that.'

A myriad of emotions flitted across his face, very few of which I could decipher. What I couldn't fail to notice, however, was his pain. My heart contracted. 'We were friends once,' he said quietly. 'Even when there was something else between us…' His voice tailed off then he cleared his throat. 'I know I've lied to you before, and I know you've never been able to trust me fully. But you can open up to me now. Saffron, what aren't you telling me?'

'I don't know what you're talking about.'

'Yes, you do.' He drew in a breath, an intense urgency lighting his eyes. 'You walked away from me after I told you what I'd done. You became a different person. Now I don't believe I'm seeing the whole picture. Tell me what I'm missing.'

Jasper reached into his pocket and took out his wallet, flipping it open to reveal a small pressed dandelion behind the transparent plastic window. It was the one I'd dropped into the box of his belongings just before I'd walked out of the Office of Faery Godmothers for the last time. 'Why did you leave me this?'

'I...' I swallowed. *Because I think I love you. Because I don't want you to forget me. Because I still hope that somehow we'll get past these dark days and tangled lies and have a future together. And yes, I knew I was a fool for wishing that.* I dropped my head. 'Just because,' I said aloud.

'Do you hate me?' he asked.

My eyes flew to his. 'No!'

'I keep thinking about that night in the restaurant,' he said. 'We came so close, you and I. I understand that my past is complicated and that I've done things you might find hard to stomach.'

Regardless of my other motivations, I couldn't permit Jasper to feel bad about that. He'd killed a man when he wasn't even a man himself. He'd been burned up by hatred, revenge and grief for his dead sister and he was still making amends for what he'd done. It had been an appalling thing to do but it was understandable. His magic had overtaken him and he'd been out of control. I knew exactly how that felt; it was my magic that had killed Art Adwell.

'I don't hate you, Jasper. I could never hate you. What you did to your sister's killer...' I sighed. 'I don't know anyone who wouldn't have done the same, given half the chance. I know you'll take that guilt with you to the grave, but you shouldn't.'

For a moment anguish flickered in his eyes. Then he snapped his emotional wallet shut and tucked it away, shuttering his eyes at the same time. He began to turn away and I put out my hand to stop him.

'You'll find out about this sooner or later,' I said. It was true. And telling him wouldn't change anything or affect our plans for the Director. Not right now. But he deserved to know. 'I might as well tell you. I was there. I was there when Figgy died.'

Jasper froze. 'What?'

I swallowed hard. 'I went to confront Adwell, and Figgy was already there. She...' Fuck a puck. I hadn't thought this through. I couldn't blurt out the whole truth and reveal that she'd been lured there because of a note that was seemingly written by the Devil's Advocate. I'd have to fudge some of the details.

'Adwell was manipulating her and he ended up attacking her. In return, I snapped. Just like you did. My magic...' I forced myself to continue. 'My magic flew out of me and I couldn't contain it. It slammed into Adwell and he fell out of the window. I'm the same as you, Jasper.'

I clicked my fingers, making the pretty plant close to us momentarily burst into full bloom then lapse back into dark foliage again.

Jasper stared at it and then at me, shock and horror and sympathy written all across his face. 'Saffron,' he whispered.

'Yeah.' I forced a laugh. 'I don't need a wand to grant wishes. I'm exactly like you.'

His expression didn't change. 'I'm sorry.'

A lump rose in my throat. He got it. Of all the people who knew my secret, Jasper was the only one who understood. I took more comfort from that than I could ever get from a tequila bottle. The power I now held was great – but what had happened in order for me to gain that power threatened to overwhelm me whenever I thought about it.

I'd done the right thing by telling him. The weight that had settled across my shoulders hadn't gone, but it had eased somewhat.

He shook his head. 'I wish you hadn't told me.'

I recoiled. What?

'I'm the Devil's Advocate, Saffron. I'm tasked with keeping

law and order amongst all faeries. God knows, I don't always do the best job. In fact...' He looked away and changed tack, squaring his shoulders. 'Never mind that now,' he muttered. He raised his eyes back to mine. 'There are strict procedures that have to be followed and questions that have to be answered. The bureaucracy around something like this is on a level that you've never experienced before, even in the Office of Faery Godmothers.'

I stood up a little bit straighter. 'I can accept that,' I said honestly. 'Along with whatever censure or punishment you think I deserve.'

'It's not about...'

I held up my hands. 'I know. But it's worth saying anyway.' It was probably better that this truth was out, even if other secrets had to stay hidden. I'd woman up and deal with the consequences. I wouldn't allow myself to be like the Director and conceal my misdeeds. I was better than that. I would always be better than that.

I glanced at the drawing room and prayed this wouldn't mess up our plans for the agency. 'If you need to take me into custody, then so be it. I'm not going to resist.'

Jasper pressed his lips into a thin line. 'Hopefully it won't come to that. But I will need to call a meeting of all the departmental heads and inform them about your confession. Tomorrow, or the day after at the latest. They'll discuss how best to proceed.'

That meant the Director would find out. I could well imagine what her reaction would be and what she'd recommend for my future.

'So be it.' I nodded.

Jasper reached out and touched my arm. 'I'm sorry,' he said. 'For all of it. For you.'

I bit my lip. 'Thank you.' I wanted to ask him for a hug, for his safe arms to wrap themselves around me and hold me close, but I didn't dare. Instead I looked into his eyes. 'Thank you for not hating me.' I reached onto my tiptoes and brushed my lips against his cheek.

Jasper closed his eyes for half a beat before cupping my face with his hands. 'Saffron...'

No. I pulled away, trying not to dwell on the flicker of hurt in his expression. This couldn't happen; it would only give the Director an opportunity to level even harsher accusations against Jasper. She'd use the hint of any relationship between us to persuade the rest of the faery leaders that he couldn't be trusted. It would spell disaster for him and for all our plans.

'I'll wait to hear from you,' I said formally. 'And I'll keep you informed of every step of Wish Inc's progress to ensure that appropriate supervision is maintained.'

Jasper's face shuttered. 'Okay,' he said, all trace of emotion gone from his voice. 'Okay.' Then, without another word, he twisted round and walked away.

CHAPTER

NINE

The next morning I still hadn't been carted away in handcuffs. I decided I'd take that as a positive indication that things might go my way and maintained a smile that was almost genuine. Equally, I did an excellent job of acting like I'd had a wonderful night's sleep and hadn't tossed and turned for several heartbroken hours.

I didn't fool Pumpkin, who refused to stray more than a few inches from my side, but no-one else noticed. To a faery, the others were remarkably buoyant – and matters were moving far faster than I'd anticipated. Angela was on the ball; less than twenty-four hours after our meeting, she'd already found us an office to rent.

'I like this place,' Rupert declared, looking around. 'The rooms are a good size and the location is perfect. I'll take the corner office. As the only faery godfather around here, it's only fair.'

Billy coughed loudly. 'I'm a faery godfather.'

'Yeah,' Rupert said, clapping him on the shoulder, 'but you don't deal with clients. You're the office janitor.'

'You don't deal with clients either.'

Rupert just grinned. 'This is the perfect time to start.' He rubbed his palms together. 'In fact, I'd like my first client to be a twenty-something blonde woman. I can sort out her love life for her.'

'This,' Billy said with a sniff, 'is exactly why you need to be kept away from real people.'

'You misunderstand me!' Rupert protested. 'I want a client like that so I can prove I've changed and that I can be perfectly professional.'

'I'll believe it when I see it.'

Alicia raised her eyebrows at me and I shrugged. 'Everyone should get the chance to turn over a new leaf,' I said, as Rupert's delighted smile grew. 'But we also need procedures and rules in place to make sure that we are *all* professional.'

At that, Billy beamed. 'I've taken the liberty of swiping the rulebooks and operating procedures from the Office. The Devil's Advocate has already done most of the work for us. He recommended we streamline all of them into a simpler document. So far the Director's ignored that idea but I managed to get a copy.' He waved a folder. 'I've got it here. I'm already working on altering the wording to suit us.'

Alicia's expression didn't change. 'Perfect.'

Vincent bounced towards us. 'Which office is mine?'

I gazed at him, befuddled. 'What do you mean? You don't work here. You've already got a job.'

He twirled round. 'This place is awesome, Saffy. The last thing I want to do is miss out. If you're inviting a troll to work here, then you also need someone to provide a human perspective.' He nodded happily. 'I'll make an excellent consultant.' He waggled his eyebrows. 'For the right price.'

'In two days' time,' I reminded him, 'I might not even be here. I might get carted away to faery gaol and the rest of you will have to cope without me.'

'All the more reason for me to get a job at this place,' he said. 'I can be the eyes and ears on the ground that you can trust.'

Alicia snorted. 'Nothing bad will happen to Saffron. It can't. We need her – at least until we can arrange for a supply of magic wands for those of us who are normal faeries.'

I glanced at her, wondering whether that was another barb. 'At which point I can be thrown out on my ear?'

She waved a hand. 'You know what I mean. No matter what anyone says, what happened to that Adwell bastard was entirely justifiable. No-one would have done differently and every faery in the land will see that.' I blinked, genuinely surprised at her words. She flicked a look at Vincent and raised her voice pointedly. 'And Saffron knows she can trust us. *We* can't trust *you.*'

He winked at her. 'Of course you can. Besides, I have the inside scoop on all things human.'

Alicia pointed at Pumpkin, who allowed himself a tiny wag of his tail. 'Just like the dog's got the inside scoop on all things furry? Should we give him a job here too?'

Vincent shrugged. 'That's your prerogative.'

At that point the door opened and Melissa, wearing a suit of all things, marched through, her head held high. I hadn't been expecting Ethan to come himself; as the leader of the trolls, he wouldn't have the time to dedicate to another full-time job. But Melissa was one of the more vocal faery godmother opponents, and I doubted she was pleased at her new posting.

'It smells peculiar in here,' she said. 'There might be damp.'

'The surveyor's given the place a clean bill of health,' Alicia said. 'We won't find anywhere better at such short notice. Are you going to be our troll rep?'

'I am.' Melissa glanced round, her mouth turning down.

Keen to ensure that she was made welcome, I raised my

voice. 'Melissa doesn't need a wand to use magic. None of the trolls do. So if I do end up in chains…'

'You won't.'

'If I do,' I continued firmly, 'then she can fill the gap. I'm not integral to Wish Inc's success.'

Melissa gave a curt nod. 'Although I'd like to take this opportunity to inform you all that I wholly disapprove of faery godmothers, wishes, improving the lot of ungrateful humans and magic wands. In general.' She pursed her lips. 'I'll take the corner office.'

'Saffron can have the corner office,' Alicia said casually.

Everyone turned to her then to me. Even Pumpkin seemed surprised, but that might have been because he'd spotted a squirrel edging its way up the tree outside.

'Uh,' I shuffled my feet. 'Thanks. It's not really necessary, though. I can fit in anywhere.' I felt oddly embarrassed. I almost preferred it when Alicia was being her usual mean faery self.

'What's wrong with you?' Melissa enquired. She pointed to my face. 'Your eyes are all bloodshot and you look like death warmed up. Are you doing drugs? Because if you are, then I'll have some too. I need something to get me through this.'

Vincent looked at her, suddenly animated. 'I can help you with that,' he said.

'You will not,' I snapped. I realised the tone of my voice was overly harsh and softened it. 'And I'm fine. Thank you for thinking of me.'

Melissa curtsied before smiling with sudden, unexpected glee. 'Maybe this will be fun after all.'

Billy tapped his foot. 'This is all well and good but I should point out that we're missing someone.'

I grimaced. I'd been hoping that Mrs Jardine was merely running late.

'I don't know if Miranda will join us,' Alicia said with a

frown. 'I invited her because I knew she was having a hard time and we could do with her kind of experience, but it's a big leap for her to leave the Office of Faery Godmothers and come here. She's worked there for decades and her loyalties have always been unshakeable. She might end up telling the Director everything. She has a stern demeanour but deep down she's always been something of a yes woman who has jumped to the Director's every command.'

I'd had my doubts about Mrs Jardine in the past but she was a strong lady who knew her own mind, and she'd helped me when she'd had no reason to do so. Plus, I'd seen how she'd blanched at the truth about Figgy's death. 'She's only come across as a yes woman because she's been under the Director's thumb for so long,' I said. 'And it's not easy to say no to someone like the Director.'

The door opened and Mrs Jardine appeared. We all stared at her and she faltered. 'Yes?' she asked haltingly.

We burst out laughing. Even Melissa cracked a smile. In that moment, I knew that, whatever the outcome of this venture and whatever happened to me, we were going to get along fine.

'I don't see what's so funny,' Mrs Jardine snapped.

She walked towards us, her lips pursed. Now that she was here, I wondered what the atmosphere at the Office of Faery Godmothers was like this morning given that both she and Billy hadn't turned up to work. The loss of Angela and Alicia could be managed – there were plenty of other HR managers and faery godmothers. But Billy and Mrs Jardine were the cogs that made the whole machine turn, even if they'd never been given the respect they'd deserved. I'd have liked to be a fly on the wall of the Director's office about now.

'The reception desk should go out by the front,' Mrs Jardine said with a sniff, 'facing the door. And I'd like to have some input on the colour scheme. I find lilac a very soothing colour.'

'I'd prefer pink,' Billy said. 'It's evocative of the original faery godmother cloaks and a more welcoming colour than people realise.'

Melissa frowned. 'Black would be better.'

Vincent waved his hand. 'How about a Disney theme?'

They lapsed into a round of good-natured bickering. I breathed out and met Alicia's eyes. For a moment we smiled at each other; maybe Wish Inc would pan out after all. Then we joined in with the argument.

WITH THE MOVING-IN process well under way, I left the others and returned to the supermarket to complete my last shift. Despite the bonhomie at Wish Inc, I wasn't prepared to scrape along on hands and knees and beg Alicia for an advance so I could pay the last of my bills.

She'd made mutterings about some investment fund that would easily recoup any losses the new agency accrued, and she didn't seem to find the financial situation any sort of burden. Truthfully, I suspected that she was delighted that it was her idea and we hadn't laughed her out of her own house. It also helped that Ethan and Rupert had agreed to make contributions. But I still had some pride; besides, I'd made a commitment to stack shelves for a few hours more so that was exactly what I was going to do. Hopefully on this occasion there would be no vomit involved.

When I donned my branded apron and headed onto the supermarket floor, I spotted Albert in the café with the same woman whose aid I'd encouraged him to leap to. I felt a glow of pride. I wasn't a bad person, I told myself. Not all the time.

Once I'd finished replenishing the shelves with fresh fruit, I armed myself with a spray gun and ambled over to the large glass windows to wipe away the sticky finger marks. As I rounded the corner I registered Ben, my new neighbour, perusing the shelves of magazines. I was sorely tempted to pretend I hadn't seen him and avoid the trauma of more painful small talk but I was better than that. At least, for today I was.

'Hey, Ben.'

He looked up, his face clearing when he saw me. 'Saffron! How lovely to see you!'

Ah. We were back to lovely again. 'It's lovely to see you too, Ben. How are you?'

He grinned, a tiny dimple forming in his cheek. 'I am fabulous. I have to tell you that I wasn't sure about moving here. I don't really know anyone in this part of the country. But it's already working out. I even have an audition tomorrow.'

'You're an actor?'

'A musician. I play the violin.' He mimed for me without a shade of embarrassment. 'My ultimate ambition is to play with the London Philharmonic but I want to cut my teeth with a local orchestra first.' He was surprisingly earnest. 'They don't get enough recognition. I want to change that.'

'Good for you.'

'How about you? I take it you work here?'

I smiled. 'This is a temporary job, alas.' Then I thought some more and took a deep breath. 'I'm actually in the process of setting up a new agency with some friends.'

Ben seemed intrigued. 'How lovely! Doing what?'

'Uh, life coaching,' I answered. It was close enough to the truth.

'Fascinating. I'd love to know more about how you go about it. Do you have many clients?'

'Not yet. We're just getting started,' I explained. I waved my window cleaner at him. 'I'll tell you about it some other time. I'd better get to work.'

'Of course, of course! Lovely to bump into you, Saffron.' He wiggled his fingers at me in farewell.

I left Ben to his magazines and focused on the window, rubbing distractedly at a few of the more stubborn streaks. He was a nice chap, I decided. Overly effusive perhaps, but thoughtful and pleasant. He was quite good looking, although obviously not a patch on Jasper whose brilliant green eyes could pierce a person even from the other side of a streaky supermarket window...

I blinked and did a double take, dropping my spray gun. What the hell was he doing here?

I stayed where I was, my feet rooted to the floor, while Jasper walked through the sliding doors and strode towards me. His grim expression didn't augur well.

When he reached me, I held out my wrists towards him in mock surrender. 'Are you taking me in now?' I asked, trying to make light of the situation.

Jasper didn't smile. 'I've met with the other faery department heads,' he said. 'They would like to question you to find out more before coming to a decision.'

That sounded ominous. 'Now? But I'm working,' I said pathetically.

'I can see that. It's taken me a while to track you down.' Jasper looked round. 'Does this mean that the agency is no longer a viable option?'

'No, I'm simply fulfilling my other commitments first,' I told him. 'We've already found an office space and Wish Inc is on its way to opening its doors. We'll be located on Honeysuckle Avenue, if you need to check it out.'

'I'll do that.' He nodded formally at me. 'The interview with the department heads will be at nine o'clock tomorrow morning. The Director has said we can use the Office of Faery Godmothers.'

How kind of her, I thought sourly. 'I can't wait. Should I bring a lawyer?'

Jasper frowned. 'That's up to you.' He started to turn away. 'I'll see you there.'

That was it? I gazed after him. 'Wait!'

Jasper glanced back. 'Yes?'

'Is that it?' I squinted at him. 'I mean, you could have telephoned.'

'I could have,' he said quietly. He raised his shoulders in a shrug before appearing to make some sort of decision. 'I guess I wanted to see your face.' My mouth went dry and I stared at him. 'Don't worry about the meeting tomorrow,' he continued. 'You've got more friends than you realise. As long as you tell the truth, you'll be fine.'

Easier said than done. I couldn't tell the whole truth without the evidence to back it up. Unfounded accusations wouldn't help my cause. I'd do my best, however. 'Thanks, Jasper. And,' I licked my lips, 'thanks for coming in person.' I took a deep breath. 'It's good to see your face too.'

He gave me a long look. 'I've never met anyone who blows as hot and cold as you do, Saffron,' he said finally.

A flickering shape caught the edge of my vision as I tried to think of an appropriate answer. I would have ignored it and kept my focus on Jasper if it hadn't been for the loud scream from one of the nearby shoppers. I started to turn, just as the window I'd been cleaning shattered into a thousand pieces, glass spraying everywhere.

The man on the other side raised the baton he was holding and grinned. His pupils were dilated but his gaze was focused on me. 'Hi,' he said. He swung the baton and I ducked just in time. 'I've been looking for you.'

CHAPTER

TEN

Jasper's reaction time was faster than mine. He leapt in front of me, shielding my body from the crazed attacker, raised his hands and shot enough magic to blast him backwards. The man flew through the air, landing on his back at the edge of the small supermarket car park.

'Human,' Jasper grunted. He looked at me. 'Who is he?'

I gazed at him, shocked and baffled. 'I don't have a clue. Mistaken identity, maybe?' We exchanged a look. That was highly unlikely.

Brenda ran over, her apron flapping. She stared at the shattered window and the fallen man in horror. 'My goodness, Saffron,' she gasped. 'Is he on drugs?'

'Uh,' I scratched my head. 'I guess so. Someone should call the police.'

'Alistair is already on it.' She turned away and headed for the information desk, waving a hand at the pale-faced woman behind it. 'Turn on the tannoy,' she said, grabbing the microphone and holding it to her mouth. 'Ladies and gentleman, there is no need for alarm. For your own safety, please make your way calmly but quickly towards the back of the store. The police are on their way.'

For a moment nobody moved, then, as if everyone had taken a collective breath, there was a stampede as shoppers from all directions ran down the aisles away from us.

'I think it's okay,' I said. 'He's out for the count.' I hoped the man wasn't dead; he'd had quite a heavy landing and his body was sprawled across the tarmac in an awkward position. I raised my foot to step over the sill of the window and check on him.

Jasper's arm shot out, preventing me. 'Wait,' he said.

'It's fine. He's...' My voice faltered as my assailant moved. First his arms and legs twitched as if of their own volition, then he sprang to his feet in one lithe movement and shook himself, sending more shards of glass flying.

'What the fuck?' I whispered. Was that sheer adrenaline that was propelling him?

Jasper's hands bunched into fists. 'Magic,' he said darkly. 'That's magic.'

Swallowing, I waved a frantic hand at Brenda. 'Get to the back!' I yelled. 'Run!'

'But...'

The man was already advancing, his flickering eyes fixed on me.

'Go!' Thankfully, I didn't have to tell her again. She darted away, her fear getting the better of her.

Brenda wasn't the only one who was scared but I couldn't run away. Not only was he here for me, but I had the power to stop him. Or so I hoped.

As my attacker drew closer, he appeared to grow in stature, his muscles straining within the confines of his clothes and threatening to rip his shirt open at the seams. He bared his teeth in a snarl and started to run. I drew in a breath and threw out a wave of magic. Throwing him to the ground hadn't worked; the next best move was to contain him.

My magic encircled him, creating an invisible wall designed to keep him in one place. But this wasn't like Rupert's three-breasted conjuration; as Jasper had said, this man was totally human, regardless of what power he'd been imbued with. In theory, that should mean he was easier to contain.

His body bounced backwards, away from my magic wall, and his face contorted with rage because I'd stopped his approach. When Jasper saw what I'd done he copied my movements, strengthening my barrier further.

The man twisted, slamming out his fists and searching for a way out. He tried the left, the right, and then behind him, but he was definitely trapped. Leaning his head back, he opened his mouth and howled, a keening, inhuman sound that filled the air.

At that very moment, we heard the sirens of an approaching police car.

Jasper glanced at me. 'Are you okay?' he asked gruffly.

I nodded, although I was shaken to my core by what had happened. 'Are you?'

His expression was grim. 'Yes.' He jerked his head at the man, whose face had turned an apoplectic purple as he continued to rage. 'We need to find out who he is and what's going on.'

The police car pulled up, its tires screeching. 'Too late,' I muttered.

Two police officers jumped out of the car, frowning when they caught sight of the man. They advanced towards him, their batons raised. 'Get down on the ground!' the male officer yelled.

The man stopped howling and twisted his head towards them. A slow, unpleasant smile crossed his swarthy face. He dropped his hands by his sides and muttered something. I tried to read his lips. I couldn't make out what he was saying but I had a deep sense of foreboding.

'Something's not right,' I said. 'We need to put him down.'

'I'm open to suggestions,' Jasper told me.

I cast around, trying to think. I left it too long. A moment later, the invisible wall of magic started to glow, emitting a faint blue light. The man's lips continued to move – and the more they did, the deeper the glow became.

'Jasper…'

The man lunged towards me, swivelling round so that his back was to the broken window. I gasped as the entire sky seemed to light up. A beat later there was a deafening boom and both Jasper and I were flung to the side, smacking into a neatly constructed display of Halloween goodies. Sweets and plastic pumpkins scattered everywhere, spinning across the super-market floor.

Jasper landed on top of me, effectively pinning me to the ground. For a few seconds my vision went blurry and a strange sound surrounded me, penetrating everything. When I managed to blink away my confusion, I realised it was my ears ringing. An explosion, I thought dully. That had been some kind of explosion.

'Jasper,' I croaked.

He didn't move.

'Jasper!'

I tried to shake him. His body was a dead weight on top of mine. Panic clawed at me. I raised my hands, clutching his shoulders and trying frantically to rouse him. Eventually I rolled him off me before hunching over him and checking his airway. His skin was pale and his eyes were closed but he was still breathing. Praise be.

I stirred up a sprig of magic, unwilling to hit him with too much but desperate to bring him back to consciousness.

Then I heard a low whistle.

I turned my head. Standing less than five metres away, and now wholly free, was the psychotic bastard who'd done this. He was slapping his baton into his free hand over and over and over again. When I didn't move, his eyes slid to Jasper's unmoving body and I understood instantly. It was him or me.

I rose slowly until my gaze connected with his and forced his attention to me. He was still smiling. That made it even worse.

'I don't know who you are or why you're doing this,' I whispered. 'But you're not in control of yourself. Stop. Think.'

'I've been looking for you.' He started to advance.

I side-stepped, not to get away from him but to ensure that he stayed away from Jasper. From the corner of my eye, I could see the bodies of the police officers splayed out beyond the supermarket's walls. The female officer was moving her arm and trying to reach her radio. She was alive, then. That was good.

I lifted my hands again, not to defend myself but to attack. I didn't want to kill him but I would if I had to. If it meant protecting Jasper and the people crowded into the rear of the supermarket, I'd do it a thousand times over. There was just one thing I wanted to know first. 'Who's controlling you?' I asked. 'Who sent you here?'

'I've been looking for you.'

He seemed incapable of saying anything else. I hissed under my breath and looked deep into his eyes. Somewhere behind that glazed sheen of craziness was a human being. An innocent. He drew closer. 'I'm sorry,' I told him. 'I really am.'

A second later I hit him with everything I had, drawing up every ounce of energy from the pit of my belly. Jets of magic slammed into his body and he froze – before rising half an inch off the ground as if he were floating. That wasn't supposed to happen.

I thrust my palms forward again, spewing out more magic. His body juddered as it exploded into him and his eyes rolled back into his head. It wasn't pain or horror on his face, however. It was ecstasy.

I stared down at my hands. The more magic I sent his way, the more he seemed to feed off it. I had to try something else. I had to stop him.

He started to lower himself to the ground, his feet planted firmly. His eyes bored into mine. 'I've been looking for you.'

'So you keep saying,' I said. I crouched down and grabbed a shard of glass. Its sharp edges cut into the fleshy parts of my palm, drawing blood that dripped onto the white floor. I ignored it and brandished my weapon. 'Come on, then. What else have you got?'

He grinned, raised his baton and swung it hard in my direction. I tried to duck but the edge of it caught my temple, sending me reeling backwards. I swiped the shard of glass forward, snagging his shirt and tearing it open. Beads of blood appeared on his skin but it was little more than a flesh wound.

I stabbed the glass towards him again, this time embedding its sharp tip in his torso. I pushed forward, prepared to force it into his soft body. He immediately dropped the baton and reached for my wrist, squeezing hard until I heard my bones crunch. I screamed and released my grip on the glass as I stumbled to my knees.

The man glanced curiously at the lethal shard sticking out from beneath his ribs before gripping it with his thumb and forefinger and sliding it out. There was an unpleasant sucking sound as it left his body. He frowned at it and shrugged, throwing it aside before bending down and grabbing hold of his baton again.

'I've been looking for you,' he told me for a final time. He raised the baton high in the air, preparing to swing it down onto my skull.

There was a glimpse of a shadow in my peripheral vision and a sudden crunch. The man's eyes widened before he fell to his knees and keeled over. Behind him stood my neighbour Ben, holding what looked like a frozen leg of lamb in his right hand.

'Sorry,' he gasped, his face pale. 'I tried to get to you sooner.'

FIVE MINUTES LATER, the supermarket was surrounded. There were blue flashing lights everywhere that were doing nothing for my already wavering consciousness.

'Everyone's alive,' Brenda said, her hands fluttering at her neck. 'Even the bastard who attacked you.'

I shook my head dully at the venom in her voice. 'It wasn't his fault.' Something – or rather *someone* – had turned magic in on itself and used it to control him. He was a tool, nothing else. I had no idea how they'd done it but I had a good idea who was behind it. Yet again, however, I had no proof.

I staggered over to the ambulance where Jasper was being attended to. He blinked blearily while one of the paramedics shone a light in his eyes. 'You don't seem to have suffered any serious damage,' she said. 'But there's a good chance you've got concussion. We need to get you to a hospital so you can be seen to properly. Don't worry, though – I think you'll be fine.'

Jasper glanced at me, his meaning clear. I nodded and summoned up my last few dregs of magical energy. While the paramedic glanced to the side, her attention caught by the camera flashes from the journalists who'd started to arrive, Jasper was transformed. Using glamour, I healed his injuries and camouflaged the worst of the resulting bruises. He inclined his head gratefully and stood up.

'Thank you,' he murmured to the paramedic, who jerked in surprise at his miraculous recovery. 'I'll make my own way to the hospital with my friend.'

Before she could argue, I put my uninjured arm round him and we walked round the corner and out of sight. 'I'm not sure I've done enough,' I said anxiously. 'I didn't have much left in me after—' I swallowed '—after all that.'

'I feel fine.' He looked down. 'But your wrist doesn't look particularly healthy.'

He could say that again. It had swollen to twice its normal size and was sporting a glorious rainbow of bruises. Jasper's fingers brushed against my skin and I shivered as the bones healed at his touch. The swelling would take longer and the bruises would remain for days, but that was nothing compared to what could have been. And there were far more important things to worry about.

'I'm not covered by memory magic,' I said urgently. 'There are CCTV cameras all over the supermarket and the car park.' There would be no explaining away what had just happened to anyone who'd seen – and remembered – the truth.

'It's okay,' Jasper said. 'I was here on official business so I'm covered. All the public and the police will see is a man off his head attacking random passers-by. You don't have to worry on that score. And the fact that it was a human who saved the day makes it easier to manage.' He stepped back, checking on Ben who was in deep discussion with a plain-clothed policeman. 'Is he really your neighbour?'

'Yeah,' I said. I smiled slightly. 'He's lovely.'

Jasper frowned but didn't comment. 'You're sure you don't know who the attacker was? You've never seen him before?'

'No.'

His expression grew more intense. 'Who do you think was behind this? You must have some idea.'

Fuck a puck. 'I don't know.' I ran a hand through my hair. 'I guess I have a lot of enemies.'

Jasper's eyes narrowed. 'If you won't talk to me,' he said eventually, 'maybe our poor psychotic fellow will.' He spun on his heel and marched towards the organised chaos of the emergency services. I grimaced and trotted after him.

The man had been taken to a secure van where he could be locked up and checked over for injury. Magic flickered round Jasper's body as he approached the police officer guarding the van and held up his wallet. 'I want to talk to him.'

The police officer squinted at the wallet, immediately fooled by the glamour Jasper had conjured up. He nodded and stepped back, allowing us inside. Glamour or not, we wouldn't have long before the van took our assailant to the hospital and then to the police station. I hoped that we could get some answers quickly.

'I need a minute,' Jasper said to the older of the two paramedics who were leaning over my attacker. He was on his back and clearly out for the count. He was also tightly cuffed; nobody was taking any chances.

'We have to take him to St Cuthbert's,' the paramedic protested.

Jasper's gaze turned hard. 'One minute.'

He received an eye roll and a loud tut before they left us in peace. Jasper wasted no time in snapping his fingers and forcing the man into consciousness. 'What's your name?' he demanded.

'Alan Kennedy.' The man blinked. 'I don't understand. What's going on?'

Jasper clicked his fingers again. 'Why did you come here?'

Kennedy jerked his hand and the chain on the cuffs rattled.

His face remained clouded with confusion but the compulsion to answer overcame everything else. 'I was following you,' he said. 'I had to follow you because you were going to lead me to her.' He looked at me. 'Sorry. I didn't want to hurt you. I don't know why I did.' His eyes filled with tears.

'Shhh.' I placed a hand on his forehead. 'Don't worry. This wasn't your fault.'

I could feel Jasper shaking with fury beside me. 'Who?' he asked. 'Who told you to do this?'

Alan Kennedy paused before answering. 'A man,' he said almost dreamily. 'Blond hair. Maybe thirty years old. Good looking. He has a tiny scar at the edge of his mouth and...'

Jasper didn't let him finish. 'Ethan,' he spat. 'This was all down to Ethan.' He pulled back and threw open the van door before storming out.

I cursed and gave Kennedy a quick smile of reassurance. 'We will fix this for you, Alan,' I said. 'Don't worry.' Then I darted out after Jasper.

CHAPTER
ELEVEN

Jasper was already halfway down the street, his spine ramrod straight with fury. I ran after him, forcing my legs to move quickly and ignoring the still-throbbing pain in my wrist. 'Jasper, wait!'

He ignored me and continued marching.

'Jasper! Think about this for a moment! It can't have been Ethan. It doesn't make sense!' He wasn't listening to me. I put on a final surge of speed, caught up to him and grabbed his arm. 'Look,' I said, desperation colouring my words. 'Ethan wouldn't...'

'I'm going to kill him.' His face was a mask of unadulterated rage.

'You need to stop this. Don't jump to conclusions. You're supposed to be the level-headed one, remember?'

Jasper wasn't hearing a word I was saying. His anger was overcoming every other emotion – and every rational thought. I shook him. It was imperative that he calmed down. If he confronted Ethan like this, goodness knows what might happen.

'Let go of me, Saffron.'

I shook my head. 'No.'

'He tried to kill you. He'll pay for this.' His face contorted and then I felt his arm grow insubstantial beneath my touch.

Alarm lit through me. Oh no. 'Wait!' It was too late. A moment later, Jasper's body dissolved into a haze of red and he was gone, leaving me standing there holding nothing but air.

I ground my teeth. Regardless of what poor Alan Kennedy had said, it seemed implausible that Ethan was behind this attack. He had no reason to come after me.

I stared at the spot where Jasper had disappeared. I knew where he was going. If I followed on foot I'd arrive far too late but I'd never tried to use my magic to transport myself. I might mess it up. I had to try, though. If Jasper went for Ethan with all guns blazing and Ethan fought back, it would be catastrophic for all of us.

I drew in a breath and closed my eyes. I'd already used up almost everything I had, firstly in trying to stop Kennedy and secondly in healing Jasper's wounds. But I had to find sufficient traces of magic within myself to do this. Nothing was more important.

I stayed where I was, splaying out my hands and widening my stance as if stronger contact with the ground beneath my feet would help me. 'Come on, Saffron,' I whispered. 'You can do this. It can't be that hard.' Then I squeezed the last of the magic out of my body and prayed.

A cold breeze rippled against my face and ruffled my hair. I heard a faint whoosh and my stomach lurched. Gasping aloud, I stumbled and collided against something hard. I opened my eyes, blinking rapidly to regain my balance.

I was in front of a grand old house, surrounded by fields and trees and very little else. I'd transported myself somewhere –

but was this somewhere the right place? There was no-one in sight. For all I knew, I'd ended up in France and was about to hammer down the door of an unsuspecting French landowner. Then I heard raised voices and I knew my magic had proven itself. I was in the right place – and there was no time to waste.

I sprang forward, unwilling to waste time knocking on the door. Instead I burst through it, a small part of my brain noting the splinters in the woodwork and realising that Jasper had just done the same thing. Fortunately I didn't have to go racing round the house to find the pair of them; they were right in front of me, encircled by a large group of very angry trolls.

Jasper had his hands up and was clearly ready to attack at a moment's notice. The look on his face was disturbingly similar to Alan Kennedy's when he'd been in the throes of his magically-induced psychosis. Ethan's expression was also angry but there was a hint of wariness behind his clever eyes. Don't do anything rash, Ethan, I prayed. Please.

I forced myself into the fray.

Jasper flicked a look in my direction. 'Your magic is increasing, Saffron,' he said through clenched teeth. 'Stay back. Don't let him near you.' He returned his attention to Ethan and glared with such venom that a shiver of fear ran through me. 'Why?' He bunched his hands into fists. 'Why did you do it?'

'Saffron,' Ethan said, his tone deceptively mild, 'what is he talking about?'

Jasper took a step towards the troll leader. 'Don't talk to her,' he spat. 'Don't so much as look at her.'

'You broke into my house,' Ethan said. 'You're looking for a fight.' His eyes sparked, hinting at the rage he was also feeling. 'I will do whatever I fucking feel like.' He waved a hand. 'You're obviously outnumbered, so perhaps you ought to calm down and start explaining what's going on.'

'Answer my questions,' Jasper hissed, 'or we're done talking.'

Ethan simply folded his arms. 'I have nothing to answer for.'

Jasper lunged forward with a raised fist. One of the watching trolls streaked forward and hauled him back before the punch could land. I suppose I should have been grateful that he wasn't using magic – at least, not yet.

'Try that again,' the troll yelled in Jasper's face, 'and I will end you.'

Ethan held up his right hand. 'No,' he said. 'Stay back. Whatever this is, it's between the Devil's Advocate and me. The rest of you stay out of it. Understood?' None of the trolls reacted. 'Understood?' he repeated.

They nodded reluctantly. The one in front of Jasper moved away, a tight snarl on his face.

Jasper went on as if nothing had happened. 'She's the one faery who stuck up for you, despite everything that you've done. She was on your side – and this is how you repay her?'

'Jasper, wait...' I said.

'I'm dealing with this, Saffron!' he snapped.

'Not very well.' I moved forward between the pair of them. When Ethan opened his mouth to speak, I glared at him. 'You're not my boss,' I reminded him gently. 'You can't tell me what to do either.'

'Then explain to me what the fuck is going on!' Ethan exploded.

Suddenly, I realised how close to the edge he was. I stretched out my arms, one towards Jasper and one towards Ethan. Ethan's eyes dropped to the bruises around my wrist and his eyes narrowed but he didn't say anything.

'Just now,' I said calmly, despite the hammering of my heart, 'someone tried to kill me.'

Ethan went preternaturally still. 'A troll?'

'No, you fuckhead!' Jasper snarled. 'We all know you wouldn't risk one of your own. Instead you slammed magic into some poor human bastard and got him to do your dirty work for you. You've got no shame.'

'Someone tries to kill Saffron Sawyer and you immediately think it's me?' Ethan said. 'Well, I guess now we all now know what you really think of us trolls! If a crime's been committed, we must be the culprits. Right?'

Jasper pushed forward, trying to get at him. I stood my ground and forced him back. 'We questioned the human who attacked me,' I explained. 'We asked who'd sent him and he described you.'

'Down to a fucking T,' Jasper growled. 'You will bleed for this.'

'Except,' I said, before things got worse, 'anyone who has the power to push magic into a human and compel them to do their bidding also has the power to create a glamour to look like Ethan! And anyone who wants to get me out of the way and encourage all-out war with the trolls would do that!'

Jasper opened his mouth to argue then my words penetrated his fury. He blinked and rocked back on his heels. 'Huh,' he said. He dropped his hands. 'Huh.' He pursed his lips. 'It still might have been him.'

'I trust Ethan.'

Jasper's face started to suffuse with red. 'You don't trust me?'

'I do. Only...' Fuck a puck. I lowered my voice and looked into his eyes. 'I don't trust myself around you. It's one thing to trust your actions and another to trust your heart.'

'Have I wandered into a Hallmark film?' Ethan enquired. He glanced round. 'We need a violin or a harp or something? Where's the orchestra?'

Jasper stared at me for another long moment then at the troll leader. 'Where have you been today?' he asked with less aggression than before. 'Can you account for your whereabouts? Do you have an alibi?'

Ethan shrugged. Some of his earlier tension seemed to have left his body but we weren't out of the danger zone yet. 'I've been here all day,' he answered simply. 'Any one of my trolls will attest to that. But then,' he smiled faintly, 'of course they would back me up.' He turned to me. 'I'm sorry about what happened to you. But you must remember what I said to you at the church.'

'That you wouldn't hurt me,' I answered. 'Regardless of what happened between the trolls and faery godmothers.'

He inclined his head. 'Indeed. I haven't broken that promise. Nor will I.'

'I believe you because I also remember that you were there when I almost snapped the first time,' I told him. 'If it wasn't for you, I could easily have killed a human being. I'm not saying I always agree with your actions or your words, Ethan – though to be fair, I don't always agree with my own actions and words. But I don't think you did this. I never did.'

'Thank you.' He moved sideways to get a better view of Jasper. 'I would have nothing to gain and everything to lose by attacking her. This wasn't me.'

Jasper didn't answer immediately. When he did he spoke stiffly, but there was no denying the regret in his expression. 'I apologise. I didn't question what I was told and I rushed to the wrong conclusion. I can see that Saffron doesn't believe it was you, and that is enough for me. But the fact that someone is inciting trouble in this manner needs to be looked into urgently. I apologise to all of you for coming here. I apologise especially to you, Ethan.' He turned on his heel and walked out.

I looked at Ethan too. 'I'm sorry too,' I said.

Ethan nodded, although his eyes remained troubled. 'If *she* did this,' he said, 'she's escalating matters dangerously. You have to take care, Saffron.' He rubbed the back of his neck. 'All of us do.'

'I know,' I said. I didn't have to ask who the 'she' was that he was referring to.

Ethan glanced at the door through which Jasper had departed. 'Trolls kidnapped him and he didn't react like that. Trolls infiltrated the Office of Faery Godmothers and he didn't react like that. I've never seen anyone, let alone the Devil's Advocate, prepared to throw away peace so quickly. I think his feelings for you are deeper than even he knows.'

I stared at him. For some reason, I couldn't speak.

'You have to watch him, Saffron. If he finds out who's really behind this attack...'

I found my voice. 'I know.' I licked my lips. 'He won't hear it from me. Not until we have absolute proof and we're able to manage the situation.'

'Good.' Ethan kept his eyes on mine. 'Once upon a time, I would have found the prospect of civil war delightful. I don't feel that way any more. You need to take care of yourself. And the Devil's Advocate.'

'I will.' I half-turned. 'I should go after him.'

'I can send people with you, if you need them.'

'No.' I raised my chin. 'I'll be fine. *We'*ll be fine. And thank you for your restraint.'

Ethan regarded me. 'It was a close-run thing.'

I bit my lip. 'I know.'

THIS TIME JASPER hadn't gone far. He was sitting on top of a fence in front of Ethan's property, his back to me as he gazed at the fields. I knew he'd heard my approach although he didn't turn around.

'It still could have been Ethan, you know,' he said when I drew close.

'It wasn't.'

He sighed and ran a hand through his inky-black hair. 'Yeah.' He paused. 'But you have your suspicions as to who did this.' He glanced at me. 'There's no point denying it.'

I didn't answer. Instead, I hopped onto the fence beside him, took his hand and squeezed it. His fingers gripped mine with such fervour that I wasn't sure he'd ever let go. I wasn't sure I wanted him to.

'There's only been one other time when I've lost it like that,' he told me, returning his eyes to the field and fixing on a distant tree. 'I didn't think I'd ever react to anything in that way again. My sister was the dearest person in my life. I loved her so much – I'd have done anything for her. I didn't think I'd ever feel that same level of emotion again for anyone.'

I stopped breathing, unsure what he was telling me and too scared to ask. 'For what it's worth,' I said quietly, 'I'd do anything for you.'

Jasper's fingers tightened even more round mine. For a long time, neither of us said anything else. We remained as we were, perched on the fence, staring at the green fields as the remnants of the day's sunshine dappled the long shadows. Every now and then a small breeze kicked through the grass, sending billowing waves through the tall stems.

Eventually Jasper broke the silence. 'You think it's the Director.' It wasn't a question. 'You think she's coming after you. She certainly has the power and the magic to pull off that sort of feat.'

'I can't answer that.' I said it so quietly that my words were barely audible. Regardless of what I'd said to Ethan, I couldn't maintain the lies any longer – but neither could I tell the truth without risking Jasper, along with everything else.

His jaw clenched. 'I was sneaking round her house for a reason. There was nothing unusual there and I've not started an official investigation, but there's something about the Director that's not right. And it's not because she's delayed implementing my audit recommendations. There's the whole business with Figgy. And you. Not to mention some strange hints that her right-hand woman has dropped in my direction.'

I swallowed. Adeline? I hoped she was going to be careful and not say too much. It wouldn't go down well with the Director if she did. 'Stop,' I said. 'Stop what you're doing. Don't investigate her, even quietly.'

'Why not?' he challenged. 'Do you think so little of me that you assume I'll make a mess of things? Or are you afraid she'll find out and try to stop me?'

I looked away.

Jasper wasn't finished. 'If you won't answer that, then answer this. Why did you walk away from me after I told you about my sister and what I did after she was killed?'

'I can't answer that either.'

'Why did you resign your job?'

'I can't...'

Jasper pulled his hand away from mine. 'You can't answer that.'

I drew in a breath. 'I'm not in a position to make demands of you and I can't force you to do my will. But,' I swallowed hard, 'please do this for me, Jasper. Please stop thinking about the Director. Please stop focusing on who was behind today's attack. When I can tell you everything, I promise that I will. You have my word. Until then, don't pursue this. I'm safe and I need you to be safe as well. Stay out of this until the time is right.'

His eyes narrowed a fraction and he took a long moment before answering. 'I'm not sure I can agree to that.'

I persisted. 'You have to oversee the new agency. You have to fix what happened to Alan Kennedy this afternoon. You have your other duties. For now, focus on those and leave the rest to me. Just for a while.' I waved a hand between us. 'Right now this can't happen.'

'This?'

'Us.' I tugged at a loose curl and wished things were different. 'You need to be seen to be above reproach. Without bias.'

His shoulders stiffened. 'I'm perfectly capable of...'

'I know that,' I interrupted. 'But not everyone else does. Humour me, Jasper. Maintain a professional distance. It's not because I don't want you – it's because I do.' Now I was pleading with him. 'I know you've got more questions than answers and I know this goes against the grain of who you are as a person. But do this for me.'

A muscle jerked in his cheek. 'You ask a lot.'

'Yes. If there was another way...'

'Fine,' he said. 'I'll hold back on this – on all of this. But only because it's you. And I can't do it for long.'

I closed my eyes with relief. 'Thank you. Thank you so much.'

'What about the meeting tomorrow with the faery department heads? I won't be able to keep quiet if it turns sour.'

'You have to stay away.'

He shook his head. 'I don't think I can do that.'

'Jasper.' I touched the back of his hand lightly.

'It's my job to be there.'

'Something urgent might call you away.'

Several seconds passed before he spoke again. 'Something might.' He pushed himself off the fence. 'I have to go. I can't stay here with you when things are like this.' His emerald eyes darkened. 'Don't wait too long, Saffron. I can't restrain myself forever.'

He kissed the back of his fingers and held them out to me. I was still gazing at them, the ache in my chest threatening to cleave my heart in two, when he invoked his magic once again and left.

CHAPTER

TWELVE

Harry adjusted his tie and looked nervously up at the building containing the Office of Faery Godmothers. 'You know, I've never been inside this place,' he said.

'I'd like to say it's not impressive inside,' I told him, 'but I'd be lying.'

'Are you sure you don't want a real lawyer with you? I mean, I know I'm fabulous and all that, but I've never been in a situation like this before.'

'None of us have.' I smiled down at Pumpkin, who was growling loyally at the front door. I was glad he was coming with me; between Harry and Pumpkin, I'd have all the moral support I needed, especially during Jasper's absence.

I'd spoken to the others, making sure they knew what had happened yesterday as well as ensuring that plans were made in case I couldn't return to normal life after this meeting. Jasper had provided precedent, of course; he'd been in this very situation and had become the Devil's Advocate as a result. The faery world had no need for more than one of him, however, and I was a very different person.

I sucked in a breath. 'Let's go. Once more unto the breach.'

Harry cleared his throat conspicuously and nodded. 'Bring it on.'

With Pumpkin trotting beside me, we headed into the lobby. Obviously I knew it wouldn't be Mrs Jardine behind the reception desk but it was still jarring to see a different face in her usual spot. Fortunately I recognised him, and I was fairly certain he wasn't one of those faeries who hated me. All the same, a shadow crossed his face when he saw me and he hastily picked up the phone to announce my arrival to those waiting upstairs.

'Ms Sawyer,' he said formally. He glanced at Harry. 'Your guest will have to remain here and wait for you until the meeting is over.'

Not a chance. 'I am fully entitled to representation.'

The faery's eyes flicked anxiously from side to side. 'I was told you'd be alone. I'm only following orders.'

I wasn't beyond a little intimidation when required. I leaned forward and gave him my nicest nasty smile. 'So you're willing to break the law?' I asked. 'To be hauled in front of a tribunal of your own?' I reached into my pocket and drew out my phone, pressed record and held it up. 'Why don't you repeat what you just said? I want to be sure I have it on camera.'

His cheeks turned red and he stammered, 'I … uh … I…'

I sniffed. 'That's what I thought. My representative is coming with me and there's nothing you can do about it.' Pumpkin gave a small bark and I smiled some more, this time showing my teeth. 'My dog is coming too. He's my emotional support animal.'

'But…'

'Bye!' I said brightly as the three of us strolled towards the lift.

Once we were inside and the door had closed after us, Harry

expelled a rush of air. 'Man, Saffron. You can appear pretty damn scary when you want to be.'

I was no longer smiling. 'Let's just say I've learnt a lot over the last few months.' I glanced at him. 'Are you ready for this?'

'Not even slightly.'

I grinned and punched his arm. 'You'll be fine. Shoulders back, head up and don't take any shit.'

'Easy for you to say,' he muttered as the lift reached its destination and the door slid open.

The usual buzz of office chatter ceased as soon as we stepped out and every head turned in our direction. I tossed my head and tried to look relaxed. 'Hey, everyone!' I trilled out. 'Good to see you again!'

Philippa, her face set into a grim mask, marched over. 'You are in meeting room one. I will escort you there.'

'It's less than twenty metres away, Philippa,' I said drily. 'I think I can make it on my own.'

She folded her hands together neatly and gazed at me implacably. I shrugged and leaned over to Harry. 'I think they're worried that I'm going to steal a hole puncher,' I said cheerfully. Fake it till you make it, I decided. I would completely ignore the waves of nausea assailing my stomach. It wouldn't look good if I threw up all over the floor. Philippa's shoes were very shiny; it would be a shame if they ended up splattered with my vomit.

We were already halfway there when a figure stormed towards me. Delilah looked utterly furious. Her arms were swinging and her spectacles were pushed all the way up her nose in a way I'd never seen before.

'Fuck off, Philippa,' she said.

'I have to escort Ms Sawyer to the meeting room.'

Delilah's glare turned icy. 'I said fuck off.'

Philippa paled and turned tail. I raised an eyebrow. This was a side of my old cubicle neighbour I'd not seen before. I was impressed – and a little scared.

'Well?' she demanded.

I stared at her. 'Well what?'

Delilah threw her hands up in the air. 'When are you planning to invite me to join Wish Inc? Are you deliberately trying to shut me out in the cold? After all I've done for you in the past, Saffron! Why haven't you asked me to come with you?'

My mouth fell open. 'Uh… It's really Alicia's agency,' I began.

'Alicia Shmalicia! I'm highly capable, very organised, an excellent faery godmother and I would be an asset to your team. Not to mention that I don't want to spend any more time in this hell-hole.' Her glare increased in its intensity. Harry watched us, amusement written across his face. 'Ask. Me.'

'Uh…' There was no denying that Delilah would be an asset, but could our fledgling operation manage another recruit? Not to mention that I didn't want Delilah to jack in her position here and then regret it when Wish Inc folded. 'I think you'd be great,' I said honestly. 'But you have a job here and I don't know that…'

'Saffron, I want to do this.'

I sighed then I walked to the nearest cubicle and snagged a scrap of paper and a pen, ignoring the look on the face of the faery godmother who was sitting there. I scribbled down Alicia's phone number. 'Call Alicia and she can explain the arrangements. If you're still happy to get involved after that, I'd be thrilled to have you join us.'

Delilah sniffed. 'I thought Alicia hated you.'

'It's a long story.' I caught sight of Jacob peering out from the meeting room and frowning at me. 'I'd better go,' I said hastily. I sent Harry a nervous glance and he smiled reassuringly.

'Don't fuck this up, Saffron,' I muttered to myself. Then I strolled into the lions' den.

~

THE HEADS of the various faery departments were already sitting round the long table. I recognised several of them, including Jacob, Winkie and, of course, the Director. At least half of them had official-looking notepads in front of them with questions and notes already scribbled down. All of them had nameplates, stating who they were and what position they held. I had the sinking feeling this would be a lengthy interrogation but I couldn't see any torture equipment, so that was a bonus.

Putting my best face forward, I smiled confidently. 'Good morning. Thank you for inviting me in to talk to you.' Let's pretend that my presence hadn't been demanded, I decided. A few expressions soured.

Naturally, the Director took charge. She rose elegantly to her feet and glided over to me, her arms outstretched. 'It's so good of you to join us, Saffron. I know it must be hard for you, coming back here after you were forced to leave. I have to say that you're looking very well.' She took me by the shoulders, her long fingernails digging painfully into the fleshy part of my upper arms, and kissed me on the cheek. Like Judas, I thought sourly.

'And,' I said, 'it's wonderful of you to allow me into the building, even though I *resigned* my job here. You have a big heart.'

The Director's nails pressed harder into my skin for a second or two then she released me and returned to her seat. 'We like to be generous at the Office of Faery Godmothers,' she said, to no-one in particular. 'No grudges are held here.' She gave a titter of laughter, as if such a thought were completely preposterous. Yeah, yeah.

At the far end of the table, a man wearing brightly coloured clothes frowned at Harry. I couldn't see his name plate from this angle but, from the look on his face and Harry's previous description, I knew this was his boss.

'Harold Ramsworthy,' the man said. 'Why are you here?'

'I shall be acting as informal counsel for Saffron,' Harry answered instantly. His tone was light but I could feel his tension. I hoped he wouldn't get into trouble for helping me.

'My goodness,' the Director said, 'there's no need for that. This is a purely exploratory process – and a friendly one. These are hardly criminal proceedings.'

'Well then,' Harry said with a small smile, 'you won't mind if I sit in.'

Ha! Score one to us.

'And the dog?' an older male faery enquired with a faint lip curl. 'Why is it here?'

Before I could answer, a gruff-looking woman leaned forward. 'I think it's commendable. It shows Ms Sawyer's dedication and commitment. I recall being told that you were having some issues with him,' she said to me. I noted that she was listed as Pride, the head of the animal faeries. That was another tick in my favour, then. 'I'm glad to see that those have been resolved.' She beckoned and I released my hold on Pumpkin's lead. Fortunately, he didn't let me down but trotted over with his tail wagging. We were all on a charm offensive, even him.

Harry and I sat down at the foot of the table while Pumpkin enjoyed a belly rub. I shuffled and twitched, trying to sit in a manner that was relaxed but also showed I was taking this meeting seriously. Respectful, but not defensive. Easier said than done.

'So,' the Director said, 'shall we get started? We don't want to make this any more painful or awkward for poor Saffron than it already is. The Devil's Advocate has sent his apologies and won't be here.' She smirked at me, clearly hoping this would be devastating news that I'd just lost a valuable ally.

Despite being *poor* Saffron, I kept a pleasant smile on my face. Inwardly I was seething. Was she upset that I was still breathing after her attempt to kill me yesterday? If so, she wasn't giving anything anyway. She'd spent a lifetime wearing the right masks. I wasn't as skilled as she was – but I was learning.

I inclined my head. 'It's a shame that he won't be here,' I said. 'But yes, let's begin. How will this work?'

'You will explain,' the Director said, 'in your own words, how you happened to break the natural barriers of your magic. Then each one of us will ask you a related question. Once we have finished, we will decide what action to take.'

Harry twisted his fingers together and cleared his throat. We'd prepped and practised for this but it was still nerve-wracking. 'We feel,' he said carefully, 'that Saffron should begin with her experiences in this office as they offer a context to what happened.'

The Director's eyes flashed. 'We're all busy people and we don't want to be here all day. We will stick to what is immediately relevant. If we require "context" we shall backtrack.' Her tone brooked no argument although I could see a few of the other department heads frowning. That was good.

I wasn't ready to discuss the Office of Faery Godmothers at this point – but I did want to throw the Director off-balance with the thought that I might start flinging accusations her way. And if some of the others thought she was being heavy-handed by not allowing me free rein to speak, I'd gained another advantage. Right now, I needed everything I could get.

I did my best to look disappointed and gave a reluctant nod in Harry's direction. Then I took a deep breath and said, 'I am responsible for the death of Figgy Barfellow.'

There was a collective gasp from around the table. Even Jacob, who until now had been smiling at me with friendly encouragement, looked horrified. Clearly, no-one had expected me to start like this but, while I wasn't going to tell the whole truth, I *was* going to tell the truth.

The Director couldn't keep the eager glint from her eyes. 'Oh dear,' she murmured. 'Do go on, Saffron.'

I plunged ahead. 'I first became acquainted with Art Adwell when I was assigned an older client who'd had dealings with him in the past. She was very reluctant to trust anyone and I knew I'd never find out what she wished for until I could get her to trust me. However, memory magic meant that was impossible. I conducted some research and discovered that gingko biloba can put a block on memory magic and so I gave her some. Unfortunately, Art Adwell also inadvertently took some of the gingko biloba. He threw it back up afterwards and I believed there wasn't a problem. Of course, I was wrong.'

I took a deep breath. 'He managed to get hold of my magic wand. Despite being incarcerated for his crimes, he used images of it to spread the word about what he knew regarding faery godmothers. He was released after his conviction was quashed – and then he offered a million pounds to anyone who could prove our existence. I visited him in order to stop him – and I found Figgy. If I hadn't messed with memory magic, she would never have been there.'

I paused and took a sip of water from the glass in front of me. Images of Figgy's last moments replayed in my head, almost making me lose momentum, but Harry squeezed my hand reassuringly. I replaced the glass on the table and, with shaking hands, continued.

'I tried to intervene. Figgy believed that she had to help Adwell and act as his faery godmother. I didn't think that was true so I tried to stop her. She decided to call the Devil's Advocate for help but when she rang his number Adwell went crazy and killed her.'

I looked down as the rest of my words flooded out. 'I wasn't thinking logically. All I felt was horror and rage and grief. My magic exploded and the force of it sent Adwell flying out of the window onto the street below. The fall killed him instantly. At that point I went into panic mode. I turned myself invisible, seconds before the Devil's Advocate arrived and discovered Figgy's body. He, in turn, called the Director who also arrived to view the scene.'

I glanced up. The Director looked genuinely shocked. Until now, she hadn't known I was there and she was desperately trying to remember if she'd done anything – or left anything – that I could use as evidence against her.

'And that,' I said sadly, 'is how I snapped and broke my magical barriers.'

Nobody said anything. A few of the department heads exchanged looks and a few others wrote down notes and questions. More than one person looked sick. They weren't alone; reliving Figgy's death, even though I'd left out a lot of the details, was making me feel nauseous too.

It was Jacob who eventually spoke. Despite the shock in his eyes, there was sympathy too. I knew that with him at least I was on firm ground. I hadn't been sure after he'd turned me away from the dope faeries' door; it made me feel much better to know that he didn't think I was a monster.

'I have two follow-up questions,' he said, 'but they are related.' He watched me. 'Did you want Figgy Barfellow to die?'

The answer to that was easy. 'No. Of course not.'

'And did you want Art Adwell to die?'

This one was a little harder but I was still determined to be honest. 'No,' I said. 'I wanted him to pay for his past crimes but I did not want him dead.'

'Thank you, Saffron.' He nodded at me and leaned back, the expression on his face suggesting the rest of this meeting was pointless now I'd answered the salient points.

The woman next to him spoke up. From her nameplate, it seemed she was the head of the tooth faeries. 'Why was Art Adwell released from prison? Was he innocent of any wrongdoing?'

From his spot next to the animal faeries' leader, Pumpkin growled. Honestly, sometimes that dog understood a lot more than he was given credit for.

'He wasn't innocent,' I said. 'He was an evil man who deserved to be locked up. But as to why he was released, all I know is that the police decided he'd been wrongly convicted.' I didn't have any proof that the Director had used magic to engineer that decision. Unfortunately.

'Could the trolls have been involved?' Winkie enquired almost casually, although I didn't miss the quick glance she sent in the Director's direction.

'What? No!' I shook my head adamantly.

'It's possible that the trolls wanted Adwell released in order to sow chaos amongst the faery godmothers. It wouldn't be the worst thing they've done, and they have the magic to achieve it.'

Under the table Harry nudged me, reminding me to stay calm. I counted to ten before answering. When I spoke, my voice was level. 'On the contrary,' I said, 'the trolls were desperate to stop Adwell. In fact, *they* revealed that he was searching for knowledge about faery godmothers and that he had my wand. If I hadn't stopped him, they would have.'

'Hmm,' the luck faery head said. 'We know that the trolls

are insidious and clever. Perhaps they wanted to create a situation where your magic snapped so they could prove that faery godmothers are unstable. After all, their original goal was to destroy the entire faery godmother office.'

There were several grim nods around the table, including one from the Director.

'Actually,' I said loudly, 'that can't be true. I almost snapped beforehand when I was dealing with another client. The only reason that I didn't is because Ethan, the head of the trolls, stepped in and talked me down. The trolls' attitude towards faery godmothers has changed dramatically in recent months.'

The Director's mouth tightened. That was something else she'd not been expecting. She was lining up her attacks like skittles and I was knocking them down – so far.

'Let's return to something you said earlier,' interjected Harry's boss. 'You deliberately removed the memory magic safeguards. Whether you were a new faery godmother or not, you must have known how dangerous that was.'

I bit my lip. It was a good question. 'At the time,' I said, 'I thought it was a calculated risk. I didn't appreciate the full ramifications of my action.'

'Oh dear,' the Director said, looking concerned. 'There's a long section in faery godmother training about why maintaining the integrity of memory magic is vital. Did you just forget it?'

Ha. 'I didn't receive any proper training,' I answered instantly. 'I saw the start of a video on my first day, but the kidnapping of other faery godmothers took over and I didn't have the time to view it all. I had the faery godmothers' handbook, but my duties were such that I didn't have time to read that, either.'

'You should have made time,' the Director said sharply. 'It's an important document.'

Harry reached into his briefcase and pulled out the training manual so that everyone could see that it was several inches thick and more than a mere document. 'Do you mean this handbook?' he asked innocently.

Her mouth twitched in annoyance. 'Yes.'

I tried to look meek. 'With all due respect, Director, I didn't get the impression that I was expected to *read* it. After all, unbeknown to me, I'd only been appointed as a fairy godmother to act as bait for the kidnappers.'

Her gaze turned icy cold. 'You mean the trolls.'

'We didn't know that at the time but, yes, the trolls,' I said reluctantly.

The animal faery frowned at the Director. 'Is it true that she was employed as bait?'

'It's complicated,' the Director snapped. 'We were under a great deal of pressure.' She stared at me and I knew she was calculating what to say next. There was no reason for her to bring up my relationship with Jasper, especially given his absence and apparent lack of support for my cause. She could invent something, a lie that would be the final nail in my coffin. But I'd already shown that she wasn't aware of everything, and I might have more cards up my sleeve. If she were caught out in a direct lie then *her* entire house of cards could come tumbling down.

Things had gone well for me so far, but she could still turn everyone against me. The Director was a far from stupid faery.

'Oh, Saffron,' she sighed. 'While it's clear that you've made some terrible, fatal mistakes, I can't help feeling that you're a victim in all of this. If only you'd come to me sooner, I might have been able to help. You shouldn't have shouldered these burdens alone.'

She glanced round the table. 'I'm sure I speak for all of us when I say that you shouldn't be punished for your actions, despite the severity of the consequences. All we can do is ensure that such terrible events never happen again.' She offered me a cloying smile. 'We need to look after you from now on. The last time someone's magic broke forth, we were able to move the faery in question to the post of Devil's Advocate. Obviously that's not possible this time, but it's clear that you're in need of rest, recuperation and counselling. You're suffering from a lot of guilt and I can't help feeling partly responsible for that. But I have a solution.'

I bet she did.

'There's an excellent rehabilitation clinic for faeries,' she continued, 'in Canberra in Australia. It's the best there is.' And the furthest away. 'I recommend that we pay for you to go there without delay. As soon as you're well again we can discuss how to proceed, but it's your well-being that we have to consider now. We can't have any more deaths on our hands.'

Nicely played. If I ended up in Australia for counselling, not only would I be out of the way but she'd also be lauded for helping a pathetic fuck-up faery return to the straight and narrow. I didn't need the pressure of Harry's leg against mine to know that I had to tread very carefully indeed.

'My goodness,' I gushed. 'That's such a thoughtful and generous offer – but I couldn't possibly accept. In the first place, although I feel tremendous guilt for my actions and their conse-quences, my mental health is in reasonably good nick.'

Harry nodded. 'I can attest to that. All of Saffron's friends are providing her with excellent support. As her representative, I believe it would do more harm than good to distance her from the people she trusts.'

I could see the Director preparing to argue so I quickly jumped in. 'Secondly,' I said, 'it would be remiss of me to use up valuable faery resources by travelling to Australia. If I were to get a free holiday for killing a human being, I don't imagine it would go down very well.'

At that, I saw several of the faery heads nod. More important than being fair was being *seen* to be fair. The joys of management.

'Finally,' I added, 'I'm participating in an exciting new venture that I think will be an effective way for me to make amends to society for my misdeeds.'

'What new venture?' the Director asked, even though I was certain that she already knew about it.

'Some other faeries and I are forming a new agency,' I explained.

The spine of every faery in the room stiffened. Winkie's face was growing red and Jacob looked disturbed.

I elaborated hastily. 'The Office of Faery Godmothers can't possibly attend to every wish requirement, it's simply not possible. Our agency will provide much-needed support. We're privately funded, so there's no need to worry on that score, and we won't be in competition with the Office of Faery Godmothers because our approach will be different. Rather than focusing on specific wishes, we'll take a more holistic approach and work on improving our clients' lives overall.'

'Wait,' the tooth faery head said slowly. 'Isn't that the sort of thing the Devil's Advocate recommended for your office, Director?'

'He did. Obviously, we haven't implemented such sweeping changes yet but...'

'This way,' I interrupted, pointedly ignoring the way her eyes narrowed, 'you might not need to. You can continue focussing on granting specific wishes. We will attend to the rest.' I smiled sweetly. 'After all, the Office of Faery Godmothers is steeped in tradition. It would be a shame to alter it. The

Director and her faeries can take care of traditional requirements and we'll take a more contemporary approach.' I
shrugged. 'Then everyone wins, especially the clients.'

'We are already making plans to fall into line with the
Devil's Advocate's requirements,' the Director said stiffly.

'Yeah,' Jacob said, 'but if we're being honest here, we all
know that you're not very enthusiastic about them. I think
Saffron is right. This new agency provides the best of both
worlds and allows her to work for the betterment of all society
as recompense for what has happened.'

I tried to keep the delight off my face. I could tell that a lot
of the other faeries agreed with Jacob's assessment. This was
going better than I could have imagined.

The Director hid her fury well. 'Oh no,' she uttered with
tragic melodrama. 'Oh, Saffron. Oh no.'

Winkie glanced at her in alarm. 'What is it?'

She shook her head in dismay. 'It hadn't occurred to me that
this was the reason why.' She gazed at me. 'How could you do
this to the Office that you used to work for, Saffron?'

I frowned. 'I'm sorry, I don't...'

The Director stood up, ensuring that she had everyone's
attention. Her apparent distress increased; any second now,
she'd start to well up, I thought sourly.

'Several of my faeries have resigned in the last week or so. I
thought it was because the pressure of the job was too much for
them, but now I see the truth.' She pressed her lips together in
horror.

'What?' asked the head of the animal faeries, taking
Pumpkin off her lap and returning him to the floor so she could
concentrate more closely.

'Yes,' Harry's boss nodded. 'What truth are you talking
about?'

The Director folded her arms and sniffed. 'She's poached

them. She's weakening my office. Regardless of her apparent altruism, Saffron Sawyer could potentially destroy my office.' She swept her gaze around the table. 'What if the same thing happens to you? What if other faeries undercut your departments? Everything we've worked for over countless generations will fall.' She turned to me with a pleading look. 'I can see that you think you're doing a good thing, Saffron, but please stop. Please stop stealing my staff and destroying all the joy that my faery godmothers bring.'

'I hadn't thought of it like that,' the luck faery head said. 'Such an agency could have a domino effect on all our departments. Unregulated agencies could spring up all over the place.'

Winkie nodded fervently. 'The damage done to the humans would be catastrophic.'

I spoke up. 'We won't be unregulated. I've spoken to the Devil's Advocate already and he will supervise what we do to ensure that we don't mess up.'

The Director gasped. 'Are you ... colluding with the Devil's Advocate? I know you both have the same magic skills now that you've both murdered someone—'

I should have known she'd get that accusation in sooner or later. 'No,' I said flatly, 'we're not colluding. He was also concerned about our new agency but he could see its potential merits.'

Winkie got to her feet and joined the Director. 'I think it's clear that we need to nip this in bud,' she began. 'Upon reflection, this sort of thing could—'

The door to the meeting room burst open and Delilah strode in.

'This is a private meeting,' the Director snapped at her.

'Don't worry,' Delilah answered airily. 'This won't take long.' She thrust an envelope into the Director's hands. 'I hereby tender my resignation, effective immediately.' She beamed. 'I'm joining Saffron and the others at Wish Inc.'

I closed my eyes briefly. Delilah had shitty timing.

The Director looked at me. 'Now you've stolen Delilah from me as well.'

There were murmurs from around the table. Delilah, however, wasn't having any of it. 'She didn't steal me,' she said. 'I'm not a *thing*. I've got thoughts and opinions of my own. I *asked* to join. I don't want to stay in this office any more.'

'Why not?' Jacob asked.

Uh-oh. If Delilah started criticising the Office of Faery Godmothers, all would be lost. The other faery leaders would envisage themselves in the same position as the Director and they'd put the kibosh on Wish Inc before it got off the ground. Somehow this meeting had gone from my own freedom being at risk to much, much more.

'Actually,' Delilah responded, as Pumpkin trotted up to her and sat at her feet with a happy wag of his tail, 'this has nothing to do with this office and everything to do with the future. Don't you see that we've been working as a series of single companies for far too long? For the future to be a healthy one, we faeries need to show that we can move with the times and adapt to new circumstances.'

The department heads were starting to pay attention. 'Having more than one faery godmother company means that there will be less chance that groups like the trolls will feel threatened,' Delilah went on. 'If they don't agree with one group, they can work with a different one. Just because an office has a set of rules doesn't mean that there's no other way to do things. Diversifying is the future. It will allow for specialisms. And for cross-overs.'

She gestured expansively round the room. 'All your departments are large and unwieldy. Smaller agencies can offer different services, as well as challenging the original departments to up their game. There's no lose in any of this – it's all win. Our purpose is to help humans, not to jealously guard our power in gigantic monopolies. A small faery godmother agency will find it easier to work with a small dope faery agency to help a client more effectively. We can't forget our raison d'être, people! We're here for humans, not for ourselves!'

I gaped at her. I'd never heard Delilah make such an impassioned speech about anything that wasn't gossip related; furthermore, she'd come up with several very good reasons why Wish Inc really should exist. Our plan had been to use the agency to lure out the Director and force her into making an obvious mis-step that we could use as proof of her culpability. But maybe Wish Inc *should* exist because of its own merits. There was a place for us after all – and it might be a necessary one.

'Well,' the Director returned, 'in an ideal world that would be wonderful. But what happens when mistakes are made? If agencies aren't up to par?' She paused. 'What happens when Wish Inc fails the very humans it's supposed to serve? This venture is doomed from the start. We should put a stop to it now before disaster happens.'

'I have an idea,' drawled a very familiar voice from the doorway.

I stiffened and looked over at Jasper, who was leaning casually against the door frame. Fuck a puck. What was he doing here? I thought he'd agreed that it was best if he stayed away. Then he smiled lazily and my heart skipped a beat.

I knew his sharp green eyes missed nothing and he was fully aware of the tension in the room.

He spoke authoritatively. 'In fact, I've been giving it some thought since I met with Ms Sawyer. We will arrange a test, a way to judge whether the faeries at Wish Inc have the knowledge, ability and wisdom to move forward. If we approach this idea of a new agency objectively rather than subjectively, we'll have carried out due diligence.'

'What sort of test are you suggesting?' the Director enquired icily.

Jasper grinned. 'The best one that a faery godmother could dream of.'

CHAPTER

THIRTEEN

Alicia's eyebrows rose when I strolled into the new Wish Inc office with Pumpkin and Delilah in tow. Harry's boss had kept him back to harangue him for getting involved. One look at my friend's expression and I knew it was best to stay out of it. I resolved to no longer involve Harry in any of my shenanigans. I couldn't drag everyone down to the same subterranean depths of my own shame, even if lots of the daft buggers seemed determined to join me.

'You've not been locked up then,' Alicia said with a toss of her head. 'I suppose that's good news.'

Melissa gazed at her blankly. 'Is it?'

I smiled at them both. They didn't fool me for a second – I'd seen the flicker of relief in their eyes when I opened the door.

'Nope,' I said, stretching out my arms to indicate my liberty. 'I'm free as a bird. In fact, rather than spending time considering whether I should be thrown in gaol or not, we ended up discussing this place. Unsurprisingly, the Director was trying to shut us down.'

The others, who'd been busy painting the walls, stopped what they were doing and drew closer. 'She knows Wish Inc has the potential to be a real threat to her,' Mrs Jardine said, nodding with approval. 'That's good. It makes it more likely that she'll take a risk and screw up. We'll catch her out soon enough.'

'Not if she actually manages to close us down,' Billy said darkly. 'What happened?'

'They are planning to test us,' I said. 'We have one task to complete and, if we manage it successfully, we'll be allowed to stay open. If we fail, the other departments will force us to close.'

Rupert's eyes flitted anxiously. 'That's good, right? The Director will try to trip us up. We need to catch her in the act and then we win.'

'You know,' Melissa said, 'we could just kill her instead. It'll solve all your problems if she's dead.'

'The lady troll makes a good point,' Rupert muttered.

'No killing. We've got to be better than she is, otherwise what's the point? In fact,' I continued, 'I think we ought to reconsider the reasons for our existence.' I pointed to Delilah. 'As my friend here said, there are some compelling arguments why Wish Inc should exist – and none of them have to do with the Director.'

'Whatever!' Angela waved her hands impatiently. 'What's the test?'

A slow smile spread across my face. 'It's going to be amazing.'

'Saffron...'

'What's the first thing that comes to mind when you think of faery godmothers?' I asked.

'Incompetence,' Angela answered without missing a beat.

'Genocide,' Melissa offered unhelpfully.

Rupert shrugged. 'Very unsexy and unflattering cloaks?'

'A tendency towards rule breaking?' Billy suggested.

Alicia folded her arms. 'Magnificence. Obviously.'

Vincent wandered through, whistling. He caught sight of me and a grin spread across his face. 'Saffy! You're still with us!' He bounded over and hugged me. 'We should celebrate,' he said. 'How about wishes all round? Especially for me?'

I rolled my eyes. 'Vincent, what's the first thing you think of when you hear "faery godmother"?'

He pulled back and looked at me as if I were stupid. 'Duh. Cinderella, of course.'

I smiled. 'Of course.'

There was a beat of silence and then everyone exploded in a cacophony of gasps, questions and shouts. I waited until the noise died down then, with smug satisfaction, I explained. 'The opportunities for another royal wedding are all fulfilled,' I began.

Alicia tutted. 'Although it was the American faeries who took care of the last one, muscling in on our territory...'

'And they did a wonderful job,' I said, with a narrow-eyed glare in her direction. 'We'd have to wait another twenty years if we were going to perform that kind of task. As we are a modern agency, however, we'll work with modern royalty.'

Delilah started to dance, unable to contain herself. 'Celebrities!' she said, hopping from foot to foot. 'Or rather one celebrity in particular. We'll find the one true love for none other than the pop princess herself!' She clapped her hands in glee.

Rupert was immediately impressed. 'Kylie?'

'Not her,' I said.

'Billie Eilish?' Angela frowned. 'Isn't she a bit young, though?'

Vincent waved his hand around. 'Beyoncé!'

Melissa frowned. 'She's married. And she's the queen, not a princess.'

'So?' Alicia looked at me. 'Who is our target?'

Before this descended in chaos, I got to the point. 'Estrella,' I said. 'We're going to find Estrella the man of her dreams.'

Mrs Jardine pursed her lips. 'I've never heard of her.'

Vincent turned to her. 'I bet you have.' He began to sing *Sad Times,* Estrella's latest and greatest hit. Admittedly, he was off key and sounded more like a hyena in heat than an accomplished songstress, but she got the point.

'Ohhhh.' Mrs Jardine nodded. 'Gotcha.'

'We've got until the clock strikes twelve on New Year's Eve,' I said, feeling immensely proud of myself. 'Three weeks to grant the perfect wish, find the ideal man and change how faeries work forever.' I grinned. 'No pressure.'

'Three weeks?' Angela was flabbergasted. 'We can't do that sort of thing in three weeks. William and Kate took years! And that was with the Adventus room to help us. We've got nothing!' She threw up her hands in disbelief. 'Three bloody weeks? It's not possible.'

'Of course it is. How hard can it be?'

The others exchanged glances. 'I forget sometimes how new you are to all this,' Mrs Jardine murmured. 'True love isn't an easy thing to manage. The pressure of finding the right person is intense. And then, if you do find the right person...'

'The circumstances need to be right,' Billy finished. 'If Estrella is recording or on tour...'

'Or if Prince Charming, whoever he is, is still in a doomed relationship of his own...' Alicia added.

'Or if there are issues with the extended families,' Rupert agreed.

Angela grimaced. 'There are *always* issues with the families...'

I stared at them. I hadn't expected this level of pessimism. 'We don't have to reach the wedding stage,' I said. 'That would be daft. The department heads recognise that we have limited time and they don't want to drag this out longer than necessary. Our couple doesn't need to declare love for each other. All we need is the perfect kiss between Estrella and her Mr Right that creates the potential for a lasting relationship between them.'

'That's still easier said than done,' Mrs Jardine said.

'We don't have to achieve success – we only have to do a good job of *looking like* we're achieving success,' Billy said thoughtfully. 'We need the Director to keep trying to thwart us. If she tries to kill us a few more times, that would be good.'

'Kill Saffron, you mean,' Alicia said. 'Not the rest of us.'

'I've been through this with her already.' Rupert ran a hand through his hair and then twisted his body into a supermodel pose 'I'm too pretty to die.'

Angela rolled her eyes. 'All we need to do is get evidence of the Director going after Saffron in the next three weeks and we're golden.' She considered it. 'We can do it.'

'Guys,' I protested, 'I want to nab the Director as much as you do but this is also an amazing opportunity. We can find the evidence we need to deal with the Director *and* find true love for Estrella at the same time. We are faery godmothers!'

Mrs Jardine's lip curled. 'We'll need a different slogan for a start.'

'Tell me about it,' Melissa muttered.

Vincent raised his hand, clearing his throat. 'I have an answer,' he said.

'What's that?'

He smiled.

We all continued to gaze at him. 'You'll need to be clearer, Vincent. What solution?' I asked.

He pointed at himself. 'Me! I'm single. Estrella's single. I'm more than charming. She'll fall for me in an instant.' He puckered up his lips. 'Plus, I'm an excellent kisser.'

'Yeah.' I nodded. 'Sure. Um … let's hold that thought for now.'

His face fell. 'I'd be perfect for her. I'm prepared to lower my standards just this once so that I can help you out. She's only about twenty years younger than me. Stranger things have happened.'

I tried – and failed – to imagine them together. For some strange reason I couldn't picture it.

Rupert folded his arms. 'If he's a candidate then so am I. Just because I'm a faery doesn't mean I shouldn't be considered.'

'What if she's not heterosexual?' Delilah enquired. 'If she's not, I'd make an excellent partner.'

Alicia raised her eyebrows at me. Yeah, maybe this would be harder than I'd thought.

We were all clustered round our only laptop gazing at photos of Estrella Davies when the doorbell rang. As it chimed throughout the almost empty office, everyone paused and looked up. Pumpkin, paws skittering on the wooden floors, sprinted out of the room and started barking loudly.

'Is that for us?' Angela asked.

I shrugged. 'We're the only ones here. It's got to be.'

'But we're not open for business.' Alicia frowned. 'Saffron, go and see who it is.'

'Maybe it's the Director,' Rupert said hopefully. 'She'll stab Saffron in the heart and we'll win.'

I glared at him. 'That doesn't sound like much of a win to me.'

He realised what he'd said. 'I meant…'

I sighed. 'I know what you meant.' I stepped back. 'Wait here. If I scream for help then come running.'

Vincent nudged Delilah. 'Out the back door and away from here as fast as we can.'

She smirked.

Tutting to myself, I walked out. Pumpkin was leaping up at the opaque glass door that led onto the street, his claws clicking against it. His woofs were growing more and more high-pitched and excited. I tilted my head and examined the shadowy figure on the other side of the door.

'Let me in, Saffron,' Jasper said.

No wonder Pumpkin was throwing himself against the door with such gleeful abandon. A zippy kick of delight shivered through me and I almost joined him. Then I shook myself, smoothed down my frizzy curls and straightened my shoulders, before finally opening the door. 'Hi,' I said.

Jasper put his hands in his pockets and gazed at me. 'Hi.'

Pumpkin looked from me to Jasper and back again, before flopping down onto the floor and presenting us with his belly. I crouched down and gave him an absent-minded rub. At least it broke some of the tension.

'You weren't supposed to be at the meeting this morning,' I said, chiding Jasper gently. 'You said you wouldn't go.'

'Actually,' he answered, crouching down and fondling Pumpkin's ears, '*you* said that I shouldn't go. I didn't promise anything. Besides, it didn't go so badly. From what I've been told, you conducted yourself very well.'

Oddly embarrassed at his praise, I coughed. 'So did you,' I told him. 'The idea of the test is a good one. It takes all uncertainty out of the equation. Either we pass or we fail – there won't be any grey areas.'

Jasper reached across Pumpkin's happily squirming body

and his fingers brushed against mine. 'It's not going to be easy,' he warned.

I smiled ruefully. 'That's what everyone is telling me. We'll do it, though.' My resolve was pure and strong. 'I won't countenance failure.'

Something lit Jasper's expression; I could have been mistaken but I was fairly certain it was pride. 'I believe in you.'

'That means a lot,' I whispered.

He gave me a crooked smile and stood up. Pumpkin whined when I followed suit but I couldn't spend all day giving him belly rubs. 'Anyway,' Jasper said, 'I'm not here for the test. And I'm not here because I wanted to see your face or smell the scent of your skin.' He paused and looked at me for a long moment. 'You smell wonderful, by the way.'

I leaned in, allowing myself a deep inhale of his cinnamon-spiced aftershave. 'So do you.' Much more of this and I'd need a cold shower. 'Why are you here then?'

Jasper cleared his throat. 'Regardless of the test, I still need to ensure that Wish Inc is following appropriate procedures. I want to see how you're getting on.'

I pretended I wasn't disappointed. 'You've still got a job to do, right?' I said lightly. 'We're all through here. You're welcome to poke your nose into whatever you wish.' I'd prefer if he'd poke his nose into what I was currently wearing underneath my suit but I couldn't expect to have everything I wished for.

'Great,' he said.

I stepped back to let him walk past but he stayed where he was.

'What is it?'

His mouth tightened fractionally. 'I walked here from the Office of Faery Godmothers,' he said. 'I'm almost completely certain that I was followed. I was going to confront them but then I thought better of it.'

An involuntary chill ran through my body. 'Oh,' I said. 'Okay.' No prizes for guessing who was behind that. The Director would still be looking for reasons to prove that Jasper was biased towards me.

However this might be the opportunity I'd been looking for if I could turn the tables on Jasper's tracker and obtain proof of the Director's deceit. 'I think that while you're here I'll take Pumpkin out for a walk,' I said.

At the sound of his favourite word, Pumpkin rolled onto his feet and started bouncing. Jasper nodded. 'I thought you might say that.' The emerald green of his eyes deepened. 'Be careful.'

'Always.' I swallowed. 'I'm going out!' I called. 'I'll be back later.'

A chorus of answers echoed through. 'Okay!'

'The Devil's Advocate is here,' I shouted. 'Let him do whatever he wants and make sure you answer all his questions.'

This time all that rebounded was silence. Then Alicia's face popped round the corner. When she saw Jasper, she went pale. 'Oh.'

I grinned at them both. 'Have fun!'

I grabbed Pumpkin's lead and left hastily.

CHAPTER

FOURTEEN

The happy warmth that had sustained me since I'd left the Office of Faery Godmothers dissipated once I left Jasper and Wish Inc behind. The chilly wind, which had been fairly tame earlier, was whipping itself up into a frenzy, blowing my hair in all directions and making it difficult to see. I pushed it out of my eyes in a bid to scan the street for Jasper's tail but it was a wasted effort and a second later I was once again blinded by my own frizz. I'd have to hope that venturing out so soon after Jasper's arrival would be enough to draw the watcher in my direction.

I nodded at Pumpkin, who appeared to be fascinated by the skittering leaves dancing on the opposite side of the street, and turned to my right. I'd learned quite a bit from Rupert's attempts to follow me and I already had a good idea where I was heading.

In an ideal world, I'd also have had a concealed camera filming all the action. As I wasn't quite ready to audition for the role of Inspector Gadget just yet, I did the next best thing, flicked my phone onto record and slipped it into my pocket. I wouldn't get any visuals but, if I was forced to confront Jasper's tail face to face, the audio should be clear enough – assuming there was any useful audio to pick up.

Pumpkin and I wandered down the street, side-stepping the odd puddle. The little dog was proving his weight in gold. He stopped several times to take a sniff at the ground. When he cocked his leg against a grubby lamppost, I was able to stop and turn my head casually enough not to draw suspicion. Initially, I didn't see anything but then, as I turned back, I spotted some-one. A man holding a sodden newspaper had just darted into a doorway. Without any question, I knew this was the guy.

Resisting the urge to start whistling and trying to look casual, I continued strolling with Pumpkin. When we reached the first crossroads, he decided that he wanted to turn left towards a little park he knew of. I tugged on his lead. There were too many exits and potential escape routes there and I had something else in mind.

Now the Director knew I no longer needed a wand to perform magic, she'd expect my powers to be greater. Whoever was following me would be well prepared for a magical confrontation. To be successful, I'd have to rely on more than magical sprinkles.

We walked on for another half mile or so, diverting twice along the way. On the first occasion, I ducked inside a small newsagents to buy a packet of cigarettes and a lighter. When I left, I didn't waste time checking to see if my tail was still there. Instead I started moving faster until Pumpkin was jogging to keep up.

We crossed the road without waiting for the traffic lights. I ignored the angry beep of a car horn and the rude gesture from the driver who'd been forced to slam on his brakes. Twenty metres further on I stopped, opened the cigarette packet and lit one.

There was method in my madness. By altering my speed

seemingly at random, as well as nipping into shops and crossing the street in kamikaze fashion, I was ensuring that the goon following me was kept off-balance. I didn't want him to think I was on to him, hence the abrupt halt to give him the time he needed to catch up.

I was enjoying being in control of this situation. I'd clearly missed my calling as a spy. If Wish Inc and the faery godmother gig failed, I might look into setting up the faery equivalent of MI5. Espionage was kind of fun.

My second stop was at a deli, one of those new-fangled kind of places where you could purchase long sticks of dubious-looking vegan pepperoni, every flavoured hummus under the sun and odd concoctions that always seemed to involve avocado. I chatted briefly to the young woman behind the counter before purchasing some gloopy taramasalata in a poly-styrene tub as a cover for my visit. So much for my supermarket wages, I thought ruefully. Easy come, easy go. At least it was for a good cause.

Once I stepped outside again, I mimicked my previous movements by picking up speed and marching quickly away. This time, however, when Pumpkin and I reached the next crossing I swung right, heading down a narrow side street. Then I scooped Pumpkin into my arms and ran at breakneck speed.

After fifty metres, we turned right again. I didn't slow down. I kept going, my head down and my fingers crossed. If Pumpkin was bemused by this turn of events, he didn't let on. A few seconds later, I reached a fire exit halfway down the block. I threw myself inside it, pulling the door closed behind me. Panting hard, I released my hold on Pumpkin.

'Thank ... you,' I gasped.

The young woman from the deli smiled in response, although I could tell she thought I was nuts. That didn't matter;

I'd paid her well for this little excursion and, if I'd timed it right, I'd have achieved all that I wanted to.

'Sure thing,' she said.

I handed her Pumpkin's lead. 'You know where you're taking him?'

'Honeysuckle Avenue,' she recited. 'Wish Inc. I can't leave till I shut up shop in another half an hour, though.'

'That's fine.' I wagged a warning finger in Pumpkin's direction. 'Behave for the nice lady,' I told him. 'And well done just now. That was awesome.'

Pumpkin gave my nose a lick. I stroked his head and promised I'd see him again soon. Then I stepped through the staff door and back into the deli, hastily flicking my fingers and glamouring myself a different outfit – jeans and a puffy black jacket, the street uniform of thousands.

I checked on the deli assistant, whose back was turned as she busied herself with Pumpkin, then conjured up a woolly hat and stuffed my unkempt curls inside it. It wasn't a great disguise and it wouldn't stand up to much scrutiny, but I reckoned it would do the trick at a distance. I could turn myself invisible but performing that sort of spell held troubles of its own and there was no need to over-complicate matters. The end goal here was to interrogate the tailing goon and find out what he knew.

'Thanks again,' I called. I'd taken a risk by trusting the woman but it seemed like it was paying off. I straightened my shoulders and stepped out of the shop.

As soon as the cold wind hit me, I knew I'd been successful. At the end of the street, at the junction where I'd turned right before looping back on myself, stood the man who'd been following me. He was slowly turning round, clearly searching for me. The one place he wouldn't expect me to see me was behind him.

If I was lucky, he'd lead me to the Director. And if she was acting as cagey as she'd been with Alan Kennedy and wasn't revealing herself to anyone, then he might still lead me to something I could use. Either way, any bastard that thought he could tail *my* Jasper would pay for it in spades. I'd sacrificed too much to keep him safe for some sneaky prick to mess it up.

I stayed out of his line of sight until he finally decided that I'd gone for good. I'd been hoping that he wouldn't simply return to his spot outside Wish Inc and when he crossed to the opposite side of the street and headed away from me, I knew that hope had been realised. I smiled and followed, maintaining a clear distance between us.

The man took a few twists and turns but there was nothing about the way he moved that suggested he suspected he was being followed. After a good twenty minutes, he turned into a small cul-de-sac. It looked like he'd reached his destination.

I waited for a few beats and then tailed him, more slowly this time. I reckoned I had him cornered. Where the pavement began to curve round, I spotted him fumbling with the lock on the door to a small house. I grinned. Go, Saffron, go.

He disappeared inside and closed the door. I immediately doubled my pace.

I didn't knock politely on the door or ring the doorbell and wait, I simply snapped my fingers and used magic to throw open the door again. Without missing a beat, I strode inside. 'Honey!' I called. 'I'm home!'

He had faster reactions than I'd expected. I'd barely finished my sentence when I heard a click, similar to a sound I'd heard before. My eyes widened and I threw myself down to the carpet in the nick of time. A beat later, a loud crack rent the air and the plaster wall next to where my head had just been exploded in a shower of dust. Fuck a puck.

Unsure whether he'd managed to shoot me or not, the man

edged out brandishing the gun in front of him. I ignored the shock of recognition when I saw his moustachioed face and stayed where I was on the floor, jetting out a string of magic that wrapped round his ankles. As he raised the muzzle of the gun for a second attempt, I yanked on my thread. His feet flew out from underneath him and he landed on his back with a heavy thud, the gun falling from his grasp.

I sprang up, kicked it away and jumped towards him. 'Hello,' I cooed down at him. 'Long time no see.'

His brow furrowed in confusion. 'Who are you?' he snarled. 'Whaddya want?'

I remained calm. 'I think it's more of a question of what do *you* want. After all, you're the one who was following me. And my … friend.'

Even though he wouldn't remember me, I knew he was one of the goons who used to work for Art Adwell. He was one of two men who'd walked away in the moments after Figgy's death. The memory of that event didn't endear him towards me, whether he'd made the right call by leaving or not.

'Dunno what you're talking about.' He struggled up onto his elbows. 'Get out of my house before I call the police.'

I dug into my pocket, took out my phone and handed it to him. 'Go on then,' I said. 'Call them.'

His eyes narrowed suspiciously then he called my bluff. 'I will.' His finger jabbed 999. He watched me carefully. 'I'm gonna do it.'

I shrugged. 'Do it.'

His thumb hovered over the green call button. I folded my arms and rocked back on my heels, waiting.

The man cursed and threw down the phone. 'I was hired to do a job, that's all. I don't have anything against you as a person. I don't even know who you are.'

Ah-ha. We were getting somewhere at last. 'Tell me about the job,' I ordered.

His bottom lip jutted out like a child's and his moustache quivered. He really wasn't happy about this. 'I was supposed to follow the dark-haired fellow. My employer wanted photographs of what he was up to, especially if it involved you. I was told,' he continued matter-of-factly, 'that if the opportunity presented itself where I could kill him without any witnesses then I was to take it.'

I drew in a sharp breath. Fear and fury mingled inside me, threatening to overtake me. It was one thing to know that I was being targeted to die; it was quite another to hear that Jasper was in the same situation.

'When he went into your office and you came out, I reckoned that maybe I could grab you and use you as bait to draw him out. It was a good plan.' He glared. 'Until you screwed it up for me.'

I counted to ten in my head. It didn't work. Struggling to keep my breathing under control, I reminded myself that this bastard was just the hired help. I knew who was behind all this – but I needed proof.

'Before you ask,' he said, seeming to read my mind, 'I can't tell you who my employer is.'

'Oh,' I bit out, 'I think you can.' I stepped closer, raising my foot until it was directly above his groin. No, I wasn't going to kick him while he was down – but he didn't know that.

'Hurt me as much as you want,' he said. 'I still can't tell you. It's all been done by email. I don't know who it is.' He bared his teeth in a smile. 'And what I don't know can't hurt me.' He raised his hands apologetically. 'This ain't personal so you've no reason to get upset about it.'

'Not personal?' I spat. 'You've just admitted that you wanted to abduct me and kill my ... friend.'

He was entirely unfazed. 'I got bills to pay. A man's gotta eat.'

'I know a supermarket that might hire you on a temporary basis.'

He stared at me.

Calm, Saffron. Stay calm. I hunkered down beside him. 'What's your name?'

'Bob.'

'Your real name.'

'Bob' looked away.

I tutted and reached back to the small table near the wall behind me, scooping off one of the letters that lay in a messy pile on top of it. I pulled the letter out of its envelope and scanned it. 'Wow,' I said, glancing at the numbers displayed in angry red print, 'you really do have bills to pay, don't you, Samuel Francis Alwick?'

Samuel slumped back down. I nudged him with my toe. 'Get up. I want to see these emails.'

For a second or two, he didn't move then he rose to a sitting position. Before he was fully upright, however, he slammed out his foot, connecting his heel with my shin. I screeched in pain and, without thinking, zapped him with a bolt of magic. It hit poor old Samuel square in the forehead and he immediately keeled backwards. He wasn't having a great day.

'I'll thank you not to try that again,' I admonished him. 'That hurt.'

'My head,' he moaned. 'I think it's exploding.'

'You'll be fine,' I said briskly. I reached down and took him by the hand. 'Come on. Up you get.'

'What did you do to me?'

'Magic.'

He glared at me. 'It was a taser, wasn't it?' He scanned my body up and down. 'Where is it? Are you hiding it?'

'That would be telling.' I tugged harder. 'Come on, Samuel. Stand up.'

He heaved himself up, yanking on my hand far harder than was necessary. When he was standing, I realised how big he was. No wonder he'd ended up in the thug business.

'This employer of yours,' I asked. 'How did they find you to begin with?' I already had a good idea about the answer but I wanted to hear it from his own lips.

'They said my old boss had recommended me.'

'Uh huh.' I nodded. 'Your old boss being Art Adwell?'

The colour drained from his face. 'How did you know that?'

'Told you already,' I said. 'Magic.'

Samuel made a face. 'Whatever,' he grunted.

I was starting to think that I could conjure up a rainbow unicorn in front of his eyes and he still wouldn't believe in the existence of magic. That suited me; he was right that what he didn't know wouldn't hurt him – or me.

Unfortunately, it appeared that the Director was of the same opinion. No doubt she'd made a note of who had worked for Adwell so that she could employ them herself for her own nefarious ends. But if I couldn't show that the Director had met with Adwell, I certainly couldn't prove this either.

'Show me the emails your employer sent you,' I ordered.

'Okay,' he grunted. 'My laptop is in the kitchen.'

He'd given in far too easily. I saw his gaze flick downwards. Of course – he was planning to grab his gun again and turn it on me. I weighed up my options before directing a spurt of magic towards the fallen weapon.

A second later, Samuel lunged for it. 'You're a dead woman,' he spat, waving the muzzle in my face.

'Mmm-hmmm.'

'I mean it! I'll shoot you!'

'You could do that,' I agreed, 'but then you'd end up with

blood splatters all over your hallway. This is a nice carpet. It would be a shame to ruin it.'

My lack of fear baffled him. 'What are you? Some kind of psycho?'

'I'm a faery godmother. Not the best in the world – not yet – but I'm working on it.' I placed my hand on the barrel of the gun. 'You can try and shoot me, Samuel,' I said. 'It won't do you much good but you can definitely try. But I've got a better idea, one that will benefit us both.'

Conflicting emotions warred on his face. I hoped that he was far less bloodthirsty than he believed himself to be. He'd walked away from Art Adwell when things got dicey; if he was smart, he'd also walk away now. Samuel Francis Alwick had a well-developed sense of preservation and I crossed my fingers that he'd make the right choice. Either way, he could pull the trigger as many times as he wanted and it wouldn't do him any good since my magic had rendered the gun useless. But I wanted to give him the opportunity to be a better man and choose a different path on his own. I was even prepared to sweeten the deal for him.

'What do you mean you're a faery godmother?' he asked suspiciously.

'I grant wishes.' I leaned forward. 'What's your wish, Samuel? What do you want out of life?'

He thought about it for a moment then he pointed the gun directly at the centre of my chest before yanking hard on the trigger. Fuck a puck. Wrong choice.

'Bang!' I said.

Samuel stared first at the gun and then at me. 'Wh – what?'

I shook my head sadly. 'You blew it, Samuel. I like to think that everyone can have a shot at redemption and that there is more good than bad in people. Unfortunately you didn't shoot me in the heart but you did just shoot yourself in the foot.' I tutted. 'You can't say I didn't give you a chance.'

He roared and threw himself at me, fists flailing. The now-useless gun dropped to the floor but actually Samuel didn't need it. He was a better hands-on fighter than I'd given him credit for, and he landed several hits despite my attempts to ward off his blows. The metallic taste of blood rose up on my tongue. Fuck a puck. I had to switch tactics.

I spun round and retreated through the front door. As I pulled it shut, Samuel tugged violently on the handle from the other side in a desperate bid to open it and get to me. I hung on tightly to give myself a few more seconds to regain my equilibrium. A moment later, I released my hold on the door and Samuel, who was still pulling on it from inside, flew backwards and sprawled on the floor again.

'Samuel, Samuel,' I sighed. I ducked down, picking up my phone from where it lay next to him. He'd already helpfully jabbed in the number I needed. I pressed the green button and was connected almost immediately.

'Help!' I said breathlessly as he started to rise again. 'There's a man here with a gun! I'm at twenty-three Badewell Close. I think he's going to shoot me!'

I hung up before the operator could answer.

Samuel's face twisted with rage. 'What have you done?' he bellowed. 'What the fuck have you done?'

I smiled sweetly. 'You don't have long,' I told him. 'In my limited experience, the police do tend to move rather quickly at the mention of firearms.' I nodded towards the gun. 'I suggest you find a way to get rid of the evidence while you still can. If I catch a glimpse of you again, I'll do a hell of a lot more than make a phone call. You'll regret the day you ever crossed my path.' I wasn't exaggerating; to threaten me was one thing but to threaten Jasper was entirely different.

For a moment it was clear that Samuel Alwick didn't know what to do. His strongest impulse was to smash my head in and accept the consequences. But I also knew what he'd done the last time he'd faced impending doom when he'd deserted Adwell. He clenched his fists then he muttered under his breath and grabbed the gun.

I let out my breath. Thank goodness I hadn't completely misjudged him.

He stormed past me, his shoulder catching me as he headed for the door. 'You'll pay for this one way or another,' he snarled. 'I don't know who's paying me but I can tell you they mean business.'

Unfortunately, I knew he was right. 'We all reap the consequences of our actions sooner or later,' I replied calmly.

He didn't hear me; he was already gone.

I pressed my lips together. I should have planned this better and I was lucky that things had turned out the way they had. Then I strolled into the kitchen, picked up Samuel's laptop and left the same way he had.

CHAPTER
FIFTEEN

The throbbing music was getting on my nerves and the sticky sweet cocktail I'd been nursing for the last hour was starting to make me nauseous. 'Is this really the best idea we could come up with?' I asked.

Alicia, who was wearing the tightest dress imaginable and looking as if she was having the time of her life, tossed her hair and wiggled her hips suggestively at a group of men who were ogling her. 'We need to get to know our client in her natural environment. This is the way it works, Saffron. You're the person who said we should take this task seriously. That means knowing what makes Estrella tick.'

'But she isn't here,' I pointed out. Now that we were no longer part of the Office of Faery Godmothers, we didn't have access to Metafora magic to transport us directly to our clients. I missed the convenience of it more than I'd anticipated.

Alicia remained serene. 'She will be.'

I sighed. I took out my phone to check if there were any texts or missed calls, hoping that there might be something from Jasper. Just because I'd dealt with Samuel Alwick and hopefully scared him off didn't mean there weren't others on the same payroll to worry about.

'That's very rude, you know. Checking your phone in the middle of a conversation with someone else isn't a good look.'

'I wanted to see if Billy had found anything useful in Samuel's emails,' I lied.

Alicia smiled. 'If you say so. We both know that the Director is too smart to be caught out like that.' She leaned in. 'And the Devil's Advocate is stronger than you, Saffron. He's perfectly capable of looking after himself.'

I took another sip of my cocktail, almost immediately regretting it. I wasn't getting into a debate about Jasper. I knew he could look after himself but that didn't stop me worrying about him or doing what I could to protect him. 'Do you think she's *too* smart?'

Alicia glanced at me. 'The Director?'

I nodded. 'Do you think she's too smart for us to catch her out?'

'I wouldn't be doing this if I did. We'll get her.'

I was starting to have my doubts about that but voicing them wouldn't do any good.

Melissa strode up. She was wearing a skin-tight leather jumpsuit that made her look more intimidating than sexy. 'Human men are pathetic,' she said.

I raised an eyebrow and glanced in the direction she'd come from. A young bloke was doubled over and clutching his groin. His friends were gesticulating angrily at one of the bouncers and pointing at Melissa. That was exactly the sort of thing we didn't need.

'Why don't you go and keep an eye out for Estrella at the entrance?' I suggested hastily.

The troll shrugged. 'No need.' She jerked her chin. 'She's already here.'

I looked round. Melissa was right. A small crowd was already forming as Estrella and her hefty entourage strolled in.

'I told you she'd be here,' Alicia said smugly. 'I did my research properly.'

'Well done.'

'You say that as if you doubted I'd come through.'

'Alicia,' I murmured, 'the only thing I doubt when you're around is my sanity.' I clapped her on the shoulder and happily abandoned my drink. It was time for phase one.

A man in a dinner jacket led Estrella and the group trailing after her towards a roped-off area at the back of the club where they wouldn't be bothered by the hoi polloi. She was flanked by a broad-shouldered man in an impeccably tailored suit. Everyone was staring in her direction and he was glaring at them with hard eyes. A bodyguard. I sucked on my bottom lip. That complicated matters.

Estrella's expression was studiously bored but I suspected that she was actually quite irritated by the whole circus. As the man unclipped the rope to allow her into the VIP area, a young bloke approached, all swagger and bravado. He clearly fancied his chances and was being urged on by the catcalls and shouts from his mates clustered behind him.

I hung back, watching carefully; I could learn a lot from this. He was good looking in a cutesy kind of way, with blond hair, smooth skin and dimples. In another life, I probably wouldn't have turned him down myself. I hadn't always possessed discerning taste in men.

'Hey.' He stepped directly in front of Estrella and grinned. 'Nice dress.'

Oh dear. He'd have to do a lot better than that – although it *was* a nice dress, and not what I'd expected from the pop princess. It was some sort of vintage number, red with white spots, that wouldn't have looked out of place at a 1950s' tea dance. It complemented her glossy dark hair and matched her red lips perfectly. Unfortunately, right now those lips were puckered with disapproval.

She side-stepped to the right as her bodyguard immediately moved to the left to prevent her admirer from getting any closer. It was a fluid movement and one that was obviously practised. Then she climbed the steps to the VIP area while the poor bloke was dealt with. The bodyguard took his job seriously; given how the fan's face paled dramatically before he was ushered away, I reckoned he'd received more than a mild scolding. Dimples or not, it was obvious that the way to Estrella's heart didn't involve approaching her without an invitation.

I continued to watch as she drew further away, heading towards a small table in the furthest corner with a few of her girlfriends. I nodded thoughtfully. She might have made a conspicuous entrance, but she wasn't here simply to be seen.

Vincent sidled up, leaning in to my ear. 'I've got a plan.'

'Let me guess,' I said drily. 'You're going to unbutton your shirt to the waist, expose your manly chest and shout to Estrella that you're the man of her dreams.'

He tapped his mouth. 'No, but that's worth considering.' He winked at me. 'I'm actually thinking about the blonde woman. You see her? The one in the pink top?'

'Vincent, I'm not sure she'll fancy you any more than Estrella will. She's about twenty years younger than you.'

'Women go for older men!'

I glanced at the glossy crowd who were settling into their seats with grins and giggles. 'Not these women. You'd be punching too far above your weight, Vincent. Much as I love you, I don't think...'

'Pfft!' he dismissed me. 'Settle down, Saffy. I wouldn't want one of them anyway. I'm looking for someone older, someone with more experience. What I said before about me and Estrella was a joke.'

'Uh-huh.' I squinted, my eyes tracking the waiter carrying a tray of champagne glasses who was being ushered past the rope. Maybe posing as a member of staff was the best way to reach Estrella. The waiter didn't get near her, however; he was pointed to one of the unoccupied tables and it was the bodyguard who handed her a glass. I wouldn't have been surprised if he'd tested it for poison first.

'Look more closely at the blonde,' Vincent urged.

I sighed and glanced at her. 'I don't see...' I began. Then I did see. There was a tension both to her slightly bloodshot eyes and her mouth. She was skinny as a rake – and not in a diet fanatic fashion either. 'Heroin,' I said.

'If I can get to her,' he told me, 'I can get us in.'

Dismay filled me. 'You're not drug dealing again, are you?'

'No. I don't have anything on me and I haven't had for months. You know that, Saff. But it doesn't mean I don't know where to get some stuff. I recognised all the dealers within two minutes of walking in here. I can act as the go-between.'

The blonde, who'd only been sitting down for a few moments, stood up and murmured something to the man beside her. Then she walked out past the rope, heading for the ladies' toilets. Vincent flashed me a triumphant grin and started forward.

'Wait!' I lunged for his arm to pull him back but he was too fast.

When I made to dash after him, my way was blocked. 'Hi there.' The bloke who'd tried to sidle up to Estrella was barring my path. 'I couldn't help noticing that you were watching her. She's glamorous and famous but you're far more beautiful.'

Oh, good grief. After being shot down by Estrella and her entourage, he was obviously trying to salvage his ego by trying it on with lesser mortals. No wonder she hadn't been interested. Despite his good looks, up close there was a desperation about him that was incredibly off-putting.

'Don't bother,' I snapped. 'I'm not interested.'

He waggled his eyebrows suggestively. 'You should get to know me before deciding that.'

'You don't want me to get to know you. You want a quick fumble round the back.'

'Well,' he said, 'I was going to offer to buy you a drink first but if you insist...'

I rolled my eyes and pushed past him, searching for Vincent. I finally spotted him in a dark corner, his head bowed as he chatted to the strung-out blonde. I squared my shoulders and marched towards him. No matter how much I wanted us to succeed, I wouldn't allow anyone to exploit another person's weaknesses. Our job was to help people.

As soon as I reached Vincent, I elbowed my way between him and the blonde. 'No,' I said firmly. 'Leave her alone.'

'Hey!' she protested. 'This is a private conversation.'

I ignored her and glared at him. 'This is not the way to do things,' I said. 'We are better than this.'

'It's the perfect plan,' he hissed under his breath. 'Just let me do my thing!'

'Listen, bitch,' the blonde said. 'Get out of my way. I was here first and I've got the money.'

I counted to ten then slowly turned to face her. 'You don't need him.'

She gave me a flat, dead-eyed stare. 'Yes, I do.'

'You look like a smart woman,' I said softly. 'You know the damage this will do. You know that you're better than this. I'm not stupid enough to tell you that all you need is a bit of willpower, but why don't you give it ten minutes? Wait ten minutes and then see if this is still something you think you want.'

'Ten minutes won't make it go away. If I want drugs, I'll have some fucking drugs.'

I drew in a breath, preparing my counter argument but someone got there before me.

'Jayne.'

The blonde turned her head. Standing beside us was Estrella with an expression in her eyes of kindness, concern and more than a hint of steel. Right next to her was the bodyguard.

'I only need a little pick-me-up, Essie.' Jayne's hands flailed in desperate shame.

'Have a drink instead. I'll get Mitchell here to call Maggie and she can speak to you.' She smiled. 'You've got this. I'm with you all the way.'

Jayne's head dropped and she nodded then shuffled back towards the VIP area.

Estrella looked at me. 'Thank you for that.'

'That's okay.' I bit my lip. 'I've ... worked with drug users before. I know the signs. Is Maggie her sponsor?'

Estrella nodded. 'Yeah, she's great. She'll set Jayne back on the straight and narrow. At least for now, anyway.'

'I'm glad to hear it.'

Estrella tilted her head, examining me. She looked a lot younger than she did in her pictures but, despite her dewy glowing skin, there was a weariness behind her eyes. 'We're having a few drinks up there,' she said. 'Why don't you and your friends join us?'

The bodyguard, Mitchell, stiffened. 'Essie,' he began, his eyes narrowing in my direction.

'It's fine,' she said dismissively.

I pretended I hadn't noticed anything amiss. I knew he was

doing his job but there was more than an ounce of overkill in his approach. 'That would be great. Thank you.'

'It's the least I can do,' she replied simply and walked off.

Vincent, still behind me, leaned into my ear. 'Told you it would do the trick. I save the day yet again!'

Yeah, yeah. I beckoned to Alicia and Melissa. We were in.

ALTHOUGH THE VIP area was still part of the club and hovered less than a foot higher than the rest of the floor, it felt like a different world. The furniture was better quality, the walls were covered in expensive plush material and the drinks tasted a whole lot better. I could get used to this sort of lifestyle, I decided.

'So,' Estrella said, leaning across, 'what is it that you do, Saffron?'

I coughed while Alicia and Melissa sat a bit straighter in alarm. 'Uh, it's kind of embarrassing, to be honest.'

She laughed, an honest sound that made me warm to her even more. 'More embarrassing than lip-synching on a stage in your underwear?'

I knew from my research that Estrella never lip-synched but I understood the need to downplay your accomplishments from time to time. Not that I usually did. I smiled. 'Maybe not.' I shrugged. 'I'm a life coach. I help people get their lives on track and focus on what they want to do, or have, or be, in order to be successful.'

'That sounds fascinating.'

'It is,' I admitted. 'Although sometimes the hardest part is working out what people really want. Often we lie to ourselves as well as to everyone else. I work with my clients to under-stand their needs and get them to where they need to be.'

'So you're like a fairy godmother?'

Melissa choked on her drink. I just smiled. 'That's exactly what I am.'

Estrella seemed genuinely interested. 'Can you give me some examples of what you've done?'

'Well,' I hedged, 'client confidentiality is important but I recently helped an older man find a new friend. I'm keeping my fingers crossed that the relationship will turn into something more romantic, but the most important thing is that he's got someone to help him stave off his loneliness.'

'Wow. That sounds amazing.'

I nodded. 'It is. Loneliness can be a killer.'

Alicia leaned forward, getting in on the act. 'And true love can conquer it. How about you, Estrella? Do you have a partner?'

Her eyes slid momentarily to Mitchell, who remained standing less than a foot from her. 'Nah. I don't have time for any of that stuff right now. I'm not looking and I'm not interested.'

Melissa, recovered from her splutters, took a sip of her drink. 'What's your type? Tall, dark and handsome? Good sense of humour?'

Estrella pulled back. Too many questions. 'Someone who makes me laugh,' she said simply. She turned away to speak to someone else; even here amongst her friends, she was still very guarded. So was Mitchell. When the conversation had turned, he'd gone from acting dark and brooding to almost menacing.

I frowned at Alicia and Melissa, silently telling them to lay off the interrogation. This operation required kid gloves. It was still early and there would be plenty of time to get the information we needed.

I leaned over to pick up my glass, catching Vincent out of the corner of my eye as I did so. He was by the main bar and gesticulating wildly in my direction. I stiffened, glaring at him and hoping nobody else noticed. He jumped up and down, mouthing something.

Alicia nudged me. 'What's he saying?'

'I have no idea.' I shook my head, wondering if I should go and see what the problem was. Probably nothing, I decided, turning away. A second later, pain smacked me across my face and I gasped.

'He punched himself in the face!' Alicia whispered, horror-struck. 'Why would he...?' I wiped a smear of blood away from my nose and her face cleared. 'Wow. He really wants your attention.'

I gritted my teeth. 'I'll be right back.'

I left the VIP area, anger spilling through me. As soon as I reached Vincent, I put my hands on my hips. 'What the hell are you doing? You can't summon me whenever you want, Vincent! I know the magic that binds us together is annoying, but I try my best not to invoke it unless absolutely necessary. Slapping yourself in the face because you're bored is not helpful!'

'Listen to me, you daft faery! Something's about to go down. We need to get out of here.'

It was his tone of voice rather than his words that gave me pause. 'What do you mean?'

'There are about a dozen people in here who don't belong. I recognise at least four of them. They're coppers, Saffron. Plain-clothed coppers. This place is about to get raided.'

'Rai—?' Then I realised. Of course it was about to be raided. An anonymous tip would do the trick, especially from someone who wanted to put the kibosh on our plans to get to know a certain songstress who was hanging out here.

I spun round and waved frantically at Alicia and Melissa. Alicia raised a perfectly manicured eyebrow while Melissa merely smiled. I ground my teeth and prepared to stomp over to them. Unfortunately, I was already too late.

The harsh overhead lights blazed on at the same moment as several voices rang out. 'Police! Hands on your heads!' A second later the music was killed and every single punter in the place was left blinking with a mixture of panic and confusion.

I saw Estrella get to her feet and peer over the VIP balcony. Mitchell was already there, shadowing her protectively. Alicia and Melissa stood up as well and I felt a sudden wave of fear that one of them would do something daft. Fortunately, they were beaten to it – one of the other club-goers, who was probably in possession of some highly illegal substance, decided to make a break for it.

He sped for the door, perhaps thinking that if he ram-raided his way out he'd escape to freedom. He was taken down in about three seconds. Everyone else leapt out of the way, nervous of being tainted by their proximity to him. I looked round as more and more police officers entered the club. My heart sank. This sucked.

CHAPTER

SIXTEEN

Melissa's expression was sour. 'Just when I was starting to think that this godmother gig wasn't so bad, you lot end up getting me arrested. Can't we magic ourselves out of here?'

'There are too many variables,' Alicia muttered. 'And it's too messy. There are too many of us to manage the covering memory magic on our own. We're not official yet. Until Wish Inc gets the rubber stamp of faery approval, we don't have access to every magical resource.'

'Well,' I said, trying to remain bright, 'we're still faery godmothers. We're not powerless. We can still get close to Estrella and talk to her about the sort of man who floats her romantic boat.'

'I'm a troll godmother,' Melissa sniffed. 'And we can't talk to *anyone* if we're behind bars like this.' She looked round the holding cell. 'Unless someone wants to dig their way out with a spoon.'

'They have no reason to hold us,' I said calmly. 'We'll probably have to answer a few questions and then we'll be released.'

'Either that,' Melissa said, 'or your Director will have fina-gled it so that we're charged with mass murder.'

I shook my head. 'Too messy.'

Alicia agreed. 'Too many variables,' she said again.

Melissa rolled her eyes. 'I feel like I've been incarcerated with Tweedledum and Tweedledee.'

My fingertip traced around the graffiti scratched into the wall beside me. *Mat and Jenna 4 eva.* Apparently. 'We should be looking at this as a win,' I said.

'How do you figure that?' Alicia enquired.

'Can we all agree that it's most likely the Director who pulled this stunt? After all, what are the chances that there'd be a raid on the club when we're there to meet Estrella for the first time? The Director knows she's our client.' I beamed. 'What she doesn't know is that she's playing right into our hands.'

Melissa made a show of looking round the stark walls of the holding cell. 'Yeah,' she said sarcastically. 'We really pulled one over on her this time.'

At least Alicia understood what I was getting at. 'All it would have taken is an anonymous phone call. She wouldn't have had to use magic to achieve this.'

I sat forward. 'Our plan is working. We're drawing her out into the open. If our attempts to help Estrella are stymied, we might raise a decent level of suspicion among the other faeries. We need to continue meeting Estrella loudly and publicly. Even if we don't get the proof that we need, it will be obvious that someone is working against us.' I sighed happily. 'We can fulfil our remit to find Estrella the man of her dreams *and* bring the Director to justice at the same time.'

'It's hardly cast-iron proof that she's a wrong'un,' Melissa said.

'No,' Alicia agreed. 'But it's definitely a start.' She nodded at me. 'More of this and we might be onto something.'

A police officer appeared, clipboard in hand. 'Saffron Sawyer?' she asked.

I smiled confidently and got to my feet. 'That's me.'

'This way.' She unlocked the door and I walked out.

'Name, rank and serial number!' Melissa called after me unhelpfully.

'Ignore her,' I said under my breath to the police officer. 'She's just a troll.'

I was led down a narrow corridor towards an interview room. Under any other circumstances, this would have been quite interesting. I'd helped out plenty of clients who'd been arrested but I'd never been the one in handcuffs. Metaphorical handcuffs, anyway; as yet, my wrists were free.

I was directed toward a scuffed plastic chair and sat down with a complacent smile, like the good citizen I knew myself to be. An older police officer, who was already sitting opposite, scowled at me. 'Is something funny?'

What? 'No!' I wiped the smile off my face. 'I'm only trying to be friendly.'

'This is a police station, Ms Sawyer, and you're currently under arrest as part of an investigation into the sale of illegal drugs. This isn't playgroup.'

Okay, so he was the bad cop. That was alright – we all had roles to play. I straightened my shoulders and sobered my thoughts. A younger police officer sat down on the spare chair and offered me a sympathetic look. He could play good cop all he wanted; I was going to focus my attention on Sergeant Grumpy.

'You searched me,' I said. 'There were no illegal drugs on my person. There are no illegal drugs in my system. I don't take illegal drugs. You have no reason to hold me.' I spread my hands wide to indicate that it was a *fait accompli*. There was nothing more to be said.

'Mmm,' the first policeman said. 'That is indeed all true.'

'Great.' I got to my feet. 'So I take it I'm free to go.'

'Sit down, Ms Sawyer.'

There was a time and place for arguing and this wasn't it so I did as I was told. I maintained a serious expression; I didn't want to be accused of treating the entire judicial process as a joke. That sort of attitude wouldn't endear me to anyone.

'The thing is, Ms Sawyer,' the younger, friendlier police officer said, 'we have CCTV footage and information from various eye-witnesses who state that you were seen in conversation on more than one occasion with a certain Vincent Hamilton. This man is a known drug dealer.' He leaned forward. 'Can you tell me what your dealings were with him?'

Uh-oh. When in doubt go with the truth. 'He's a friend of mine,' I said simply. 'And while he has made some missteps in the past, he is no longer a drug dealer. He's cleaned up his act and should be commended for doing so.'

Grumpy glared at me. 'We should commend someone for no longer breaking the law?'

He certainly had a way with words. 'Everyone makes mistakes,' I returned. The Director drifted back into my thoughts. Did I owe her an opportunity to repent from her mistakes? I bit my lip. No, I decided, not when she kept trying to kill me. Or when she threatened Jasper.

Grumpy scratched his chin. Something about his expression made me think we were about to get to the point of these questions. 'We'll agree that there is nothing directly linking you to any drugs,' he said finally. 'But we'd like to ask you about another matter. Ms Sawyer, what is the nature of your relationship with Estrella Davies?'

That was the one thing I hadn't expected. I stared stupidly at him. 'Huh?'

'You know – Estrella,' the younger man said. 'She's a glob-ally-renowned popstar. You met her this evening.'

'Um, yes. I did meet her this evening, that's true.'

'Ms Sawyer, is it your intention to harm Estrella Davies?'

My mouth dropped open. 'What?'

'You worked with Vincent Hamilton to engineer a meeting with one of Estrella Davies' friends.'

I began to shake my head. 'No! That's not what happened!'

'You positioned yourself as a hero, rescuing Ms Davies' friend from Vincent Hamilton's attempts to sell her drugs in order to insinuate yourself into her group.'

'That's nuts!' I protested. I grimaced inwardly. Mitchell, the over-zealous bodyguard: he'd shopped me to the police. I'd bet money on it.

'Are you planning to extort money from her? Or are you just a plain, old-fashioned, garden-variety stalker?'

'Neither!'

Grumpy stared at me. 'If we obtain a warrant and seize your computer, will we discover recent internet searches for Estrella Davies?'

Fuck a puck. The answer to that was yes. 'I have nothing but good wishes for her!' I spluttered.

The police officers exchanged glances. 'Isn't that exactly what a stalker would say?'

I threw up my hands. 'How the hell would I know? I'm not a stalker!'

At that moment, the door to the interview room opened. When I saw Jasper, my heart almost leapt out of my chest. Praise be. He was dressed in his usual attire of a dark suit and white shirt but he really should have been wearing his under-pants outside his trousers and a cape round his shoulders.

His lip curled in disdain as he took in the scene. 'I am Saffron Sawyer's solicitor,' he announced. 'Without even entering this room, I can see that there are procedural concerns, gentlemen.'

Grumpy opened his mouth to protest but Jasper waved him down. 'Regardless of that, I require some time alone with my client.'

Grumpy couldn't argue about that. His eyes narrowed but he got to his feet and nodded at his colleague. Without another word, the pair of them stalked out.

As soon as the door closed, Jasper looked at me. 'I'm not kidding about the procedural errors, you know. Were they recording this?'

I sprang out of my seat and threw myself at him. I needed a hug and I needed it now. 'I thought everything was fine,' I mumbled into his shoulder. 'Then they started asking me questions and I realised that I might be in some serious shit.'

'And then some,' Jasper replied. 'Don't worry. I'll sort it out.'

'Are you alright?' I asked. 'Has anyone else been following you?'

'Not a soul. You scared them all off.' He sounded more proud than anything.

I wrapped my arms tighter round his body, pressing myself against him. A moment later, I realised what I was doing and jumped back. I coughed and looked down at my shoes. 'Sorry.'

'Don't be. I enjoyed that.'

So did I. Jasper's cinnamon scent still clung to my own clothes. It was faint – but it was still enough to send a zippy kick of unadulterated lust through my system. I felt my cheeks going red and hastily returned to my chair.

Jasper sat down in Officer Grumpy's abandoned chair. 'Well,' he said, 'this isn't a particularly auspicious start for Wish Inc, is it?'

I didn't meet his eyes. 'It could be worse.'

'Saffron.' He reached across the table and took my hands. 'I told you that I was more than able to do my job and remain unbiased, despite what has gone on between us both in the past and now.'

'Uh-huh.'

'I wasn't lying about that.'

'I know.' It was one of the reasons why I loved him. One of the many, many reasons. It was also one of the reasons why I'd tried to hide the truth about the Director from him.

'Obviously,' he continued gently, 'I will ensure that you and the others are released without charge. The same would be done for any faery under similar circumstances. But there are limits to what I can achieve, and it's imperative that this test remains fair.'

'I understand that, Jasper. It's fine. It's all fine.'

'You could have used your magic to get out of this on your own.'

'Yeah,' I shrugged. 'But we were concerned whether or not we were covered by memory magic. I've learnt my lesson as far as messing with that is concerned. Plus, it didn't seem right.'

He quirked an eyebrow. 'Didn't seem right?'

'You know – waving my hands around to save my own skin. It's not what the magic is there for. Not unless it's absolutely necessary.'

For a moment, he didn't speak. 'You know,' he said finally, 'you're a better faery than you give yourself credit for.'

'Sometimes,' I mumbled, 'I have a pretty big ego.'

'And sometimes,' he replied without a trace of sarcasm, 'you show incredible humility.'

'I'm not perfect.' I hesitated. This seemed as good a time as any to establish a mutual admiration society. 'You make a pretty good Devil's Advocate, you know.'

'Saffron, please.' He grinned at me suddenly. 'I'm the best.'

CHAPTER

SEVENTEEN

'You should have left it up to Delilah and me,' Rupert declared the next morning, as we all sat around the brand spanking new, but sparsely furnished, Wish Inc office. 'We'd have done a much better job.'

'Really?' Alicia said flatly. 'And when the police arrested you, what would you have done?'

His eyes danced. 'I've got some moves.'

Mrs Jardine frowned. 'Everyone knows that, Rupert. It's a shame the moves in question are so sleazy.'

'Hey! I'm trying to be better. Cut me some slack.'

'Did you lot have any luck with Samuel Alwick's laptop?' I asked, before we spent too long dwelling on Rupert's state of mind.

Delilah wrinkled her nose. 'He was telling the truth about the emails. He was contacted four days ago by someone calling themselves a friend of Art's. For a modest fee of a grand, he was supposed to tail the Devil's Advocate – and you, if the opportunity presented itself.' She turned the laptop round so I could see. 'Look,' she said brightly. 'There's a photo.'

I squinted, drawing in a sharp breath. 'That's my old Office of Faery Godmothers' ID.'

Vincent peered at it. 'Oh, I remember. That's the photo where you look drunk.'

Alicia shook her head. 'Not drunk. More like you've been lobotomised.'

Delilah snickered. I tutted. 'This is good,' I said. 'The Director has finally slipped up. That photo is proof that whoever sent those emails to Samuel Alwick works in the Faery Godmother office. Otherwise they'd have found a different shot.'

Billy was more dubious. 'The Director threw out all your stuff after you walked out. Anyone rifling through the rubbish could have picked up your ID.'

Our smiles faded. There was still no smoking gun pointing at the Director.

'The second email,' Delilah said, 'is the one where he's offered more money to kill the Devil's Advocate if he gets the chance. The word *kill* isn't used, though. It only says that he'll receive a considerable bonus if Jasper's taken care of for good.'

Vincent clapped his hands. 'I love it!'

I glared at him. 'You love that Jasper is being targeted for assassination?'

'I love that we've got proof that he's being targeted.' He beamed. 'Can't you take this to the Devil and let him deal with it?'

I looked at Billy and Delilah. 'Is there anything to indicate where the emails originated from or who sent them?'

Billy grimaced. 'Not so far. It's an anonymous account, probably set up for no reason other than to contact Alwick. There are no identifying characteristics in the emails, although I've managed to isolate the IP address.' We all leaned in and held our breaths. 'And the email was sent from Costa Coffee. The big one on the High Street.'

There was a chorus of disappointed exhalations. I curled my hands into fists. Fuck a puck.

'If I could get my hands on the laptop or mobile device used to send the email, I might be able to prove more,' Billy said.

Alicia frowned. 'But we have no way of knowing what device the Director used when she sent it.'

'Or,' I said glumly, 'if she used her own device. She was smart enough to avoid using the Faery Godmothers' IP address, even if she did use my old ID photo. She might have been smart enough to borrow someone else's phone or laptop to ensure that nothing can be traced back to her.'

'I guess,' Rupert said, 'that our best bet is to stick with the Estrella plan. We continue to meet with her publicly so the Director is forced to do more to stop us.'

'No-one's infallible,' Alicia agreed. 'She'll slip up sooner or later and give us something we can use as evidence against her. It's bound to happen.'

Melissa, who until now had been sitting silently in the corner listening to the exchanges with a dark look, piped up. 'Actually,' she said, 'I'm infallible. You lot can't appreciate it because you're merely faeries, but it's true.'

'*I'm* not a faery,' Vincent retorted.

'And,' Mrs Jardine snapped, 'neither of you is infallible.'

Angela rose to her feet. 'Enough of this. As Head of HR, I institute a no-bickering rule.'

Rupert blinked. 'Why? I was about to break out the popcorn.'

She tutted in disgust. 'Come on, everyone. Stand up.'

I had a horrible feeling about this. Apparently so did everyone else because nobody moved.

'Stand up!' she barked.

We all reluctantly staggered to our feet. Angela reached into her pocket and pulled out an egg. 'This,' she declared, 'is your task for this morning.'

'Angela...'

She glared at me and I lapsed into silence. 'Without using magic,' she said, 'and with contributions from the entire team, you have got twenty minutes to find appropriate materials that will cushion this egg and prevent it from breaking when it is dropped from the third-floor window onto the pavement below.'

Billy folded his arms. 'We're quite busy at the moment preventing a megalomaniac from killing Saffron and destroying all the good that every faery in this world has ever stood for. As well as finding true love for a poppy princess.'

Angela's expression was serene. 'Twenty minutes of your time, Billy. It's not going to kill you.'

'No wonder you faeries are all nuts,' Melissa said. 'I'm not doing this.'

'You,' Angela said, wagging her finger, 'are either part of this team or you're not.'

Melissa opened her mouth to speak. I nudged her sharply and she sighed. 'Fine. I'm part of the team.' She raised her fist with an obvious lack of enthusiasm. 'Go team.'

Angela flicked her wand and a giant clock appeared above our heads, hovering with grim horological intent. 'Twenty minutes,' she said. 'Go.'

The trouble was that there wasn't much in the office that we could use. We might have managed to get some tables and chairs but that didn't mean there was a surfeit of materials we could use for such a daft team-building task. Perhaps that was the point.

'Pumpkin is quite podgy,' Rupert mused. 'We give him the

egg. He eats it. Then we throw him out of the window. He'll probably bounce.'

'Pumpkin,' I ordered, 'you didn't hear any of that.'

My little dog glanced at me and yawned, then he went straight back to sleep. It was alright for some.

Mrs Jardine went to her desk, returning a moment later with one of her glossy magazines. 'According to this,' she declared, 'Estrella Davies is on a yo-yo diet in a bid to find true love. A secret source close to her stated that she's been rapidly losing weight and there are fears for her health.'

'A secret source?' I asked sceptically.

Mrs Jardine shrugged. 'I didn't write it.'

Delilah rolled her eyes. 'Meaningless gossip,' she said. Then she grinned. 'I love it.'

'Meaningless gossip or not, we can use this.' Mrs Jardine opened the magazine to its centre pages and pulled out the staples. 'Anyone got some Sellotape?'

Alicia dug into a box by her feet, rummaging around until she found what she needed. 'Will washi tape do?'

'If it's all we've got, it'll have to.'

Angela's face split into a wide smile. 'There's nothing that I love more than a good team-building exercise.'

Twenty minutes later we were huddled round the open window on the third floor. Melissa was holding the carefully wrapped egg in both hands and looking immensely proud of herself. Maybe there was something in this team-building after all. At this rate, we'd be begging Angela for more motivational posters to adorn our newly painted walls.

'Who's going to do the honours?' Alicia asked.

They all turned and looked at me. I sighed and held out my hands. 'Fine,' I said. 'I'll do it.'

Melissa passed me the egg. 'Be gentle,' she warned.

'I'll wait down at the bottom,' Vincent said. 'Only don't hit me with it. The last thing I want is egg splatter on these clothes.'

'The egg won't break,' Rupert said confidently. 'We're too good.'

I had my doubts about that. All the same, I waited until Vincent had dashed downstairs and was on the pavement outside, craning his head upwards. 'Ready?' I called.

He stepped out of the line of fire. 'Ready!'

I took a deep breath and released the egg at the very moment that red smoke clouded up from the spot directly below. As if in slow motion, the egg fell just as Jasper magically transported himself to exactly the wrong position at the wrong time. He glanced upwards in my direction – and the glossy-mag bound egg smacked him on the centre of his forehead.

The others leapt backwards as if skulking in the corner of the room would save them. I stayed where I was, gazing down at Jasper and the trickle of oozing yolk that was dribbling down towards his perfect cheekbones. Oops.

'Hi, Devil!' Vincent said brightly, pretending that nothing was amiss.

Jasper took out a handkerchief and dabbed at his face. 'Vincent,' he growled.

'Talk about bad timing,' Delilah whispered from behind me.

I pressed my lips together and tried not to laugh.

'If anyone asks,' Angela muttered, 'this was all Saffron's idea.'

I headed downstairs as Jasper entered through Wish Inc's front door. Before I could say anything, he held up a hand.

'Sometimes, Saffron,' he said, 'it's better not to say anything at all.'

Fair enough. I bit back another snorted giggle and grinned at him. 'As you wish.'

His emerald eyes glinted at me with a trace of amusement then he straightened his shoulders. 'Is anyone else here?' he asked, looking round the room. Pumpkin danced towards him and tugged at his shoelace. 'Other than Vincent and the mutt, I mean.'

'Uh, I think they're hiding upstairs.'

'Call them down,' he advised. 'They're going to want to hear this.'

I did as he asked then we waited until everyone reluctantly reappeared. Even Melissa looked rather nervous. Fortunately Jasper chose not to comment on the egg and got straight to the point of his visit. 'I have some good news and some bad news,' he said.

'Let's get the bad news out of the way first,' Angela suggested, not meeting his eyes.

'Eggcellent idea,' Vincent agreed. When Jasper shot him a sidelong look, he blinked innocently. 'What?'

I could feel another giggle threatening. I shook it off – only just – and folded my hands primly in my lap. 'Go ahead, Jasper.'

He raised his chin. 'I spoke to the faery department heads this morning. They are concerned that your actions last night put Estrella Davies in danger.'

My amusement vanished completely. 'What?'

'The police were involved. There was the possibility of drugs on the scene. Estrella had to be whisked away by her bodyguard before she was arrested. It's in all the newspapers.'

My mouth dropped open. 'None of that was our fault! I would never place a client in danger. I know Vincent might have pushed the boundaries but I put a stop to what he was doing as soon as I could.'

'I understand that,' Jasper said gently. 'But unfortunately they've decided that the test will only continue if you don't approach her directly. The rest of the test is to be conducted at a distance. You can't talk to Estrella again. Don't take it personally. A lot of them are sympathetic, but Wish Inc is an unknown quantity and they're wary of disasters that will be difficult to put right.'

'That's ridiculous!'

'Can't you use your position as Devil's Advocate and tell those stupid faeries that's neither fair nor acceptable?' Melissa asked.

'I could,' Jasper agreed.

'Then...'

'But I won't.'

She glared at him. 'Why the fuck not? How are we supposed to help Estrella find her Prince Charming when we can't go near her?'

'There are several of you,' Jasper said. 'You're all talented. Besides, time is short. You can still pass the test without approaching her.'

'Sure,' the troll said sarcastically. 'It'll be a piece of cake.'

Jasper looked at me. 'It could be argued that what occurred last night was your own fault and intervention to prevent future mistakes wouldn't be in the spirit of the test. It's a safeguarding measure. I know it's not ideal, but it's not the end of the world.'

'Easy for you to say,' Rupert muttered.

Delilah glared at Jasper. 'Whose side are you on?'

I answered for him. 'He's the Devil's Advocate,' I said quietly. 'He's not allowed to take sides.'

'Sure,' Rupert said, folding his arms. 'But what happened last night isn't our fault. It's only because the Di—'

'Enough, Rupert,' I interrupted.

Jasper looked pained. 'Let him finish.'

I shook my head. 'No.' I sniffed and changed the subject. 'Well, that's the bad news. What's the good news?'

He didn't smile. 'As I said, it's arguable that the events of last night and the intervention of the police were your fault. It could also be argued that it was merely bad luck. But,' he continued, 'it's also possible that someone is trying to sabotage the test because they don't want Wish Inc to succeed.'

'Exactly!' Rupert burst out.

'There was no tell-tale taint of magic in the club itself,' Jasper told us. 'I investigated and I'm sure of that. However, this test must be fair.' His voice hardened slightly. 'On both sides. Therefore I extracted a further agreement from the faery department heads. If anything else occurs that can be construed as similar bad luck that prevents you continuing your efforts, then this Cinderella test will be negated and you will begin again with a new client.'

Fuck a puck. This was not supposed to happen. Jasper frowned at me, obviously aware that what he'd said was not good news at all.

'What about Estrella?' I asked unhappily. 'Does she get dropped as a client for good, then?'

'We'll cross that bridge if and when we come to it,' Jasper said.

Alicia stepped up until she was shoulder to shoulder with me. 'I don't think we require that sort of caveat,' she said. 'Bad luck is a fact of life. If we suffer further setbacks, we'll deal with them ourselves. We appreciate your efforts, Devil's Advocate, but please inform the other faery heads that it's not necessary.'

I glanced at her. She was right. Not only could this mean

disaster for Estrella, who we were supposed to support, but it meant that the Director's hands were effectively tied. She could no longer try and stop us. Wish Inc had been set up to draw her out so she'd make an obvious error; Jasper was all but preventing her from doing that. She wouldn't risk letting us start the test all over again with someone new because it would raise too many questions.

'I agree with Alicia,' I said. 'Thank you for your help but we don't need that extra clause. We'll complete the test without it.'

Jasper's green eyes narrowed. 'It's too late,' he said. 'It's already been agreed and it can't be cancelled.'

Alicia turned to me. 'You need to tell him what's really going on here,' she said icily. 'Before he ruins everything for us.'

My heart sank. I was beginning to think she was right. But nothing had changed; I had no proof of the Director's culpability.

'Saffron?' Jasper asked.

I sighed. Alright already.

CHAPTER

EIGHTEEN

Jasper didn't say anything for a long time after I finished my long-winded explanation. Despite focussing intently on his face, his body language and even his breathing, I couldn't tell what he was thinking. The only thing that betrayed his thoughts was the tiny tick in his jaw – and all that told me was that he was deeply, furiously angry. At what or at whom, I didn't know.

Eventually he uncrossed his arms and spoke. 'You should have come to me at the very beginning.'

I twisted my fingers together. Pumpkin nudged me with his nose and, for my own comfort as much as his, I scooped him up and laid him gently on my lap. He gave me an anxious look with his large, chocolate-brown eyes and licked my hand. I stroked his ears and sighed.

'If I'd gone to you, you'd have confronted her directly,' I said. 'Without proof of her misdeeds, she'd have turned the tables on you. She was already threatening your position, Jasper. I couldn't let her ruin your life completely. I know how much your job means to you.'

'It's a job, Saffron,' he bit out. 'It's not my life. It was my whole life once but...' His voice trailed off.

'You can say it,' Vincent piped up.

'Yeah,' Delilah agreed. 'We all know what you're thinking.'

I frowned. 'Thinking what?'

The muscle in Jasper's jaw continued to throb. 'My job stopped being my whole life,' he muttered, 'when I met you.'

Suddenly my mouth felt dry. I swallowed as my stomach flipped over and a strange tremor ran through me.

Jasper got to his feet and started pacing. 'She blackmailed you.'

'She tried to,' I whispered.

'She took advantage of her position.'

I nodded slightly.

'I suspected a lot of her,' he muttered, 'but not this.' He stopped pacing and stared at me. 'She actually contacted Art Adwell and made a deal with him?'

'I believe so,' I said in a small voice.

'She's not going to get away with this,' he ground out. He spun round and headed for the door. Still clutching Pumpkin, I sprang up and reached it before him to stop him walking out. I knew that his magic was powerful and he could leave whenever he wanted to, but I needed him to listen to me first.

'I have no proof of anything,' I said. 'She's been too careful.'

'So,' he said, 'everything to do with Wish Inc is a ploy? Nothing about this agency is real?'

'Not initially but...' My voice faltered slightly and I looked at the others. 'I think we all want it to work. I think we're all starting to believe that Wish Inc could do great things.'

I was relieved to see that everyone agreed with me. 'There's a limit to how long my family and Rupert's can continue funding this place,' Alicia said, 'but I do believe it has genuine merit. And extraordinary potential. It feels like we're on the cusp of changing the faery world.'

Melissa coughed loudly. 'It's not just the faery world.' She pointed at Vincent. 'He's human.'

'And,' Vincent said loudly, pointing back at her, 'she's a troll.'

Jasper ran a hand through his hair. 'You should have come to me before,' he repeated. 'I could have dealt with this before anyone was killed.'

My head dropped. 'I'll feel guilty about Figgy's death as long as I live.'

'Which might not be all that long if the Director keeps trying to have you killed,' Jasper snapped.

'I've got no evidence that it's her.'

He turned slowly and stared at us. 'Is there anyone here who thinks that someone other than the Director is responsible?'

Nobody answered. Jasper glanced at me. 'You should have trusted me, Saffron.'

'You can't confront her,' I warned him. 'You can't accuse her of anything because we can't *prove* anything.'

'So what happens if you never get that proof?'

I hadn't allowed myself to think that far. 'Then,' I said in a tiny voice, 'she continues as head of the faery godmothers.'

'But Wish Inc will continue too,' Mrs Jardine interjected. 'We might not have the evidence we need to destroy the Director, but we still have the potential to be bigger and better than her office. I wouldn't have signed on if I didn't believe that.'

'Amen,' Billy said.

Jasper shook his head out of frustration more than anything else. 'So what's the plan now? You'll continue trying to pass the test?'

Alicia sniffed. 'Of course. Estrella Davies is still our client.'

I shot her a grateful look.

Delilah raised her chin a fraction. 'We will do whatever we can to make all her wishes come true.'

Vincent cleared his throat. 'There's still the possibility that I can be her knight in shining—'

Rupert punched his arm. 'Careful,' he warned. 'There's a danger that you're going to sound as bad as I do.' He stood a little straighter, a challenge in his eyes. 'Saffron has forced me to confront the person I am – the person I was. She's a good person.'

'I'm not denying that,' Jasper said.

'She's making me a better faery,' Rupert insisted. 'And she's only done what she thought was right.'

I gave him a soft smile. 'You could say the same about the Director.'

'Actually,' Billy said, 'I don't think you could.'

'As faeries go,' Melissa said grudgingly, 'Saffron's not too bad.'

My gaze dropped. 'At the end of the day, none of this is about me.'

I felt Jasper's eyes on me. Eventually, he lifted his head. 'I'd like to talk to Saffron alone,' he said finally.

They all nodded and filed out, heading upstairs to give us some privacy.

'You too, Vincent,' Jasper said.

'Aw, but...'

'Please.'

Vincent stopped arguing and followed the others. Before long, only Jasper and I remained. And Pumpkin too, of course. I returned him to the floor and he whined slightly, disturbed by the continuing tension. But he seemed to understand that we needed to do this. He gazed at us both for a long moment then wagged his tail, just once, almost hopefully. A second later, he trotted off after Vincent.

Jasper gave me a long look. 'You hurt me,' he said.

I couldn't meet his eyes. 'I know.'

He stepped forward, his hands reaching for my shoulders. His grip wasn't tight but his touch seared my skin. 'You hurt me more than anyone else ever has before. Others have tried,' he said. 'Only you succeeded.'

I took a deep breath and forced myself to raise my head and confront his gaze. I couldn't run away from this. 'Maybe I should have done things differently,' I told him. 'Maybe you're right and I should have told you everything at the very beginning. But I had to protect you from the Director.'

'That wasn't your job. And there was nobody around to protect me from you.'

I felt a sharp pain in my chest at the rawness in his voice. 'I'm sorry.'

Jasper's hands moved from my shoulders to my face, cupping it and pulling me an inch closer. 'So am I. If I hadn't been so scared that you didn't feel the same way about me, I wouldn't have been so furious at what happened next. I'd have worked out far more quickly that you were up to something, that there was far more going on behind the scenes than you were telling me. I should have come to you sooner. I should have demanded to know the truth.'

'I wouldn't have told you.'

'You say it was up to you to protect me.'

I nodded.

'Well, it's up to *me* to protect *you*. The threats to your life...'

'I'm still here. I'm not going anywhere.'

Jasper growled. 'You'd better not.'

I bit my lip. 'Do you think we can get past this? Us two, I mean.'

'No more lies?'

There was a painful lump in my throat. 'No more lies.'

I felt his hands tremble. 'The trouble is, Saffron,' he said, 'I can't imagine a future without you in it. Regardless of anything else.'

He stared at me and I stared back at him then I pulled away. 'No,' I said. 'We can't. If we have a relationship – any kind of relationship – the Director will use it against you and—'

'The Director can go fuck herself.'

'That's easy to say now, Jasper, but it makes sense for us to wait.'

His expression didn't change. 'I'm done with waiting. I might be the Devil's Advocate but I'm not a saint. Or a monk. If the Director or anyone else thinks they can use my feelings for you against me, let them try. I don't have it in me to do much more of this skirting around what could be. Either we're in this together or we're not. It's a simple as that.'

He drew in a breath. 'I won't make a formal accusation against the Director just yet. I'll give you time to try and find your evidence before I get involved as the Devil's Advocate. But I won't wait for *us*. We both deserve better.'

I felt like I was about to step off a precipice. This time there would be no return – and this time I didn't want there to be. 'Well,' I said, 'then I guess we're in this together.'

Jasper dipped his head. To begin with his lips merely brushed mine as if, like me, he was scared to let go. But if we were going to do this, we would have to do it properly. Never let it be said that Saffron Sawyer went off half-cocked or didn't give it her all.

I reached up, hooking my arms round his neck so that I could draw him even closer, and I deepened the kiss. His mouth scorched mine with an intensity that sent every coherent thought flying out of the window. He tasted of spice and heat, and the cinnamon scent of his skin wrapped itself round me in the same way that his arms encircled my body. Nothing else mattered now. Maybe nothing else had mattered before.

Eventually we pulled apart, although his fingers continued to cling to mine. 'We've lost too much time already, Saffron,' Jasper said. 'Let's not lose any more.'

'Yes.' I could barely speak. 'We should leave now.' I traced the tip of my index finger along his collarbone and enjoyed feeling his muscles bunch and tighten under my touch. 'We should forget everything else for a couple of hours.'

He smiled at me. 'We should.' He lifted his eyes and looked over my shoulder. 'But your next-door neighbour with a penchant for hitting people with frozen produce wants something.'

I turned round. Ben was right there, a sheepish grin on his face. He really did possess the most bizarre sense of timing.

'Sorry,' he said, 'I didn't want to interrupt.' He shrugged awkwardly. 'I was just looking for some life coaching.'

BAFFLED that a potential client had come to us of his own accord, Delilah sat opposite him taking notes while I peppered him with questions and tried to stop my eyes from continually drifting over to Jasper. He was sitting in the corner, discussing more of Wish Inc's set up with Alicia.

'This is a judgment-free zone,' I told Ben. 'So don't hold anything back. What are you actually hoping to improve in your life?'

'I shouldn't complain,' he said. 'Compared to other people, I have a lovely life.'

'Comparison is a common problem that's responsible for all kinds of unhappiness,' I said, primly. 'You can't focus on what other people are doing with their lives. You can only focus on your own, otherwise you'll never succeed and you'll never feel true contentment.'

Ben beamed. 'I knew I was doing the right thing coming here to see you. The thing is that, even with a new flat and a new job, I still feel restless. It's like something is missing.' His expression grew more earnest. 'To be honest, Saffron, I think I'm just going through the motions. When I walked in here and saw you with your boyfriend, I was so jealous and sad and upset all at the same time that I almost had to walk out again.'

I raised my eyes to Jasper. A single, adorable dark curl was falling across his forehead. I had to sit on my hands to stop myself springing up and gently brushing it away. Was he my boyfriend? A delightful warmth spread through my body. I supposed he was.

'Jealous?' Delilah questioned.

Faint alarm crossed Ben's face. 'Oh!' he said. 'Oh! No, I don't mean like that. I don't fancy Saffron or anything. I'm not interested in her.' He paused, thinking about what he was saying. His cheeks began to turn red. 'Sorry, Saffron. You're lovely, truly lovely. I think you're a wonderful person. It's just that your life is all sorted. Not only is your professional life perfect, but your romantic life is too. Whereas I'm a complete mess.'

'Sometimes,' I said drily, 'things aren't what they seem. There's very little about my life that's perfect, Ben.'

'That's not how it looks from where I'm standing.' He shuffled his feet. 'I failed the audition. Forget the London Philharmonic, I can't even get a spot with a small local orchestra. I'm a complete failure.'

'Oh, Ben, I'm so sorry.'

His shoulders drooped. 'Thanks. You're so lovely for saying that.' He sighed. 'I don't have a job. I don't have a girlfriend. I don't have a cute dog like you do.'

I patted his shoulder. 'Have you tried online dating?'

He pulled a face and dropped his voice to a whisper. 'To be honest, I'm a bit scared of it. You hear stories, you know. I'm sure most people online are lovely but what if I ended up with a stalker?'

Given that's what the police had accused me of being, I almost laughed. In a way, I supposed, faery godmothers were the ultimate stalkers – just with better intentions. If only I could persuade Estrella of that.

'What is it?' he asked anxiously, registering that my thoughts were drifting off.

'Nothing,' I said, managing another smile and getting to my feet. 'Thank you for coming in, Ben. You've come to the right place! I think that Wish Inc can do a great deal to help you. We'll go through our notes and consider the best way to proceed and I'll be in touch in the next week or so. Bear in mind that we're only just getting started, so we haven't quite found our groove yet. But we'd be thrilled to have you as a client.'

'Definitely,' Delilah grinned. 'We'll be in touch, Ben.'

He sniffed loudly. 'You're all so lovely. It's so lovely to know that there's someone out there who can help. Thank you so much for your time.'

Her smile grew. 'It's what we're here for.'

Once he'd gone, she turned to me. 'Saffron! I know we've got other shit going on but we can easily manage him as a client as well. *He* came to *us*!' Her eyes shone. 'That's never happened before! Can you imagine the possibilities? If he pays us, Wish Inc might even end up being self-funding and then we won't have to bow and scrape to Alicia. You know she'll end up being insufferable because of the money.'

Alicia's head snapped up and she offered Delilah an icy glare. 'Last one in,' she said. 'First one out.'

Delilah nudged me. 'See? She's already threatening me.'

I frowned at Alicia then stood up. 'We've got serious potential. Wish Inc could be the start of something truly amazing. We can definitely help Ben and we can definitely get more clients like him. Before we do any of that, though...'

Delilah's face fell. 'We have to pass the test.'

'And deal with the Director,' Alicia said.

I nodded. 'Yep.' I flashed them a grin, noting Jasper watching me. He had faith in my abilities. I had faith in my abilities. My Wish Inc colleagues – Alicia included – seemed to believe in me. It was time to get shit done.

I straightened my shoulders and raised my chin. Vision. Plan. Action. Success. Angela would be proud. 'Fortunately,' I said aloud, 'I might have an idea about how we can achieve both.' I looked at Jasper.

He understood my meaning. 'You want me to go before you say anything.'

'It's for the best.' I knew he would prefer to stay but his role as Devil's Advocate would compromise everything. He was smart; he understood that.

'Will you walk me out?'

I licked my lips. 'It would be my pleasure.'

He held out his hand and I didn't hesitate. I walked over and took it whilst Delilah clutched her chest and sighed happily.

Once outside, Jasper took one of my curls and wrapped it around his index finger. 'Your hair never ceases to amaze me,' he murmured.

'Because you've never seen anything like it before? Its frizziness surpasses the ken of all mankind? It will allow no smoothing product or hair-straightening treatment to sully its manic curls?'

He smiled slowly. 'It's strong and beautiful and nothing will hold it back. Much like the rest of you.'

I looked into his eyes. 'You,' I whispered, 'can come back to Wish Inc any time.'

His smile grew. 'I could stay.'

'The only way we pass the test is if we do it on our own. We both know that.'

Jasper's green eyes were watchful. 'Will the restraining order be a problem?'

I shrugged. 'We can work round it. We have to.' I gave him a tiny nudge. 'Go on. I'm sure you've got things to do. Just...'

'Stay away from the Director.' His expression darkened. 'So you keep saying.'

'She's dangerous.'

Jasper growled. 'So am I.'

I gave him a lustful side glance from underneath my eyelashes. 'I know.'

'Keep looking at me like that and I'll do whatever you want for the rest of my life.'

I smirked. 'That's the plan.'

He kissed the tip of my nose. 'Witch.'

'When I find evidence to convict her, the Director is all yours,' I promised.

'I'll wait,' Jasper reluctantly agreed. 'For now.'

I glanced at the steamed-up windows of Wish Inc. 'Do we have your best wishes?'

He squeezed my fingers. 'Always.' He leaned in. 'No more eggs though.'

I was still smiling when I walked back into the office. Mrs Jardine raised her eyebrows knowingly. 'I'm so glad the two of you have sorted out your problems.'

Alicia snorted loudly. 'That amount of smug happiness should be illegal.'

I blinked then I saw her wink at me. I still wasn't sure where I was with her. The events surrounding Figgy's death had softened her edges but the original 'mean girl' occasionally reappeared.

'It's good to stay on your toes, Saffron,' Alicia murmured, as if she knew what I was thinking. She pulled up a chair and sat down. 'Anyway, enough about Saffron's love life. What's this plan you've been talking about?'

'Ninja faery godmothers.'

Rupert blinked rapidly. 'Ninja faery godmothers?' His face split wide with delight. 'I love it already.'

'And,' I said, 'we start now. We need to stop reacting and start acting. Until now, we've been the ones who've been stalked. We need to become the stalkers.'

Billy's expression was wary. 'What do you mean by that?'

'If these were ordinary circumstances,' I said, 'we would use the Adventus room to help us come up with a list of potentials for Estrella.'

'But we don't have access to the Adventus room,' Delilah said.

I acknowledged her words with a nod. 'We would also try to get hold of whatever device the Director used when she emailed Samuel Alwick,' I continued.

'Except,' Melissa pointed out, 'we don't know what she used and, even if we did, we don't know where she would keep it.'

'Where's the Adventus room?' I asked innocently.

Rupert frowned. 'In the Office of Faery Godmothers.'

'Where does the Director do all her work?'

'In the Office of...' Mrs Jardine's face dropped. 'Oh no.'

I grinned. 'Oh yes.'

'This is a very bad idea. It'll take months of planning.'

'Most of the planning has already been done.' I looked at Melissa. 'Right?'

She started. 'What?'

'You and the other trolls watched the Office for weeks. You planned different ways to break in. You know the weak points like the back of your hand.'

Vincent coughed. 'You might be right, Saffy, but didn't the trolls get *caught* when they broke in?'

'They were unlucky,' I dismissed.

Billy shifted in his seat. 'We implemented new security after that,' he said.

I had an answer for everything. 'And *you* know what those changes are. We break into the office. We get the information we need. We get out. And,' I smiled, 'we win.'

'I've never been a criminal before,' Mrs Jardine whispered.

Vincent shrugged. 'I can show you the ropes. It's easier than you think.'

'We,' I said with as much drama as I could muster, 'are going to break into the most lauded faery building in the land.'

'Been there,' Melissa said. 'Done that.' She grinned suddenly. 'Looking forward to doing it again.'

CHAPTER

NINETEEN

'I seem to recall,' Vincent murmured to me several days later, once our plans were about to be put into play, 'that not so long ago, you were quite set on the notion of morality. This will be the second time in a month that you've broken the law.'

I'd been wondering when he was going to bring that up. 'Pardon? I can't hear what you're saying through that balaclava.'

His head turned towards mine. Although only his eyes were visible, his thoughts were quite clear. 'Saff,' he chided.

I sighed. 'I know, I know. I guess it's just as well the Director is my only nemesis or I'd find myself compromised at every turn.'

He held his hands up. 'Hey. I'm not judging.'

'We're breaking in so that we can get information to help our client.'

'Uh huh.'

'And so that we can bring the Director to justice.'

He continued nodding. 'Yup.'

'Those are selfless reasons.'

'Mmm-hmm.'

I grimaced. 'Okay, now that you've said that and we're actually here, I don't feel quite so confident.'

Melissa growled, 'There's always a right and a wrong. This is for the right reasons. Therefore it's right.'

'Didn't your lot chop off the fingers and ears of some faery godmothers?' Vincent asked innocently. 'Was that right?'

Melissa's eyes slid away. 'It felt right at the time.'

A little bile rose up in the back of my throat. I swallowed it down. 'Look,' I said, 'if anyone wants to back out, feel free to do so. I mean it. I'm not forcing anyone to do this. Breaking and entering isn't exactly the stuff of dreams.'

'Actually—' Vincent began.

I thumped him.

'I'm in,' Alicia declared. 'I was from the start. I think this is a good idea. It's not as if we're harming anyone. Nobody is in the building – we made sure of that.'

Delilah nodded. 'And it's not like we're sneaking into the Bank of England and blowing up a safe.'

Billy rubbed his hands together. 'I'm in. I think I might even be a little excited.'

Mrs Jardine stared at us all. 'Now that I've had time to think about it and prepare, I'm a lot excited. Let's do this.' She coughed, her cheeks flushing pink. 'What I mean to say is, it's for a good cause so I think my conscience will remain clear.'

Vincent rubbed his palms together. 'A life of crime for us all, then!'

Alicia leaned in towards me. 'Does he have to come along?'

Vincent stuck his tongue out at her. Before this venture descended into anarchy, I straightened my shoulders and crossed the shadowy road to the Office of Faery Godmothers. 'Come on then, team.'

At that time of night there wasn't even a glimmer of light

coming from the shrouded building, although I could feel the slight buzz of magic before I drew close to the front door.

Billy, whose magical senses were far keener than my own, stayed close to my side. When we reached the plate-glass front, I double checked that the street behind us was empty then nodded to him. He swallowed and placed his palms flat against the door. 'The magic's not been altered,' he said to me in a low voice. 'We proceed as planned.'

I exhaled shakily then I raised my hands. The easy thing to do would be to blast the entire façade into smithereens and step inside but we didn't want to advertise our presence. Everything about this operation had to be sneaky and unobtrusive.

My first stream of magic was gentle, testing the barrier without damaging it. I closed my eyes briefly as I checked for weak points. Nothing jumped out at me. Then I probed the hinges on the main door with one hand, while carefully jetting out a coil of magic to the latch with the other.

The door jiggled in its frame, rattling the glass. A moment later there was a click and I stepped back, satisfied. 'Okay,' I murmured. 'Phase one is underway.'

Billy moved forward, pushed open the door and slid in. I followed. The others jogged over from across the street and joined us. Within seconds we were standing on the familiar marble floor and inhaling the sweet scent that clung to the air.

The door closed gently behind us. Vincent strode ahead with Melissa on his heels. Nobody else moved.

'I need a moment,' Alicia said quietly.

I glanced at her. Her face was pale and her jaw was set. She wasn't the only one struggling; Delilah's eyes shone with unshed tears and even Rupert looked disturbed.

'I know I chose to leave,' Delilah whispered. 'But coming back is—' She didn't finish her sentence.

'I know,' Mrs Jardine replied.

Billy nodded. 'I feel it too.'

From across the lobby, Vincent and Melissa turned to see what the problem was. For once they both held their tongues. The faeries amongst us needed this. I waited a few beats, keeping my eyes on my friends.

'It's just hard,' Angela said, 'when you place so much importance on something and pour your heart into making it work.'

'Most of my life has been spent inside these four walls,' Mrs Jardine agreed. She sighed. Then her spine stiffened and her voice rose. 'What is *that*?'

She strode forward to her old reception desk, her arms swinging and her face set into a furious mask. 'Unbelievable,' she muttered. 'Un-freaking-believable.'

The rest of us exchanged glances then jogged after her.

'Look at this!' she scowled. 'Look at it!'

I scratched my head. 'Uh...'

'First impressions are vital!' She stalked round to the receptionist's chair. 'All sorts of faeries come in through that door. Godmothers are supposed to be the crème de la crème. We're supposed to be the best!' She put her hands on her hips and glared. 'Do the *best* decorate their work spaces with frilly cushions?' She grabbed the small back support from the chair and waved it at us. 'This colour is offensive to my eyes! And look at those flowers! The arrangement is completely wrong. Whoever did this is some sort of idiotic heathen who clearly doesn't understand a thing!' Her fingers twisted into the fabric of the cushion.

'Uh, Mrs Jardine?' I hedged.

She glared at me. 'What?'

'We don't want anyone to know we were here. It's probably best if you don't destroy the small furnishings.'

Her chest heaved. 'But this is sacrilege!'

'Yes.'

'Standards should never have slipped this far.'

Melissa stared at Mrs Jardine. 'Are you nuts? It's only a cushion.'

From behind Mrs Jardine's back, I frowned and made a cutting motion with my finger across my throat. To the troll, it was only a cushion; to Mrs Jardine, it was a reminder that she was replaceable and that whatever pride she'd taken in her job didn't mean diddly-squat once she'd gone. It wasn't the cushion, it was what it symbolised. I sighed; this entire venture was already proving to be far harder than I'd imagined.

It was Angela who walked over to Mrs Jardine and gave her a quick hug. 'It's not fair,' she whispered.

'No.' She sniffed and the look in her eyes hardened. 'Let's get a move on,' she said, replacing the offending cushion on the chair. 'I don't want to spend any longer here than is absolutely necessary.'

We continued the rest of the way in silence. I'd been here in the middle of the night before – but that was when I still worked here. Stepping through the shadows and making our way up to the main office floor as intruders was a particularly eerie experience.

We trooped silently up the stairs, avoiding the lift. It seemed to take an age to reach our destination. Before we opened the last door, I had a sudden feeling of dread that the Director would be waiting for us on the other side, a nasty smile of triumph on her lipsticked mouth. The place was empty, however; there was nothing to greet us but a darkened room.

I glanced at my old desk. It lay bare and empty, which somehow hurt me more than if there'd been evidence that it was now occupied by someone else. But this trip wasn't about nostalgia; I didn't belong here any more – perhaps I never had.

Without saying a word, I gestured at my followers. Rupert nodded and led most of them towards the Adventus room.

Vincent, Angela and I peeled off towards the Director's office. We had a plan and we were going to stick to it.

Using a sneaky splice of magic, I jimmied the lock. It swung open at the very moment a loud, guttural shriek rent the air. My eyes widened and I spun round. A second later, there was a stampede of running feet careening in our direction. Angela leapt behind me while the others pelted for cover.

'What?' I asked in alarm. 'What is it?'

Rupert gasped, heaving in a breath and trying to speak. I didn't have to wait for an answer – a split second later, I saw what the problem was. Fuck a puck. It was massive.

'That,' Billy whispered, 'is definitely new.'

The magical monster, whose presence had no doubt been triggered by Rupert and the others' attempts to get into the Adventus room, towered over us. Its head scuffed the ceiling while its bony shoulders hunched upwards and its glowing, narrowed eyes searched for victims.

'Saffron,' Alicia hissed from where she was hiding under a desk. 'What the hell do we do?'

I watched as the conjuration took another step forward. While I had no doubt that we could take it on, destroying it would alert the Director to the fact that we'd gained entrance to the Office of Faery Godmothers. Evidence of our own wrongdoing was the last thing we needed.

I gritted my teeth. 'We hide.' I pointed to the Director's office. 'Everyone in here. Now.'

Vincent was the first to move. When the magical monster swung its head to the left, he ran from the right, skidded across the floor and landed by my feet before scooting through the door. Spurred on by his success, Delilah followed. One by one, the others did the same until everyone was in.

I closed the door just as the monster's head turned in our

direction. It roared once and for a heart-stopping moment I thought it had seen us. Then everything fell silent again.

'Shit.' Billy bunched up his fists. 'We've never had a magical gatekeeper inside the Office before. Why now?'

Melissa's mouth flattened into a grim line. 'That's easy. Your Director expected us to try this. She wants to catch us out.'

We exchanged dark glances. 'Why put it here?' Mrs Jardine wondered aloud. 'Why not downstairs in the lobby where it could stop anyone who entered?'

I mulled it over. 'Because there's a door in the lobby to the outside world and we could escape easily if we needed to. The Director wants to catch us in the act.'

Rupert's eyes were wide. 'It didn't appear until we approached the Adventus room. It's like it was lying in wait.'

Of course. The Director would be well aware how hard it was for us to come up with a list of names of suitable candidates for Estrella's heart. Although the Adventus room was far from foolproof – after all, it only contained details of those people who had already made wishes – it was the obvious place for us to start looking.

'There could be another reason to expel that amount of magical energy and create such a thing,' Alicia whispered. 'Maybe the Director has something to hide.'

I thought about it. The room was shrouded in darkness, the Director's desk forbidding in its size. 'We can't get to the Adventus room,' I said. 'But we're still here and we still have a chance to find the device she used to contact Samuel Alwick. Take a look around. Between us, we can scour every damn corner of this place.'

We wasted no more time. Alicia and I took the desk while Mrs Jardine and Billy headed for the filing cabinet in the corner. Delilah and Rupert scanned the walls, checking the various paintings and objets d'art for anything out of the ordinary.

Angela got down on her hands and knees and checked the floor before moving to the wastepaper basket and pulling out crumpled bits of paper.

Vincent and Melissa merely sat down and watched. 'Why are you really here?' he asked her conversationally. 'Is it because your boss made you come?'

'I volunteered,' she said. 'Ethan doesn't make us do anything we don't want to. He asked, I answered.'

I paused in the middle of my rummage and glanced up, surprised. 'You wanted to come?'

'It wasn't top of my list of things to do.' Her eyes slid away. 'But I thought I might learn something.'

'And how's that working out for you?' Vincent enquired.

'So far,' Melissa answered, 'all I'm learning is what *not* to do.' She glanced at him. 'What about you? Are you here because she forces you?'

I assumed the troll was referring to me.

Vincent grinned. 'Nah. All this magic business is pretty cool. I thought that drugs provided the best buzz – but magic?' He whistled. 'It's something else. Plus,' he shrugged, 'I'm holding out for some decent wish granting of my own.'

She frowned at him. 'You want to grant wishes?'

He smirked. 'No. I want my own wishes granted.'

'So it's a selfish thing.' Melissa tossed her head. 'I might have guessed.'

'Darling,' Vincent drawled, 'we're all selfish. It's just that few of us admit it.'

They lapsed into silence as the rest of us searched. Eventually Angela rocked back on her heels. 'There's nothing here,' she said. 'Nothing useful.'

'Not even a secret safe hiding behind any of these pictures,' Rupert agreed mournfully.

I abandoned my search of the desk drawers and wrinkled my nose. So much for my grand infiltration plan. I sighed. 'We should get out while we still can.'

Delilah suddenly looked scared. 'Past that thing again?'

I considered. I didn't think my burgeoning ability to magically transport myself would transfer to this number of people. I might manage to take one person with me but there was no way I could take them all.

I tiptoed to the door, opened it an inch and peered out. The creature was still there, hovering in front of the door leading to the stairs. The lift was only a few metres away. Unless the monster moved, we'd never get out of here without being noticed.

My gaze drifted to the right. The sparkly Metafora room lay in that direction, completely unhindered by any crazed conjuration. The trouble was that the Metafora magic wouldn't work without an authenticated ID. Then I had a thought.

'Alicia,' I said, 'open that top drawer on the left again.'

She did as I asked. 'There's nothing in here. Just a few pens and the Director's ID.'

I looked at Billy. 'Can we use her ID to invoke the Metafora magic?'

He pursed his lips. 'For all of us? I guess it could work. Her pass is unrestricted so she can bring in visitors if she wants to.'

'And,' I persisted, holding my breath, 'can we use her ID to see where else she's visited recently?'

They all looked at me. 'If it takes us to Estrella, we'll have evidence that she's interfering with our test,' Angela said, her expression betraying her delight. 'That might be all we need.'

Alicia went very still. 'The Director visited Art Adwell. If we can use her Metafora history to prove *that* then we've won.' Delight lit her eyes. 'We've got her!'

Billy shook his head. 'It doesn't work like that. I can only use her pass to take us to her last destination. It won't hold any more information.'

Alicia visibly deflated. 'Shit.'

I shrugged. 'It's something though, right? Where it takes us will dictate what we do next. If it takes us somewhere innocuous, I can use my own transportation magic to bring me back here and return the pass so the Director doesn't notice that it's missing. If it takes us somewhere incriminating, we've got the evidence against her that we need.'

Vincent got to his feet. 'Sounds like a plan.'

'Come on then,' I whispered. 'Let's go.'

I opened the door again. The magical monster hadn't moved. I put my finger to my lips and hunkered down. If we stayed low and moved quickly, we should make it.

I led the way. Crawling army style, which was far harder than it looked, I scrambled across the office floor. What seemed like an age later, I reached the Metafora door. The monster hadn't so much as twitched.

I turned round. The others were all behind me. Mrs Jardine was struggling the most, but she'd kept going and we'd all made it.

I was reaching for the handle of the Metafora room when suddenly there was a strange huffing sound from the creature. I froze. I couldn't see it from this angle but I could hear its lumbering footsteps as it shuffled forward. Panicking, I pushed the door open and nudged Vincent inside. The others followed, just as the monster rounded the corner and stared.

I flattened myself on the floor, praying that it wouldn't notice me. One second passed, then another. I didn't dare look to see what was happening in case the flicker of movement caught the creature's attention. It huffed again and then, thankfully, pulled back.

Breathing hard, I slid into the Metafora room. It was a tight squeeze with all of us in there. Billy took the Director's ID and held it upwards, muttering something under his breath. I squeezed my eyes shut as a sweaty palm reached for mine and held it tightly. Then the familiar swirl of Metafora magic started to do its thing and we were all transported away. Praise be.

The first thing I felt was the cool night air on my skin. By its very nature, Metafora magic would never transport a faery godmother directly into a building; as a safeguarding approach, it deposited you outside where you needed to be. I opened my eyes, praying that my plan had worked and we were in a place that would put another nail in the Director's coffin. At this stage, I'd take whatever scrap of proof against her I could get.

'Wait,' Vincent said. 'Isn't this—?'

'Yeah,' I muttered, looking round the familiar street and feeling sick. 'It's my place. The last place the Director visited using Metafora magic was here.'

Melissa, whose hand had been gripping mine, released me and stared. 'Shit. She really has it in for you.'

My mouth was dry. I looked round, absorbing the ramifications of the fact that the Director had been sneaking around my own home in much the same way I'd sneaked around hers. A moment later, sudden fear took hold of me.

I darted across the road, flung open the front door and dashed down the corridor to my flat. With fumbling fingers, I unlocked it and leapt inside. 'Pumpkin!' I yelled. 'Pumpkin!'

In a heartbeat the dog was on me, leaping upwards and licking my face in ecstatic delight. I hugged his small body and looked round. Everything seemed untouched – but that didn't mean much. I held Pumpkin for another second before releasing him. I wasn't staying here for a moment longer than necessary.

'You can come and stay with me,' Alicia said from the hallway. 'I've got plenty of rooms.'

'Or me,' Vincent chirped. 'You know I can cook!'

'You can always share a bed with me,' Rupert smirked.

I shook my head. 'Thank you all, but I've got somewhere to go. I'll just grab some stuff and head off.'

Mrs Jardine touched my shoulder. 'He'll be thrilled to have you.'

I bit my lip and nodded. I hoped that my presence wouldn't put Jasper in danger again but there was nowhere else for me to go that made sense. Not now.

Billy handed me the Director's ID. 'You have to return this.' His expression was set into a mixture of fear and anger. 'She's still coming after you, Saffron. Be careful.'

I nodded. 'I will be. Don't worry about me.' All the same, a trickle of terror ran down my spine and sent a deep chill into my bones. The Director was still several steps ahead of us and she was still targeting me. And Jasper.

WHEN JASPER OPENED his door and saw me standing there with Pumpkin in my arms and my bag on my shoulders, he didn't look surprised. A slow smile spread across his face and I felt some of my worries from the last few hours slide off my shoulders.

'Hi,' he said softly.

I smiled shyly in return. 'Hi.'

He stepped back to let me in. 'I was just thinking about you. Then again,' he said, 'I'm always thinking about you.'

My eyes met his. 'Is it okay if I stay—?'

I didn't get the chance to finish my sentence before he said,

'Yes.' He swallowed. 'Would you like a glass of wine while you settle in?'

'I'd love one,' I said honestly. 'But I have to nip out again. I won't be long.' I looked at him anxiously. 'I hope that's alright.'

'Whatever you need, Saffron. I wouldn't dare argue with you.' Jasper reached for Pumpkin, who licked his cheek. 'Are you alright?'

I set my mouth into a thin line. 'I will be.' I dropped my bag. Then, because I knew I'd never want to leave if I didn't go now, I snapped my fingers. This time I used my own magic to transport me back to the office. I heard Pumpkin's brief whine and then the marble-floored lobby of the Office of Faery Godmothers coalesced in front of my eyes again.

Now that I was on my own and didn't have to worry about the others, I wasn't taking any chances. I flicked magic at my body, ensuring I was wholly invisible, and moved towards the stairs. I planned to drop the Director's ID back into its rightful place; with any luck, the presence of her magical monster meant that she'd have no clue we'd ever been here.

The monster had vanished by the time I reached the office floor, probably back to its spot in front of the Adventus room. I slipped quietly into the Director's office and slid her ID into her drawer, ensuring it was in the same position it had been in before. A moment later, I let myself out and locked her office door again.

I was raising my hands, preparing to click my fingers and return to the safety and warmth of Jasper's apartment, when there was a faint ding. I recoiled as the lift doors opened and the Director strode out.

I checked the clock on the wall. It was gone midnight. There was no good reason as to why she would be here at this hour unless... I tensed and stared at her through the gloom. She swivelled slowly, taking in the silent office and its dark, eerie shadows. From the corridor beyond, the magical monster heaved itself towards her. When it reached her, she stretched out her hand and touched its head briefly.

A satisfied smile lit up her face and, although I knew she was unaware of my presence, my blood turned to ice.

CHAPTER

TWENTY

'We have to forget about the Director and concentrate on Estrella,' I told everyone. 'She's too smart to leave any incriminating evidence so passing the Cinderella test has to be our focus. We're agreed that we want Wish Inc to genuinely succeed, right?'

They all nodded but every one of them looked doubtful. I pretended not to notice. 'It's settled then.' I smiled, wishing I also felt more confident. 'After all, our success will mean the Director's failure.'

It was Rupert who spoke first. 'The thing is, Saffron, it won't be easy to find the right man for Estrella. We can hack into dating websites. We can talk to people on the street and do our best to find someone appropriate, but without the Adventus room it's going to be really hard.'

'And,' Delilah added, 'even if we do find her a Prince Charming, how can we be sure that she'll fall for him? True love is about more than losing a glass slipper or two.'

'We'll have to do the best we can,' I said briskly. 'We're an amazing team and I have every faith in our abilities. Besides, I reckon we might already have the right candidate.'

'Already?' Mrs Jardine frowned. 'Who?'

Vincent straightened his shoulders.

'If you say him,' Alicia began, flicking a derisive look in his direction, 'then...'

I smiled. 'Not Vincent. I've got someone else in mind.' I pointed towards the glass windows. Standing there, humming diffidently to himself, was Ben.

Delilah gasped. 'He's a musician. Estrella is a musician.'

'He's good looking,' Melissa said grudgingly. 'And he seems nice.'

'I've met him,' Alicia said. 'He's quite nice – for a human.'

'Not as nice as me,' Vincent pouted. Nobody responded.

Rupert folded his arms. 'I don't know,' he said slowly. 'I mean, isn't he a little too good to be true?'

I winked at him. 'Let's find out, shall we?' I walked to the window and knocked on it, gesturing at Ben to come inside.

He flashed me a wide grin and did as he was told. 'Hey!' he waved. 'I'm Ben. It's so lovely to see you all again.'

I smiled at him. 'Why don't you take a seat and make yourself comfortable, Ben? You know that you're our first real client, so that makes you super special?'

His cheeks coloured slightly. 'I'm not sure I deserve that accolade.'

'You do. You definitely do.' I sat next to him. 'We've come up with a life-coaching plan that is tailored specifically for you. I reckon it will suit you down to the ground.'

He leaned forward. 'I'm all ears.'

I beamed. 'From what you've told me, you're looking for a job – and perhaps some romance, too.'

He nodded vigorously.

'I think we need to concentrate on the job first,' I told him. 'Once your employment is sorted, you'll feel more confident and better able to pursue success in your love life.'

Ben chewed on his bottom lip. 'That sounds reasonable.'

'Good.' I gave him my best professional I-mean-business-but-in-a-good-way look. 'How do you feel about pop music?'

Ben looked alarmed. 'Uh, classical is usually my thing.'

'But?' I prompted.

A cheeky expression crossed his face. 'I do have a secret passion for a good pop song.'

I knew it. 'Excellent. I love it when a plan comes together.' I shoved some sheets of music into his hands. 'Go away and practise these,' I told him. 'We'll deal with the rest for now.'

He gazed blankly at me. 'That's it?'

'For now,' I said cheerfully. I gave him a little nudge. 'Off you go. In a few days' time you'll need to be note perfect.'

'No coaching?' Ben asked. 'No tips on how to get my life together?'

I nodded at Angela and her brow creased momentarily in confusion. Then she seemed to realise what I was asking of her. 'Laundry today,' she said, drawing into her bottomless bank of motivational quotes. 'Or you'll be naked tomorrow.'

Ben scratched his head. 'Huh?'

'Wise words, Angela.' I smiled. I opened the door and all but shoved Ben out of it. 'Practise that music and do that laundry!' I closed the door after him and turned to my colleagues. 'Operation Cinderella is a go.'

'IT'S DONE,' Delilah said proudly. 'Using my fabulous powers of magical persuasion, I got Estrella to decide that she needs orchestral backing for her next album. And I got Ben onto the audition list. It doesn't mean he'll get the job, of course – he's still got to step up to the plate and prove he can actually play.' She smiled. 'I will accept your plaudits and congratulations now. Barring any disasters or interference from outside, the plan is underway.'

'There won't be any disasters,' I said. 'Or any interference.'

'How can you be so sure?'

I shrugged my shoulders vaguely.

'Will Estrella be at the audition?' Alicia asked.

'We can assume so,' Delilah said. 'She gets involved in all aspects of music production.'

I settled into my chair. 'Their eyes will meet across the stage,' I said dreamily. 'He'll be nervous and over-awed by her presence. He'll smile shyly at her, revealing his dimples, then he'll wow her with his command of the violin. She'll melt into his arms...'

Alicia pursed her lips. 'That won't work.'

'Why ever not?'

She shook her head. 'It's not the stuff of dreams or magical wishes. We need to create the sort of legendary first meeting that will be talked about for generations to come. If this is to be the love story of the century, he can't just be another starstruck fan who happens to play the violin.'

'He's more than a fan,' Delilah objected. 'If all goes well, he's going to be part of her band for at least some of her songs.'

'You know what I mean.' Alicia waved her manicured fingers. 'When they meet for the first time, we need drama. Flair.' She tossed her head. 'It's got to be the perfect atmosphere for romance to flourish. This has to be something that faery godmothers all around the world will remember.'

'It'd be good,' I added drily, 'if Estrella and Ben remember it too.'

'Yeah, yeah.' She looked at me. 'We're *professionals*, Saffron. We can do better than an audition, even if that's where they get to know each other properly. We need to set something up beforehand that involves fireworks and passion. This has to be epic.'

We fell silent, brows furrowed as we tried to think of something. Rupert was the first to speak up. 'On the way to the audition venue,' he said, 'she hits him with her car. She ends up giving him a ride and they realise they're both heading to the same place.'

'No.' Alicia tapped her fingers against the arm of her chair. 'There are too many variables to consider. For one thing, what if she seriously hurts him?'

'Then,' Rupert said, 'I take his place and get Estrella to fall in love with me instead. Everyone wins.'

'Apart from Ben,' Delilah pointed out.

Rupert shrugged.

'He's good looking and he works out,' Alicia mused. 'We put them both in the same hotel. He goes to take a shower, hears a knock on the door and goes to answer it. He gets locked out of his room while he's naked and she shows up and helps him.'

I considered it. 'Why would either of them be in a hotel when they have homes nearby to go to?'

'And,' Rupert said, 'why would she be staying on the same floor as a struggling musician? Wouldn't she be in the penthouse?'

Alicia grimaced. 'Bugger.'

I snapped my fingers. 'We arrange for them to be in the same shop at the same time. She's a famous popstar so she doesn't carry any money on her. She has a sudden craving for chocolate so Ben lends her the money to get some.'

Delilah exhaled loudly. 'It's kind of ... dull. Don't we need some drama?'

'It's got to be realistic as well,' Alicia said. 'What do we know about Estrella? What does she care about?'

I picked up the file in front of me and flicked through it. Melissa wandered up and listened in. 'She's vegetarian,' I said.

Rupert brightened. 'Ben saves her from eating a burger by mistake!'

I didn't look up at that one. 'She's also an advocate for a children's charity,' I continued.

'Oooh,' Delilah said. 'We get Ben to busk show tunes from *Annie*. She hears him when she passes him in the street and she can't help but join in.'

'I've got a better one,' Rupert suggested. 'We throw an orphan at them and they have no choice but to move in together and adopt her.'

I took in a deep breath. 'She also loves animals.'

'Kittens,' Melissa said. 'Throw some kittens at them and everyone wins.'

'We can't—' I stopped. 'Actually. We can,' I said. I grinned. 'Kittens it is.'

AT PRECISELY ELEVEN thirty-one in the morning, Ben got off the bus and walked towards the old theatre where the auditions for Estrella's orchestra were due to take place.

It was possible that this wouldn't work. Not only was timing key, if Ben chose to ignore our set-up then all our careful planning would be for nothing. I crossed my fingers. Please work, I whispered to myself. Please.

Rupert's voice appeared in my ear. 'I've cleared the traffic. Estrella's car is approaching. You've got about thirty seconds.'

I breathed out and started counting down in my head. Alicia nodded at me from the other side of the street. 'You've put the appropriate protections in place?' I muttered, using magic to project my voice to her. The last thing I wanted was a squashed kitten on my conscience.

'Yes, Saffron,' Alicia said. I could virtually hear her rolling her eyes.

'It's only a freaking cat,' Melissa said. 'There's plenty more where that came from.'

I didn't deign to answer. I glanced to my right. 'Ben's moving too slowly. Get him to pick up the pace.'

Melissa huffed but did as I asked, flicking her fingers and sending a powerful gust of wind in his direction. His feet moved faster.

I tightened my grip on Pumpkin's lead and directed my magic, ensuring that we were invisible to any prying eyes. He whined, jerking suddenly in surprise. 'Don't worry,' I told him. 'You'll be fine.'

I lifted my chin and raised my voice. 'Okay, everyone. In five, four, three, two...'

The traffic lights changed to red just as Estrella's car pulled up at the crossroads. A heartbeat later, Alicia released the kitten. We'd deliberately chosen it for its bold personality. It wouldn't be fazed by any of this, even if it did look scrawny and scared. Appearances could be very deceiving.

The kitten danced across the road, pattering its way along the tarmac. It was about halfway across – and almost directly in front of the wheels of Estrella's car – when Ben appeared at the corner.

'Has he seen it?'

'Can't tell,' Rupert whispered. 'He's not going after it.'

I gritted my teeth. 'Melissa...'

'On it.' Her voice was calm and didn't betray an ounce of tension. Regardless of any doubts I had about her, I had to admit that the troll followed every instruction to the letter. She was proving to be a particularly useful member of the team.

When she wandered up behind Ben and shoved him into the road with her elbow, I both winced and cheered inwardly.

Ben staggered forward. His face spasmed in shock and anger and his violin case went crashing to the ground. Under normal circumstances he'd probably have spun round and sought out his attacker but, fortunately for us, the kitten was now directly in his line of sight.

His eyes landed on it. For a second I had the sinking sensation that he was going to ignore it and leave the mewling fur-baby to its fate – and the wheels of Estrella's posh car.

Pumpkin barked once, his doggy instincts coming to the fore. If he couldn't get to the kitten then nothing else was allowed to either. Ben's head snapped up at the noise but we were shielded from his view by the invisibility. His brow creased with confusion while the kitten went into full defensive mode, raising its hackles and spinning round in search of this new threat.

I tensed, wondering whether to use more magic to nudge Ben in the kitten's direction. Then his expression cleared and he nodded. He picked himself up and reached for it.

Estrella's car door opened and she got out, followed quickly by Mitchell. 'Oh my goodness!' she clapped her hand to her mouth. 'The poor thing! We could have run over it.'

I twisted my fingers, sending a bolt of calming magic in the kitten's direction. It immediately stopped squirming and nuzzled Ben's hand. He held it up towards his face and it licked his chin delicately.

'How lovely!' he smiled. 'I think it's saying thank you.' He stroked its ears. 'Where have you come from then?' he cooed.

Estrella reached out to stroke the kitten while Mitchell turned and frowned at the line of cars forming behind them.

'Alicia,' I muttered, 'the lights.' Any moment now they'd

turn green again and chaos would ensue – especially once the other drivers recognised Estrella.

'Don't worry, Saffron. I've delayed them another thirty seconds. There's still time.'

Come on, Ben, I whispered to myself.

As I watched, his face creased with worry. 'I don't know where it came from,' he said. 'And I'm not sure what to do now.' He checked his watch. 'I've got an audition in twenty minutes and I don't want to be late. I can't walk in with a kitten in my arms. Lovely as this fuzzball is, I really need the job.'

Estrella's gaze dropped to the violin case. 'You … have an audition?'

'I'm a violinist,' he explained. 'Although the audition is for a pop singer rather than an orchestra.'

'Essie,' Mitchell growled. 'We need to get back in the car.'

She gave him a reassuring smile before turning her attention to Ben. 'Who's the pop singer?' she asked casually. 'Anyone I'll have heard of?'

'Estrella Davies,' he said. He dipped his head, touching his nose to the delighted kitten's.

A smile spread across Estrella's face. 'It's nice to meet you,' she said softly.

Ben glanced up. 'Pardon?'

'I'm Estrella Davies.'

His mouth fell open. 'You're kidding me.'

Her smile grew wider. 'Nope.' She gestured to the car. 'Come on. We'll give you a lift.' She winked. 'We're heading that way too.' She stroked the kitten again. 'And I want to get to know this little cutie.'

Behind her, Mitchell glowered darkly. I beamed.

'Stage one complete, Pumpkin,' I told him. Then, because I could, I did a little jig.

Rupert's voice sounded in my ear. 'I know he prefers classical music,' he said, 'but how in this world did Ben not recognise Estrella? Her face is everywhere.'

'It's refreshing,' Alicia answered.

'It's weird,' Rupert said.

I watched as Ben and Estrella clambered into the back seat of her car together, kitten safely cradled between them. I sighed happily. 'It's wonderful.'

TWENTY-ONE

'So,' Harry said, with a knowing glint in his eye when I met him in the Stagger Inn a few days later, 'you're staying with Jasper again, are you?'

'Mmhmm.'

'How's that working out for you?'

An image flashed into my head from that morning, when Jasper and I had been entwined together with sweaty limbs.

'Good.'

Harry raised an eyebrow. 'Just good? Because the expression on your face right now suggests far more than good.'

My cheeks reddened.

'I'd describe it more as orgasmic ecstasy,' Harry continued.

I coughed.

Harry leaned forward. 'You smell different too.' He sniffed the air. 'Like ... cinnamon.'

That was because I'd sneakily spritzed myself with Jasper's aftershave before leaving the flat.

'I knew things would work out for you both.' He smiled with deep satisfaction. 'I can just tell when a couple are meant to be together. It wafts off them. Like a...' he searched around for the right word '...a mutual fart.'

I made a face. 'Eugh! Harry!'

He raised his glass towards me. 'You know I'm right.'

That was quite enough of that. 'How's work?' I asked, changing the subject. 'Has your boss given you any more trouble?'

'Actually no,' he said, surprising me. 'I think he's decided that either I'm a genius or a madman for hitching myself to you. Until you prove otherwise, he's going to go with genius, and I've been given more responsibility as a result. Of course,' he added with an arch grin, 'if everything goes tits up with you, my star will fall at the same time. Until then, he's hedging his bets.'

I shook my head. Faery politics: it didn't matter which department it was, they were always nuts. 'It will be fine,' I said. 'Wish Inc will pass the Cinderella test with flying colours.'

'So how is lovely Ben?'

I smirked. 'Lovely.'

'And the Director?'

My smirk vanished. 'Dangerous.' I sighed. 'Very dangerous and very clever.'

Harry looked concerned. 'No more attempts on your life?'

'No. Jasper stopped all that – but she'll have something up her sleeve.' My fingers drummed on the table. 'She always does.'

'You've got this,' Harry said.

I wished I could be as confident as he was.

'Especially,' he continued, 'when you've got tall, dark and handsome by your side.'

All at once, I felt a familiar pair of arms wrap around me. I didn't need to turn around to know who was there. 'Hey, you.'

Jasper's lips brushed against my temple. 'Hey.'

I got to my feet and turned towards him. We grinned at each other for a long, daft moment then heat flared in his eyes and I yielded to the inevitable, pushing myself up onto my toes and going in for a kiss. My skin tingled with delicious anticipation. When Jasper's hands reached for my waist and pulled me in closer, I actually groaned.

His teeth nipped at my bottom lip and his thumb found the gap between my jeans and my top, caressing bare flesh while he deepened the kiss. I reached up for his chin, enjoying the feel of the five o'clock stubble underneath my fingertips. A warm glow suffused my body; colours were dancing in the air. The gods themselves were smiling down upon us. Nothing had ever felt so right. It was as if...

I blinked, pulled back, then glanced at Harry. 'An indoor rainbow?' I enquired.

He fanned himself. 'It seemed appropriate.' He flashed us a grin. 'And one of my better efforts, even if I say so myself.'

I took another look at the arc that framed Jasper and me perfectly. 'Not bad,' I said grudgingly.

'You two should get a room,' Harry told us.

Jasper smiled lazily. 'Don't worry. We will.'

This was why faery godmothers existed, I decided. Everyone deserved to feel this happy. Then I froze and checked my watch. Fuck a puck. 'Sorry,' I muttered. 'I've got to go.'

'Work?' Harry asked.

I bit my lip and nodded, giving Jasper an apologetic look. 'It's Ben and Estrella's first date,' I explained. 'Some of the others are taking the night off and it's only Delilah, Vincent and me who are making sure it goes alright. You know, hearts and flowers and passionate fireworks. That sort of thing.'

Jasper smiled. 'Don't worry. Harry and I will keep each other company.' He planted another brief kiss on my mouth. 'Be good.'

I grinned at him. 'I'll be a lot better than that.'

'WELL?' Delilah asked when I arrived.

I wrapped my arms round myself. 'He's perfect,' I told her. 'I can't believe that every person in the world isn't in love with him too. It's not merely that he's good looking – although obviously he is. Or that he knows how to dress. It's that he's thoughtful and caring and kind and that, when you get to know him and you see how vulnerable he really is, you know that he's the right man. He couldn't be *more* right.'

Delilah gave me a suspicious look. 'We're still talking about your neighbour Ben, right?'

I started. 'Uh...'

She laughed. 'Now your personal life is the stuff of dreams, Saffron, let's make sure your professional life matches up.' She nodded across the road. 'A lot hinges on this.'

I followed her gaze. Ben was standing in front of the small restaurant. He'd done well for himself; not only had he charmed Estrella on the drive to the studio, but he'd also performed well enough in his audition to get the job and ask her out afterwards.

He didn't look nervous at all, which bothered me slightly. I'd just have to hope that he turned on the charm for this first date. At least he'd dressed up in a sharp suit with a crisp, white, open-necked shirt. He'd nailed smart casual and he didn't look like he was trying too hard – something that I suspected Estrella experienced far too often.

Delilah turned her head, glancing down the street. 'She's almost here.'

We pulled into the nearest doorway, using the shadows to hide us rather than bothering with magic. A moment later, Estrella's sleek black car appeared. As soon as it drew up at the pavement, Mitchell got out and walked round to open the door for her. I let out a low whistle. Ben wasn't the only one who'd made an effort. Her sparkly dress was perfect.

Ben leapt forward, ignoring Mitchell and thrusting out a single long-stemmed rose. Cheesy but effective. Estrella's face transformed into a smile and she leaned in for an air kiss. To my horror, Ben misunderstood and turned his head, as if attempting a snog. Their foreheads collided and they both bounced back. Mitchell's hand snapped out, steadying Estrella so that she didn't fall over.

Ben grinned sheepishly. 'I'm so sorry!' he apologised. 'You look so lovely and I'm so clumsy!'

Estrella gave him a shy smile. 'I thought it was kind of cute.' She pointed to the restaurant. 'Shall we?'

He nodded eagerly and took her arm.

'That bodyguard fellow isn't going in with them, is he?' Delilah asked.

I watched as Mitchell took up position next to the car, his arms folded and his face studiously expressionless. I smiled. 'Nope. It's about time our star couple had some alone time.'

Delilah smiled at me. 'Indeed.'

This wasn't the sort of place where you went to be seen and the chances of any paparazzi dropping by to take unwelcome shots of Estrella and her new beau were unlikely. All the same, the table they'd booked was towards the back rather than by the window. It made it more difficult for us to see what was going on from outside but it was a move I fully endorsed.

I shifted position, trying to get a better look, and glimpsed Ben pulling out a chair for Estrella before taking his own seat. He reached across the table and took her hands in his. Things were looking up.

My phone buzzed in my pocket. At first I ignored it, but when it continued to vibrate I gave in and pulled it out, checking the screen and frowning.

'Vincent,' I said answering it. 'What's the problem?'

'You told me to check on Samuel Alwick,' he said.

I stilled while Delilah looked at me anxiously. 'Yes. Is everything alright?'

'He's on the move, Saffy. He left his house about twenty minutes ago.'

Wariness flooded through me. Samuel would get far more than he bargained for if he attempted to broach the Stagger Inn. Whether Alwick knew it or not, it was a faery pub so if he was after Jasper again, he wouldn't have any luck. In fact, he might well end up dead. It didn't stop me from worrying, though.

'Where is he now?' I barked.

'Brunswick Place,' Vincent said.

At first I was puzzled. 'That's nowhere near the Stagger Inn.' Then a chill descended across my shoulder blades and my fingers tightened round the phone. Unbelievable.

This time I wasn't going to let him walk away. 'That's just round the corner from here,' I whispered. 'He's not going after Jasper, he's coming for Ben and Estrella.' I hissed.

I'd expected a lot of shit from the Director, even after Jasper's intervention, but sending someone to mess up the lives of humans as well as faeries was several steps beyond unacceptable. Hell, it was so far into the realm of pure shittiness that I could barely believe it. Destroying the lives of innocents was not what faery godmothers were created for. I cursed. This was never going to end.

'Stay here,' I told Delilah, 'and make sure those two are safe. Call the others as well in case we need them.'

Her eyes widened fearfully. 'Saffron...'

'Just do it.' I squared my shoulders. I'd let Alwick off once before; I wouldn't make the same mistake again.

Spinning round, I stormed off towards Brunswick Place. I'd

head him off at the pass and prevent him from getting close, then I'd have his damned guts for garters.

I whizzed down the road, my furious thoughts colliding with one another. So much for no more sabotage, I thought sourly. The Director couldn't leave well alone, I huffed to myself, pumping my legs as fast as I could. The cool night wind whipped at my hair and I passed more than one person who stopped in their tracks to stare at me. I didn't care that I looked like a crazed dervish; I was on a mission.

I wheeled round the corner without slowing down – and smacked straight into a hard body.

'Ow!' A split second later, another wave of pain hit me. I rubbed my nose where it had collided with the other person and blinked away involuntary tears.

Vincent gazed at me. 'Are you okay, Saffy?'

I gritted my teeth. I'd hurt myself by smashing into him and then received a second crash of agony as I absorbed his pain as well. No wonder the practice of binding humans had fallen out of favour.

I did my best to shake off the hurt. 'Where is he?' I demanded. 'Where did he go?'

Vincent chewed on his bottom lip, giving his best hangdog impression. 'Uh...' He scratched his head.

'Vincent, so help me God. Where did Alwick go?'

He made a face and shrugged. 'I'm sorry. I was right on his tail and then he vanished.'

I clenched my fists. 'Vanished? As in someone used magic to spirit him out of sight?'

Vincent's head dropped further. 'Not exactly. I was trying not to get too close to him – after all, you said that he had the potential to be dangerous. I guess I stayed too far back. He was about fifty metres in front of me and then,' he waved a hand at the street beyond, 'he disappeared round a corner. It might have been magic. Or he might just have been really fast.'

I bit back my reply. It wasn't Vincent's fault; I had indeed told him to avoid getting too close to Alwick. I turned round. There were no prizes for guessing where the bastard was heading but, as he hadn't passed me, I had to assume that he was taking a less direct route to the restaurant. Perhaps he was swinging round toward the rear.

Tension tightened my bones. Then, from somewhere behind me near where I'd left Delilah, there was a guttural shout. Fuck a puck.

Without saying any more to Vincent I ran again, heading back the way I'd come. There was another shout and I saw a small crowd of people leaving the restaurant and spilling out onto the pavement. An alarm wailed and I saw a man wearing chef's whites and holding a fire extinguisher through the steamed-up windows.

'Saffron!' Delilah caught my arm. 'Apparently the kitchen is on fire. I heard someone say that a pan spontaneously set alight.'

I bared my teeth. Spontaneously, my arse. I swung my head from side to side, searching the small crowd for any sign of Alwick. Ben and Estrella were standing to one side, holding themselves apart from the others. She was shivering and he hastily shrugged off his suit jacket and draped it round her shoulders. Atta boy.

'I can't see him.' I raised myself up onto my tiptoes to get a better look. 'I can't see Alwick.'

The restaurant was filling with smoke and I could hear the sirens of an approaching fire engine. The chef burst out of the front door, coughing and spluttering. Estrella stepped back, her hand automatically reaching for Mitchell who was, as usual, directly behind her. The bodyguard apparently decided that the situation was far too dangerous and tugged her towards the car. Ben followed.

My eyes tracked them until they were safely inside and driving away then I squared my shoulders. The fire brigade would be here shortly. They were more than capable of dealing with the fire. I pursed my lips. They shouldn't have to deal with it, though. I headed for the restaurant door.

'Lady!' someone yelled. 'You can't go in there!'

I ignored them and kicked open the door, pulling my coat off my shoulders and holding it up to my face to ward off the worst of the smoke. As soon as the door slammed shut behind me I flicked my fingers, using magic to dissipate the worst of the black, oily smoke around me so I could breathe. Until I found the source of the fire, I wouldn't be able to do very much.

There was a loud bang from behind the restaurant's counter, as if something had exploded. I sucked in a breath and marched in that direction. I could already feel the heat – this wasn't just a chip-pan fire. I grimaced and concentrated, swirling as much magic as I could from deep inside myself. When I'd built up enough power, I used my shoulder to shove open the kitchen door.

As soon as the wall of heat hit my face, I slammed out my magic and forced it back. I took one step, then another. Fire was licking the walls of the kitchen. A calendar hanging from a nail was scorched through, and a pile of cardboard boxes on a shelving unit was already ablaze. There was a large oven, which seemed untouched, and a preparation area that was sooty and black but currently fire free.

I still couldn't see the source of the flames. I swivelled slowly round, eventually spotting a grill on my left-hand side. I couldn't tell for sure – the flames leaping off it were intense – but surely that had to be where the fire had started. Or where Samuel Alwick had started it.

Tightening my muscles, I shuffled round a large metal sink. I used magic to push back the fire a little more so that I could get closer to the grill. I had to get nearer to the source even though every instinct was telling me to cut and run.

Alongside the acrid stench of burnt oil, I could smell singed hair. I wouldn't emerge from this unscathed. For some reason, that only made me more determined to put a stop to it.

I side-stepped. There, now I had it. I squared my shoulders and focused on the grill. *I'm going to get you, sucker,* I promised silently. I drew in a deep breath, regretting it the instant I felt the smoky air hit my lungs, then I pushed out every last ounce of magic I had.

Frigid air whooshed forward. The worst of the fire was sucked back, the flames pushing away from me as if they were trying to escape. A moment later, as if someone had merely turned off a switch, they were extinguished and the kitchen was plunged into near darkness.

I gasped, my knees suddenly giving way as the energy left my body. I'd done it. Everything would be fine now. Then my gaze fell on a glow in the far corner; a few remaining flames were crackling towards a large gas canister. Oh no.

Something – or rather *someone* – bowled into me. 'Stupid fucking faery,' Melissa grunted, her arms hooking under my armpits. 'You got a death wish or something?' She dragged me backwards, away from the gas and the grill and out of the kitchen.

'It's going to explode,' I whispered. I started resisting her efforts to pull me away and lunged towards the kitchen again. 'It's going to blow up.'

Melissa tutted. 'No, it's not.' She elbowed me sharply in the ribs and I cried out and fell to the floor. Instead of picking me up, she strode forward and went back into the kitchen. I felt a surge of cool magic pulsating out before she reappeared, tossing her head as if nothing had happened. Once again she scooped me up and hauled my limp body towards the exit. This time I let her.

The firefighters were already jumping out of their fire engine and heading into the restaurant. Fortunately they wouldn't have any fire to worry about.

I breathed in the fresh air and glanced up at Melissa. 'Thank you,' I gulped.

She frowned at me. 'If you'd started to think about what you were doing before you did it, there wouldn't have been a problem. You're far too impulsive.'

Perhaps the troll had a point. I started to nod, then another thought occurred to me. 'Hang on,' I said, 'what are you doing here anyway? I thought you were spending the night getting reacquainted with your troll buddies.'

Melissa sniffed. 'For some reason, I couldn't rid myself of the feeling that you might need my help. I thought I'd drop by and check.' She looked at me pointedly. 'It's just as well that I did.'

'Samuel Alwick,' I said. 'This was him. Vincent saw him nearby. The Director must have sent him to mess up Ben and Estrella's first date. I didn't think she'd dare to try and sabotage us again, not after Jasper made everyone agree that the test would be negated if we had another bout of supposed bad luck.'

Melissa didn't look surprised. 'She gets away with a lot. It's a wonder that none of you have confronted her in person yet.'

I met her eyes. We'd been moments away from disaster tonight. If that fire had reached the gas canister, everyone inside the restaurant could have died in the explosion. Melissa was right. Whether we had the evidence or not, the Director had to be stopped.

I staggered to my feet. 'Look for Alwick,' I said. 'You, Delilah, and Vincent. If you find him...'

Melissa nodded. 'Got it.'

Vincent appeared at my side, looking worried. 'Saffy, are you alright?'

'Fine.' I heaved myself away. I hurt all over and I smelled like a bonfire but by the time I reached the Director's house I'd have recovered.

'Where are you going?'

I turned my head and gazed at him. 'To confront the drag-on,' I said finally.

CHAPTER

TWENTY-TWO

The Director's house was shrouded in darkness but I could see a glimmer of light peeking through the heavy curtains that draped the lower windows. She was still awake, and for that I was thankful. I wasn't in the business of confronting anyone in their pyjamas, regardless of who they were or what they'd done.

I pulled my shoulders back and took a deep breath. There was still an odd smoky taste in my mouth but my lungs felt clear and my energy had all but returned. I felt clear-headed and eminently capable. This might work.

I strode up the short driveway to the front door and rapped sharply on it. Something prickled along the back of my neck and, as I looked up, I spotted the camera in the doorframe above me. I was certain that hadn't been there when I'd sneaked in before. The Director had grown more wary in recent days – and with good reason.

I gave the camera a little wave and fixed a grin to my face. A few seconds later, the Director's disembodied voice floated out to me. 'What do you want, Saffron?'

'To talk,' I answered, feeling a bit strange that I was speaking in such a fake friendly manner to a door.

'If you're looking for a fight, you should know that I have numerous magical abilities at my disposal. You might think you're strong now that you don't need to use a wand but I can assure you that I am stronger.'

I wasn't so sure about that. After all, she used other people to do her dirty work. I wasn't even convinced the Director believed what she was saying. It didn't matter, though. I meant what I'd said: I only wanted to talk to her. Attacking her physically wouldn't improve my situation or hers – and I had morals, even if she didn't.

And I already had enough blood on my hands to last a lifetime.

'I told you,' I said loudly, 'I'm only here to talk.'

There was another beat of silence then a click. A moment later the door opened. Standing there, on her own doorstep, was the Director. For the first time since I'd known her, she didn't have on a scrap of make-up and she was dressed casually in jeans and a loose jumper. It humanised her; like this, she looked far more approachable and considerably less stern and stand-offish. She didn't look like the sort of faery who'd come close to sending an entire restaurant load of people into oblivion. But that didn't matter; her appearance wouldn't change what I wanted to say.

She gave me the once over, sweeping her eyes from my head to my toes. When she was satisfied that I wasn't carrying any obvious weapons, she inclined her head. 'I've just opened a bottle of wine. Would you like a glass?' She didn't wait for an answer but turned on her heel and walked inside, leaving her front door open.

I stared after her then shrugged and followed. I left the door ajar, however, just in case.

The Director opened one of the cupboards in her large, impressive kitchen and took out two glasses. She returned to the table and poured us both a generous measure of red wine.

'Chin-chin,' she said, raising her glass. I didn't move and she laughed. 'It's not poisoned. I don't keep cyanide hidden in my cupboards on the off-chance that my nemesis will stop by for a chat.' She sipped of her own wine as if to offer proof. I pursed my lips and did the same.

'Director,' I began.

'Actually,' she said, interrupting me, 'it's Elizabeth. I think it's about time we worked on a first-name basis, don't you?'

If she was trying to throw me off balance, she was succeeding. It was tempting to continue to paint her as a monster but here, in her own home, drinking wine and in casual clothes, she could have been any successful suburban woman. There was still a part of me that couldn't help admiring her, despite everything she'd done. Because of that, I wasn't sure I could ever call her Elizabeth.

'Look,' I said, 'the reason I came by...'

'Wait.' She held up her hands, stopping me again. Yep: she was definitely letting me know that she was in charge. She stepped back, opened a drawer and drew out a thin wand. I stiffened slightly but stayed where I was. While I wouldn't initiate an attack, I would defend myself if need be.

Fortunately there wasn't a hint of aggression in the Director's movements. She swished her wand once in the direction of my body and I felt a faint shiver of electricity as the magic passed through me.

She smiled. 'I had to be sure that you didn't have any recording devices on you.'

If I'd thought for a second that a ploy like that would work, I'd have tried a conversation like this long before now.

I kept my expression studiously blank and watched her

carefully. 'You're afraid of being recorded and the truth being revealed?' I asked.

Her lip curled. 'I'm not afraid of anything.'

I could believe that. She leaned forward and gazed into my eyes. 'How about you, Saffron? Are you afraid of much?'

'Lots,' I answered honestly. 'For one thing, I'm afraid that the people I love will be hurt.'

'Ah yes.' She seemed amused. 'I assume that includes the Devil's Advocate. There was a frisson between you from the start. I wonder how different things would have been if you hadn't felt anything for him.'

My eyes narrowed. I didn't think they would have been any different at all. 'I'm also afraid,' I said, as if she hadn't spoken, 'that I'll make more mistakes. And that those mistakes will lead to more disaster. Like,' I added pointedly, 'the death of someone entirely innocent.'

There was a trace of sadness in the Director's expression. 'What happened to Figgy was a tragedy. I will carry it with me to the grave.'

'Because she died as a result of your actions.' It wasn't a question.

The Director tilted her head. 'And yours.'

This time I didn't have a ready answer.

When it was clear I wouldn't say anything else on the matter of Figgy's death the Director said, 'You're here because you want to confront me with my wrongdoing. You want to tell me that I'm evil and that I don't deserve to be the head of the faery godmothers.'

I remained silent.

She raised her eyebrows. 'But that's because you have a simplistic view of the world, Saffron. You look on it as a child would. You think everything is black and white and there's nothing in between. You have no regard for what has gone before. And if you expect me to believe that what you've done so far has nothing to do with your own self-interest and ambition, you must think I'm even more stupid and naive than you are.'

This time I found my voice. 'You've been playing with fire.'

She laughed coldly. 'And?'

She was more heartless than I'd realised. 'You tried to have me killed.'

'You have no-one to blame for that other than yourself,' she sniffed. 'If you'd been a good girl and slunk away into the shadows where you came from, I wouldn't have had to worry about you. I'd have left you alone if you'd left me alone.'

'I tried!' My fingers twisted tightly round the delicate stem of the wine glass. 'You wouldn't let me!'

'You're referring to what happened with the dream faeries, I take it,' she scoffed. 'You forget I've been in this business for a long time. I understand how faeries like you work. You'd have kept your head down for a while and then the resentment would have started to build. You'd engage in gossip with your new co-workers, they'd ask about my office and you'd pour oily poison in their ears. I won't have my faery godmothers denigrated by *anyone*.'

'It's all about power with you, isn't it?' I said bitterly. Whether she'd always been as cold as this, or whether Figgy's death had pushed her over the edge into manic dictatorship, I didn't know. I'd hoped that there was a chance she could see what she'd done, that we could find a way out of this mess. I'd always believed in redemption – Ethan and his trolls had proved it was possible in almost any situation – but the mad glint in the Director's eyes told me that she was too far gone for that.

My shoulders dropped. 'You don't really care about the faery godmothers. You only care that you're in charge of them. You're a power-hungry maniac who won't take advice from anyone and who refuses to change with the times, to the point where you're prepared to commit murder to maintain the status quo.' I was shaking with anger. 'Where you'll meddle with humans and invite bloodshed.'

She stared at me. 'You have no idea. You dreamed of being a faery godmother for all those years and finally achieved it, you worked alongside us as part of the team – and you *still* don't get it. The Office of Faery Godmothers is the pinnacle of our entire existence. If it's diminished, then *all* faeries are diminished! If our work is criticised, if our motives are questioned, how long will it be before all of this falls apart? I will not allow us to become superfluous!'

'So you think violence is the fucking answer?'

'I have not committed any acts of violence.'

'No,' I spat, 'you've just incited others to do them.'

The Director rolled her eyes. 'Such melodrama is pointless. As long as the end result is what we want, who cares how we get there? The ends justify the means.' She paused. 'And our continued existence is more important than anything else. We've been clinging to our role in this world for decades. The only way we can maintain it is to continue as we have done in the past and stick to our traditions.'

'Traditions of bullying and hurting people? Traditions of jobs for old networks? Traditions of pretending you're better than everyone else just because you're faery godmothers?'

'We *are* better.' The Director's eyes sparked and I knew that she was barely keeping hold of her temper. Good. I wanted her to be angry because I was furious. 'Look at what happened to the trolls. They slid out of existence in a blink of an eye. Until they began their terror campaign against us, most faeries didn't even know they were real. If we change too much, that will happen to us too! Empires fall on far less, Saffron. It will not happen on my watch.'

'None of that excuses what you've done.'

She examined me coolly. 'If you take yourself out of the equation, then what have I done that's so bad? Tell me what makes me the epitome of evil.'

'You struck a deal with Art Adwell that could have destroyed the Office of Faery Godmothers far faster than anything else.'

She tutted. 'Please. I had that little man completely under my thumb.'

'If that were the case, Figgy wouldn't have died!'

'Her death was due to your interference.' She wagged her finger at me. 'And don't forget that Mr Adwell was only a threat because of *your* mistakes.'

I glared at her. 'I owned up to that.'

She laughed coldly. 'So that makes it alright?'

'I didn't say that.' I folded my arms. 'What about the Office? Why do you think so many faeries have jumped ship to come to Wish Inc? It's certainly got nothing to do with the happy atmosphere that you've created!'

'Happy atmosphere?' she sneered. 'We've had to deal with kidnappings. We've had to deal with troll incursions. We've had to deal with the death of one of our own. We've had the bloody Devil's Advocate sticking his nose into our business and trying to tell us how to run our affairs. That man is a cold-blooded murderer and he thinks he's better than we are? Huh. As if.'

'He *is* better,' I answered quietly. 'He's better than all of us.' I sniffed. 'Step down. Step down from your job, allow someone else to be appointed in your place and I'll forget what's happened. I won't pursue my allegations against you, regardless of how serious they are. I won't reveal what kind of faery you really are.'

'If you were going to do that,' she returned, 'you would have done it already. You've no proof against me and I won't step down until I decide it's time to do so.'

'Wish Inc will...'

'Whatever happens with this ridiculous Cinderella test, your pathetic little agency will fold within the year. There's more to running an effective faery business than good intentions. You have no idea what it's like to be in charge of world-changing wishes and faeries of all backgrounds and beliefs.'

'You're wrong.' I picked up my wine glass and drained its contents. 'I came here thinking we could come up with a solution. That you could see your future is untenable and admit the things you've done are wrong. I know I've made mistakes but I've learnt from them and I've changed. You don't care about anyone other than yourself.'

'I care more than the likes of you will ever appreciate.'

I gazed at her sadly. 'No, you don't.' My mouth twisted. 'I'll see you on New Year's Eve. May the best faery win.'

She smirked. 'It's already a done deal.'

I walked out of the Director's house. The chill descending through my bones had nothing to do with the cool night air. She genuinely believed that she was in the right and that she was fighting on the side of good. She couldn't see beyond her own fallacies. Maybe I should have pushed aside my better instincts and attacked her then and there. Maybe I wasn't being sensible by refusing to become a vigilante and dispensing my own justice. Maybe I was a coward. I stomped down the driveway, wondering if there was anything I could have done or said that would have achieved a different outcome.

When I hit the dark street, I glanced to my right. A faint

smile crossed my face and I raised my head. 'You don't have to hide,' I said aloud.

Jasper stepped out from the shadows. 'I wasn't sure if you'd be happy that I was here. I'm not checking up on you, I only wanted to make sure you're alright. You've been gone a long time. Delilah told me that you'd had trouble tonight and you might be here.'

'I'm alright,' I answered honestly. 'And you can do whatever you want, Jasper. You can check up on me if you need to. Sometimes I need you to do just that. I'm not perfect and neither are my methods. I'm trying to be the best that I can be, but I've come to realise that this isn't all about me. I can't think like that. I'm not the most important person in the world.'

'You are to me,' he said quietly.

My heart flipped. I walked over to him and leaned into his body, feeling his arms wrap round me. 'You know what I mean,' I mumbled into his chest. 'No one person is more important than another. No one faery is better than another. The wishes of one human aren't any less valid than the wishes of their next-door neighbour. Everyone deserves a chance and everyone deserves a voice.'

'Keep talking like that,' he said, 'and one day you'll change the world.'

I pulled back and gazed into his eyes. 'I don't want to change the world,' I told him. 'I want to give others the tools to do it for themselves.'

He smiled gently down at me. 'You're amazing, Saffron Sawyer.' He glanced at the house. 'What happened with the Director?'

I sighed. 'I tried to talk to her, to get her to see who she really was and what she'd done.' I dropped my eyes. 'I failed.'

'It's not over yet. It's almost New Year's Eve. Speak to the other faery heads. Lay out everything on the table and tell everyone what you know.'

'I don't have any proof. It's my word against hers.'

'You're not alone,' he reminded me gently. 'Stop thinking that you are. There are plenty of others on your side.' He placed his fingers under my chin and gently tilted my head up again. 'Tell the truth – the whole truth – and everything will work out. I can remove the Director from her post, if it comes to it.'

'Not without evidence. Not if your own job is to remain free from accusations and suspicion.'

He gave me a crooked grin. 'That's for me to worry about.' He slipped his hand into mine. 'Come on. Let's go home.'

TWENTY-THREE

Alicia looked me up and down. 'That's the same dress you wore to my party,' she said.

I raised my eyebrows at her. 'And?'

She opened her mouth to say something then seemed to think better of it. 'It suits you,' she said finally.

'Thank you.' I dipped into a mock curtsey. 'You scrub up well yourself.'

She let out a mild snort. 'That goes without saying.'

Delilah walked over. 'Estrella is already here,' she breathed. 'So is Ben.' She gripped her clutch bag even tighter. 'Everything is ready. Their first date might have been a bust, but I think tonight will be perfect. It's New Year's Eve. It will be a new beginning for all of us.'

I wished I had her optimism. My stomach lurched with a sudden spasm of nervous energy. 'No matter what happens,' I said quietly, 'we've done the best that we can. Regardless of what the Director pulls out of her hat, we're good faery godmothers.'

Alicia rolled her eyes. 'We're not good. We're the best.'

We exchanged glances. I nodded decisively. I was confident,

strong and more than capable of pulling this off. 'Then,' I said, 'let's do this.'

As soon as I entered the ballroom, I instinctively sought out Jasper. I needn't have worried; my gaze was drawn to him almost immediately. He already had a glass of champagne in his hand and he raised it in my direction before taking a sip.

Vincent appeared by my side and passed me a glass of my own. I took it, belatedly realising that my hands were shaking too much to hold it. I gave it back to him and he shrugged, then drank it himself.

Jasper sent me a quick smile of reassurance and then his eyes flicked to the side. I followed his gaze and quickly spotted Estrella and Ben. A few feet behind them stood Mitchell, his face expressionless. My eyes drifted down and I spotted his hand jiggling restlessly against his thigh.

Melissa came over. 'Before all this goes down,' she said stiffly, 'I want you to know that I think you're alright. For a faery godmother fuck-up, that is.'

I started, surprised. 'Uh, thanks.'

'You have everyone's best interest at heart, even if you don't always go about things the right way.' She raised her eyebrows. 'You should listen to Jasper. He's a good influence on you.'

'I...'

Melissa strode off before I could get half way through my sentence. I scratched my head. Well, that was weird. Then Jasper moved back into my line of sight and strode towards me. Damn, he looked good. I swallowed hard.

'You look fabulous, Saffron,' he murmured. He passed me Pumpkin's lead. I glanced down at my wee dog, smiling at the bowtie that was fastened to his collar.

'So do you,' I said.

'Are you saying that to me or to Pumpkin?'

'Both, of course.' I fiddled with my bracelet and gave Jasper an anxious look. 'What if this doesn't work?'

He leaned in. 'It'll work.'

'You don't know that.'

Jasper grinned. 'I do. You're the best faery godmother in the world, Saffron. If you can't pull this off, no-one can.'

I met his eyes. 'I'm not the best,' I whispered. 'But thanks for saying it.'

Alicia reappeared, blithely unaware of the sweet moment Jasper and I were sharing. 'The room is all set up,' she declared. 'It's one of the security areas. There's a two-way mirror so we can watch the action in the ballroom. The other faery heads are already there. Even Ethan has come along, although I'm not sure who invited him. We're just waiting for you two before we get started.'

A tremor ran through my body. I glanced again at Ben and Estrella. Something about the way they were looking at each other seemed ... off. There was less affection in their eyes and more tension. Estrella shifted slightly, moving back until she was almost treading on Mitchell's toes.

'It's going to go down to the wire,' Alicia said, watching me. 'But then we knew that.'

I nodded. 'Deep breath.'

Her mouth crooked up. 'We are faery godmothers.'

Yeah. 'We are indeed.'

~

'IN THE INTERESTS OF FULL DISCLOSURE,' Jasper intoned, 'and before we formally convene this meeting, I should tell you all that Saffron and I are living together.'

Every single faery head snapped in his direction. So did mine.

He smiled at me. 'I'm in love with her.' His green eyes swept the table. 'And if anyone has a problem with that, now is the time to speak up. I'm perfectly capable of separating my romantic life from my professional one and remaining fair and unbiased, but if you want someone to take my place tonight then I am prepared to step back.' His jaw clenched slightly and his expression hardened. 'But know this,' he continued in a colder tone, 'either I am fit to be Devil's Advocate or I am not. If you don't believe that I can be impartial in this matter, you should strip me of my position. My relationship with Saffron Sawyer is far more important than my job will ever be.'

Ethan grinned. 'Is this your way of saying that I should buy a hat?'

I coughed. 'I think that's a little premature.'

Jasper looked at me. 'Is it?'

I felt my cheeks heat up. Next to me, Pumpkin wagged his tail, thumping it against my leg with enthusiastic vigour.

'If you make that dog matron-of-honour instead of me,' Alicia said in a low voice, 'I will hound you for the rest of my days.'

Delilah frowned. 'Oy! If anyone is going to be matron-of-honour, it should be me.'

Harry spoke up from the corner of the room. 'I've been Saffron's friend for far longer than either of you.'

This was making me feel distinctly uncomfortable.

At the head of the table the Director got to her feet. 'Let's get to the point, shall we? Saffron Sawyer's life isn't what's important here. We're focused on that young lady out there. The test is objective: either Estrella Davies has fallen in love or she hasn't. The Devil's Advocate is almost superfluous. In any case, I think it's wonderful that you have found each other. Who are we to stand in the way of true love?'

Under the table, my hands slowly curled into fists. At this

rate, she'd be angling for a wedding invitation. She walked towards me, her arms outstretched. 'Let me be the first to congratulate you properly, Saffron.'

I stood up, allowing her to embrace me briefly. She leaned into my ear. 'Enjoy this while you can. From now on, sweet Saffron, it's all going to be downhill. And when you go down, you can be sure that your precious Devil's Advocate will go down with you.'

I pasted on a smile. 'You say the nicest things,' I murmured.

She patted me on the shoulder and returned to her chair.

'Well,' Jacob said, looking genuinely delighted, 'I for one have no issue with the relationship. I am confident that the Devil's Advocate can remain unbiased. He has proved himself time and time again in the past.'

There was a chorus of nods and I exhaled.

The dread that was pinching my bones tightened its grip.

I glanced at the two-way mirror. I could only just see Estrella and Ben in the corner of the ballroom. His arm was casually draped round her back and they looked close.

'That's settled then,' Jasper said. He pulled back his cuff and checked his watch. 'There are only a few minutes to go until midnight. At that point, when the new year dawns, we will know whether Wish Inc has passed the test or not and whether they will be allowed to continue operations.' He turned his head, indicating the ballroom. 'I'm sure none of you need me to point out Estrella Davies.'

Everyone watched her and Ben as the music changed and they sashayed across the dance floor. I sneaked a look at the Director. A tiny smile was playing around the corners of her mouth. She actually appeared to be enjoying this.

'Who's that?' Winkie enquired. 'The blond-haired fellow? Is he the candidate?'

'His name is Ben,' Alicia said, glancing at me.

The head of the animal faeries bobbed her head. 'They make a handsome couple,' she said approvingly.

'Why don't you describe the process you went through to select him?' Winkie suggested.

I didn't answer immediately. Something about Estrella's body language had altered; she was holding herself more stiffly and it looked as if her eyes were glittering with tears rather than with joy.

The Director gasped ostentatiously. 'Oh dear,' she said, putting her hand to her mouth. 'Is it all going wrong?'

Mitchell, who hadn't taken his eyes off the couple, pushed his way through the crowd heading directly for them. It was too late, however. As we watched, Estrella drew back her hand, slapped Ben hard across the face and stormed off in the opposite direction.

The Director hissed.

'Well,' Winkie murmured, 'I guess that's that. So much for true love.'

'Mmm.' The Director did a good job of looking sad. 'We all agreed the terms of the test. Unfortunately, there is no doubt that Wish Inc have failed.'

The gathered faeries swivelled towards me. Some, like Jacob, had nothing but sympathy on their faces; others seemed positively gleeful that we'd messed up so spectacularly and that the faery status quo had been maintained.

Ethan, who'd remained separate from the rest of the table, hadn't taken his eyes away from Estrella. 'I do believe,' he said, 'that the test isn't over until midnight. It's not the new year yet.'

The Director tittered. 'That's kind of you to allow them a few extra minutes but I hardly think there will be another candidate for Estrella's heart at this late stage.' She rose to her feet. 'We are done here. And, as we are all assembled, I think it's time that we examined Saffron Sawyer's recent actions more closely. She might have had the best of intentions but she's clearly not cut out to be a faery godmother. Truthfully, I'm not convinced she's cut out to be a faery at all. She's broken the heart of that poor girl out there and dragged several of my own previously successful faeries into her schemes. I vote that we…'

'Wait.'

Her head snapped towards mine. 'What?'

'As Ethan, the leader of the trolls, said, it's not midnight yet.' I remained calm. 'We should wait.'

'You're drawing this out needlessly! I'm sure we all have better things to do than hang around here. Saffron Sawyer is not fit for purpose.'

Jasper also stood up, walked round to the back of my chair and placed his hands on my shoulders. 'The test is not over yet. There are still four minutes left.'

'This is preposterous!'

'Elizabeth.' It was Winkie. 'Look.' She pointed to the dance floor. 'Look at them.'

Mitchell was holding Estrella. His head was dipped towards hers and he was dabbing gently at her cheeks with a handkerchief. Estrella's lips moved as she said something to him. He responded by drawing her closer. He cupped her face with one hand and smoothed away a loose curl from her face with the other.

'We could really do with some sound,' Jacob muttered.

I smiled and flicked my fingers. 'Your wish is granted.'

The sound of Estrella's teary sniff filled the room. 'I suspected he was an arsehole but I didn't think he was that bad. He seemed too good to be true. How many times can one man use the word "lovely" in one sentence?' She shook her head. 'And he was so *keen*. I wanted to give him a chance even though I knew deep down that he wasn't the one for me. I just … I just don't want to be alone.'

Mitchell's response was gruff. 'Essie, you'll never be alone. I won't let it happen.'

'You have to say that because I'm paying you.'

'I'm not saying it because you're paying me.' He sighed. 'This isn't the right time to do this. But you know what? There will be never be a right time. I'd walk through fire for you, Estrella Davies. Why do you think I work so many hours? I don't need the money. But I do need to be near you.'

Estrella's mouth dropped open. Even from this distance, the hope that flared in her face was clear to anyone with half a brain.

'I don't want to take advantage of your broken heart,' Mitchell continued, 'and I'm not saying this because you might be on the rebound. I...'

'Shhh.' She put her finger to his lips. 'My heart isn't broken. And I'm not on the rebound.' She gave him a long look. 'I thought this was only a job to you. I didn't dare say anything because I didn't want to take advantage of the situation between us when I'm the one who pays your wages.'

Mitchell swallowed. 'You like me?'

She coiled her arms round his neck. 'There's a lot more to it than like,' she whispered. Then her lips met his.

'Ten seconds to go!' the DJ roared. 'Nine! Eight! Seven!'

'Cut the sound,' the Director bit out.

I shrugged and did as she said. After all, we'd already heard everything we needed to hear. While Estrella and Mitchell kissed, the room erupted around them.

I reached for Jasper's hand. 'Happy New Year,' I murmured.

He bent down, his mouth brushing against my cheek. 'Happy New Year.'

'I don't understand,' Jacob said. 'What actually just happened?'

I glanced at the Director. A trickle of blood was dribbling

down from her nose. It wasn't surprising. Estrella had walloped Ben with quite a backhand. I wondered what he'd said to her to achieve that effect. No doubt he'd been coached well.

'It's quite simple really,' I said aloud. 'Estrella Davies is in love with Mitchell Jones, her bodyguard. She always has been. She never needed our help. She'd have got there in the end, magical intervention or not.'

'And the blond-haired fellow? Who the hell was he?' Winkie asked.

I grinned at the Director. She was looking terribly pale. 'As Estrella said,' I explained, 'he was too good to be true. Although I should point out that it was my colleague Rupert who said it first.'

Harry's boss frowned. 'I still don't get it.'

'It took me a while to work it out. Ben moved into the flat next door to me very recently,' I said. 'In fact, round about the time when things couldn't have been worse for me. The first time I met him, it was in the middle of the day and I was very drunk. He didn't once remark upon it or think that it was strange. Then he showed up at the exact moment I was attacked and saved the day.'

'You were attacked?' Jacob blinked.

I dismissed his concern with an airy hand. 'It's of no importance now. Essentially, everything Ben did was too good and too convenient. He was a plant, moving in next door to me in a bid to gain my confidence and then sabotaging me in the best way possible. When this test started, it was the perfect opportunity for him. He didn't walk away from Estrella until just now because there wasn't supposed to be time for us to find her an alternative man.'

'But he's human,' the head of the luck faeries said. 'Why would a human get involved? How would a human even *know* to get involved?'

The Director broke in. 'This has been a very long evening. I think we should all depart and regroup at a later stage.' She moved decisively for the door. Unfortunately for her, nobody followed.

I picked up my phone from the table and found the number I needed. A few moments later Vincent strolled in, tossing his hair and grinning as if he were some sort of celebrity. 'Hi guys!' he sang.

Nobody moved.

'Saffron,' Winkie asked, 'who is this … human?'

'My good buddy, Vincent.' I nodded at Ethan. 'As a result of my lack of caution and my misunderstanding about memory magic, Vincent knows that I am a faery godmother. Ethan was worried about this and, as a result, I bound Vincent to me to ensure he wouldn't tell anyone about the existence of faeries and trolls.'

Several mouths dropped open in shock.

'Not,' Vincent said loudly, 'that I would ever blab anyway. I'm a trustworthy person.'

Jacob stared at him. 'You look familiar.'

Uh-oh. It was quite possible that, given Vincent's previous career as a drug dealer, Jacob had crossed paths with him. Probably the least said about that the better.

'Anyhoo,' I said brightly, 'while binding humans isn't something that usually happens in these more enlightened times, it certainly is possible. Vincent is proof of that. For those of you who don't know how the binding works, he is compelled to do whatever I tell him to. In return, if he is hurt in any way I'm the one who suffers the injury. I believe that Ben was bound to a faery in a similar fashion. A faery who wanted to use him to sabotage me.'

I linked my hands and did my best to look relaxed. 'To prove who did this, all we have to do is hit Ben a couple of times. If the faery in question is in this room, their identity will be revealed.'

Right on cue Melissa appeared, holding Ben tightly by the wrist. 'Where are we going?' he asked. 'What's going...' His voice faltered when he saw who was in the room. His eyes landed first on me and then on the Director. Suddenly, he was as pale as she was. Yeah, he knew exactly who she was.

'I think,' the Director said icily, 'the fact that Saffron Sawyer is suggesting we torture a poor defenceless human for no reason other than her own crazed conjecture is reason enough to question her sanity and her motives.'

'Saffron won't do anything,' Vincent said cheerfully. 'But I will.' He raised his hand and punched Ben in the nose.

Unable to help herself, the Director cried out sharply. Ben's eyes narrowed and he swung a punch at Vincent, smacking him in the eye. This time it was my turn to yelp. But despite the flash of pain, I was still smiling. I'd proved my point. Finally.

'What the fuck did you do?' Ben snarled at me, his handsome face contorting into a vicious, ugly snarl. 'You've ruined everything! I was supposed to get rich off the back of this!'

Several of the stunned faeries recoiled, their expressions horrified. One by one, their heads swung towards the Director.

'Elizabeth,' Winkie whispered, clearly appalled, 'why would you do something like this?'

The Director's jaw hardened. She straightened her shoulders, raised her chin and glared around the room then she slowly opened her arms wide and shook her head. 'You fools,' she said. 'You fucking fools. You think I'm the bad one here? You think I've done wrong by trying to achieve the best outcome for all of us?'

She looked at Ethan. 'I was abducted by your kind,' she spat. 'Held hostage, along with several of my faery godmothers who were maimed in the process. And now I'm supposed to act like we can be friends?'

She gestured angrily towards Jasper. 'I've been Director of the Office of Faery Godmothers for almost three decades. We've had to deal with the advent of the internet. Improved medicine. A better standard of living.' She sucked in an affronted breath. 'A *rise* in human happiness and therefore a fall in wishes! And then you swan in and think you have better ideas than I do about how to run my department?'

'Improving your business practices is hardly akin to devil worship,' Jasper said mildly.

'Fuck off,' the Director snarled.

I frowned. 'Don't talk to him like that!'

She rounded on me. 'Why? Does my language offend your delicate ears? I rue the day I ever met you, Saffron Sawyer. You were supposed to do your job, act as bait for the trolls and then realise your place and slink away. Instead you seemed to think that you were better than everyone else. That you knew better. The number of times you've fucked up...' Her lip curled. 'You're no hero.'

'I've never pretended to be,' I said quietly. 'And I know I've made a lot of mistakes. I own every single one of them. We all make mistakes, Director, but we can learn from them. Our job as faery godmothers is to improve the lives of humans but by doing so we can also learn to improve our own lives.'

'Spare me the homilies,' she snarled. 'My only mistake was you.'

'You tried to blackmail me into helping you bring down Jasper.'

She could have denied it; she'd have realised that if she hadn't been so thrown by her failure with Ben. Instead, she went hell for leather. 'So? He doesn't deserve to be Devil's Advocate! Not with the blood that stains his hands.'

I did my best to stay calm. She'd said it; she'd admitted what she'd done. I could hardly believe it. 'What about the blood that stains yours?'

'If Figgy Barfellow had been stronger and smarter, she'd never have ended up dead! That wasn't my fault!'

'And Samuel Alwick?' I asked. 'What about him? You hired him to follow Jasper and try to kill him. I'd say that's pretty close to murder. And that's before we get on to what happened at the restaurant.'

'What?' Her lip curled. 'I've got no idea what you're talking about. Who's Samuel Alwick?' I opened my mouth to spell it out for her – and everyone else – but she wasn't finished. 'You don't understand the pressure that I'm under on a daily basis. None of you understand!' She reached into her pocket and pulled out her wand. 'I'm done with this. Get her, Ben. You know what to do.'

I raised my hands, prepared to use whatever magic I could to protect everyone in the room. I needn't have bothered. All the faeries were on their feet, clutching their wands. As one, they flicked magic towards the Director.

It was over in seconds. The different threads coalesced together, binding into a multi-coloured plume that wrapped round the Director's body and held her in place. She shrieked, throwing her head back in fury. Then she dropped her wand with a clatter to the floor.

I looked at the department heads. When it counted, they'd banded together and stood against the Director. I'd begun to think I'd never reach this point – and yet I was gazing at the evidence of our teamwork and our ability to strive for nothing but good.

I turned. Vincent had wrapped himself around a struggling Ben and was holding him in place. 'A little help would be good,' he gasped.

Melissa moved to the pair of them, reached out and touched Ben's forehead with the tip of her finger. He immediately went slack, his eyes rolling back into his head.

Vincent released his limp body. 'Thanks,' he said. Then he looked round. 'Is it over now?' he asked. 'Did we win?'

Ethan stood up. 'I've said it before,' he said calmly, 'and I'll say it again. Faery godmothers are dangerous creatures.' He glanced at me. 'You've accomplished what we hoped. Don't let the power go to your head.' He nodded at us and strolled out of the room, Melissa following in his wake.

I watched them go, a sudden suspicion twitching at me. 'The trolls always wanted to see the end of faery godmothers,' I said to Jasper. 'You don't think that this was their endgame, do you? Making us fight ourselves until what's left is barely even recognisable?'

My brow furrowed and I felt a faint twist of nausea. Samuel Alwick. He couldn't have been working for the Director. If he had been, then he wouldn't have tried to interrupt Ben and Estrella's date at the restaurant. The Director already had Ben in her pocket so she didn't need Alwick – in fact, all he'd done was muddy the waters and almost destroy the test. Why hadn't I seen that before?

'Have they manipulated us all along?' I whispered aloud.

Jasper's hand slipped into mine. 'Hmm,' he said.

I turned my head and met his eyes. 'Hmm.'

EPILOGUE

I stood in the doorway of Samuel Alwick's former home and gazed round at its bare walls and empty floors.

'The Director's still denying all knowledge of him,' Jasper murmured. 'Even though she's admitted everything else.'

I nodded distractedly. 'It was the thought that he was after you that bothered me. He focused my fury and made me take risks I might not have otherwise.'

'He played his role,' Jasper replied grimly. 'We could try and find him. A bit of magic flung in the right direction...'

'No.' I turned towards Jasper. 'Whoever Samuel Alwick was, he's gone now. I don't think we'll be hearing from him again.'

He examined my face before nodding in agreement. 'The trolls have disappeared too. Ethan's house has been emptied, just like this one. There's no clue where they've gone.'

I felt a burst of sadness at the thought that we might never see them again. I'd miss Melissa's gruffness and Ethan's ability to show up unannounced. I supposed we'd never know for sure whether they'd planned for all this to happen, abandoning outright terrorism in favour of a far sneakier – and far smarter - approach.

Whatever. The Office of Faery Godmothers would be unrecognisable from here on in. What we'd started with Wish Inc would continue; rather than one main office, there would be lots of small ones, dotted all around the country. The focus would be on teams of faeries instead of one vast, dictatorial set-up.

'It wasn't a den of evil despair, you know,' I said. 'The Office of Faery Godmothers, I mean. It had plenty of good points and everyone tried really hard to make it work. And the Director meant well, in her own way.' I knew I could afford to be generous now that she'd been deposed but I wasn't lying. Sometimes we get so involved in our sense of what we think is right that we lose sight of what we should be doing.

'There was a great deal of unnecessary meddling,' Jasper said. 'But you're right. All the faery godmothers and godfathers did a lot of good and will continue to do so. And there's still hope for Elizabeth. The post of Director as we know it will never exist again – and she'll never be a faery godmother again. But there's always a chance of redemption. I think we've learned that much along the way.'

'Ben...'

'He's being taken care of. He was manipulated by the Director as much as anyone else was. He'll be fine. Besides, he's got a kitten to worry about now.' He gave me an arch look. 'You took a gamble with Estrella and her bodyguard, though.'

I smiled. 'Not really. From the very beginning, it was obvious that they looked at each other the way that I look at you. Once I stopped being so bull-headed, I realised that.'

'How do you look at me, then? Is it like a crazed woman who can't decide whether to drag me into her bed, run away from me, or wrap me up in cotton wool?' Jasper teased.

I leaned into him. 'Something like that.'

His lips brushed mine. 'What about you, Saffron? What will you do now?'

'Well,' I said thoughtfully, 'I've been thinking about setting up a competition. You know, something that will prove definitively who is the best faery godmother in the world.'

Jasper blinked and I laughed.

'I'm kidding,' I said. Maybe. 'You'll still be based in Colchester. That means I'd like to stay here too. Alicia is determined to keep Wish Inc open so I guess I'll stay with her and see what happens. Assuming that faery godmothers don't end up becoming completely obsolete, that is.'

'People will always wish for something,' he told me. 'It's human nature.'

Pumpkin pattered through from Alwick's kitchen, licking his lips. I gave him a suspicious glare, wondering what titbit he'd managed to find. 'It's faery nature, too,' I said, reaching down and scratching my little dog between his ears. 'Thank goodness. We should always strive to be more than we are. We should never stop wishing.'

Jasper smiled at me. 'What do you wish for now?'

'You and me.'

Pumpkin whined.

'And him.' I grinned and he licked my hand.

'Then,' Jasper told me, 'your wish is granted.'

About the Author

After teaching English literature in the UK, Japan and Malaysia, Helen Harper left behind the world of education following the worldwide success of her Blood Destiny series of books. She is a professional member of the Alliance of Independent Authors and writes full time, thanking her lucky stars every day that's she lucky enough to do so!

Helen has always been a book lover, devouring science fiction and fantasy tales when she was a child growing up in Scotland.

She currently lives in Edinburgh with far too many cats – not to mention the dragons, fairies, demons, wizards and vampires that seem to keep appearing from nowhere.

OTHER TITLES

The complete *FireBrand* series

A werewolf killer. A paranormal murder. How many times can Emma Bellamy cheat death?

I'm one placement away from becoming a fully fledged London detective. It's bad enough that my last assignment before I qualify is with Supernatural Squad. But that's nothing compared to what happens next.

Brutally murdered by an unknown assailant, I wake up twelve hours later in the morgue – and I'm very much alive. I don't know how or why it happened. I don't know who killed me. All I know is that they might try again.

Werewolves are disappearing right, left and centre.

A mysterious vampire seems intent on following me everywhere I go.

And I have to solve my own vicious killing. Preferably before death comes for me again.

Book One – Brimstone Bound

Book Two – Infernal Enchantment

Book Three – Midnight Smoke

Book Four – Scorched Heart

Book Five – Dark Whispers

Book Six – A Killer's Kiss

Book Seven – Fortune's Ashes

∾

A Charade of Magic complete series

The best way to live in the Mage ruled city of Glasgow is to keep your head down and your mouth closed.

That's not usually a problem for Mairi Wallace. By day she works at a small shop selling tartan and by night she studies to become an apothecary. She knows her place and her limitations. All that changes, however, when her old childhood friend sends her a desperate message seeking her help - and the Mages themselves cross Mairi's path. Suddenly, remaining unnoticed is no longer an option.

There's more to Mairi than she realises but, if she wants to fulfil her full potential, she's going to have to fight to stay alive - and only time will tell if she can beat the Mages at their own game.

From twisted wynds and tartan shops to a dangerous daemon and the magic infused City Chambers, the future of a nation might lie with one solitary woman.

Book One – Hummingbird

Book Two – Nightingale

Book Three – Red Hawk

The complete *Blood Destiny* series

"A spectacular and addictive series."

Mackenzie Smith has always known that she was different. Growing up as the only human in a pack of rural shapeshifters will do that to you, but then couple it with some mean fighting skills and a fiery temper and you end up with a woman that few will dare to cross. However, when the only father figure in her life is brutally murdered, and the dangerous Brethren with their predatory Lord Alpha come to investigate, Mack has to not only ensure the physical safety of her adopted family by hiding her apparent humanity, she also has to seek the blood-soaked vengeance that she craves.

Book One - Bloodfire

Book Two - Bloodmagic

Book Three - Bloodrage

Book Four - Blood Politics

Book Five - Bloodlust

Also

Corrigan Fire

Corrigan Magic

Corrigan Rage

Corrigan Politics

Corrigan Lust

The complete *Bo Blackman* series

A half-dead daemon, a massacre at her London based PI firm and evidence that suggests she's the main suspect for both ... Bo Blackman is having a very bad week.

She might be naive and inexperienced but she's determined to get to the bottom of the crimes, even if it means involving herself with one of London's most powerful vampire Families and their enigmatic leader.

It's pretty much going to be impossible for Bo to ever escape unscathed.

Book One - Dire Straits

Book Two - New Order

Book Three - High Stakes

Book Four - Red Angel

Book Five - Vigilante Vampire

Book Six - Dark Tomorrow

The complete *Highland Magic* series

Integrity Taylor walked away from the Sidhe when she was a child. Orphaned and bullied, she simply had no reason to stay, especially not when the sins of her father were going to remain on her shoulders. She found a new family - a group of thieves who proved that blood was less important than loyalty and love.

But the Sidhe aren't going to let Integrity stay away forever. They need her more than anyone realises - besides, there are prophecies to be fulfilled, people to be saved and hearts to be won over. If anyone can do it, Integrity can.

Book One - Gifted Thief

Book Two - Honour Bound

Book Three - Veiled Threat

Book Four - Last Wish

The complete *Dreamweaver* series

"I have special coping mechanisms for the times I need to open the front door. They're even often successful..."

Zoe Lydon knows there's often nothing logical or rational about fear. It doesn't change the fact that she's too terrified to step outside her own house, however.

What Zoe doesn't realise is that she's also a dreamweaver - able to access other people's subconscious minds. When she finds herself in the Dreamlands and up against its sinister Mayor, she'll need to use all of her wits - and overcome all of her fears - if she's ever going to come out alive.

Book One - Night Shade

Book Two - Night Terrors

Book Three - Night Lights

~

Stand alone novels

Eros

William Shakespeare once wrote that, "Cupid is a knavish lad, thus to make poor females mad." The trouble is that Cupid himself would probably agree...

As probably the last person in the world who'd appreciate hearts, flowers and romance, Coop is convinced that true love doesn't exist – which is rather unfortunate considering he's also known as Cupid, the God of Love. He'd rather spend his days drinking, womanising and generally having as much fun as he possible can. As far as he's concerned, shooting people with bolts of pure love is a waste of his time...but then his path crosses with that of shy and retiring Skye Sawyer and nothing will ever be quite the same again.

Wraith

Magic. Shadows. Adventure. Romance.

Saiya Buchanan is a wraith, able to detach her shadow from her body and send it off to do her bidding. But, unlike most of her kin, Saiya doesn't deal in death. Instead, she trades secrets - and in the goblin besieged city of Stirling in Scotland, they're a highly prized commodity. It might just be, however, that the goblins have been hiding the greatest secret of them all. When Gabriel de Florinville, a Dark Elf, is sent as royal envoy into Stirling and takes her prisoner, Saiya is not only going to uncover the sinister truth. She's also going to realise that sometimes the deepest secrets are the ones locked within your own heart.

The complete *Lazy Girl's Guide To Magic* series

Hard Work Will Pay Off Later. Laziness Pays Off Now.

Let's get one thing straight - Ivy Wilde is not a heroine. In fact, she's probably the last witch in the world who you'd call if you needed a magical helping hand. If it were down to Ivy, she'd spend all day every day on her sofa where she could watch TV, munch junk food and talk to her feline familiar to her heart's content.

However, when a bureaucratic disaster ends up with Ivy as the victim of a case of mistaken identity, she's yanked very unwillingly into Arcane Branch, the investigative department of the Hallowed Order of Magical Enlightenment. Her problems are quadrupled when a valuable object is stolen right from under the Order's noses.

It doesn't exactly help that she's been magically bound to Adeptus Exemptus Raphael Winter. He might have piercing sapphire eyes and a body which a cover model would be proud of but, as far as Ivy's concerned, he's a walking advertisement for the joyless perils of too much witch-work.

And if he makes her go to the gym again, she's definitely going to turn him into a frog.

Book One - Slouch Witch

Book Two - Star Witch

Book Three - Spirit Witch

Sparkle Witch (Christmas novella)

~

The complete *Fractured Faery* series

One corpse. Several bizarre looking attackers. Some very strange magical powers. And a severe bout of amnesia.

It's one thing to wake up outside in the middle of the night with a decapitated man for company. It's another to have no memory of how you got there - or who you are.

She might not know her own name but she knows that several people are out to get her. It could be because she has strange magical powers seemingly at her fingertips and is some kind of fabulous hero. But then why does she appear to inspire fear in so many? And who on earth is the sexy, green-eyed barman who apparently despises her? So many questions ... and so few answers.

At least one thing is for sure - the streets of Manchester have never met someone quite as mad as Madrona...

Book One - Box of Frogs

SHORTLISTED FOR THE KINDLE STORYTELLER AWARD 2018

Book Two - Quiver of Cobras

Book Three - Skulk of Foxes

~

The complete *City Of Magic* series

Charley is a cleaner by day and a professional gambler by night. She might be haunted by her tragic past but she's never thought of herself as anything or anyone special. Until, that is, things start to go terribly wrong all across the city of Manchester. Between plagues of rats, firestorms and the gleaming blue eyes of a sexy Scottish werewolf, she might just have landed herself in the middle of a magical apocalypse. She might also be the only person who has the ability to bring order to an utterly chaotic new world.

Book One - Shrill Dusk

Book Two - Brittle Midnight

Book Three - Furtive Dawn